ANOTHER CITY

WRITING FROM LOS ANGELES

EDITED BY DAVID L. ULIN

CITY
LIGHTS
SAN
FRANCISCO

Cover photography and design by Rex Ray
Book design by Elaine Katzenberger
Typography by Harvest Graphics

Library of Congress Cataloging-in-Publication Data
    Another city : writing from Los Angeles / edited by David L. Ulin.
        p.   cm.
    ISBN 0-87286-391-3
    1. American literature—California—Los Angeles.   2. Los Angeles (Calif.)—Literary
collections.   3. City and town life—Literary collections.   4. American literature—20th
century.   I. Ulin, David L.
    PS572.L6 A84 2001
    820.8'03279494'09045—dc21

                                                                              2001042122

Some of the material in this book has appeared previously in the following publications:

"Maternity," in a slightly different version, in *Santa Monica Review.*
"Enter the Year of the Dragon, 2000," in a slightly different version, in *disOrient.*
"Naked Chinese People" in *Santa Monica Review.*
"When Mother Nature Visits Southern California" in *Spillway.*
"Job's Jobs" in *LA Weekly,* and subsequently in *Other Voices.*
"Fascist Island" in *Pearl.*
"Los Angeles" in *Granta.*
"The Beach at Sunset" in *Solo.*
"Day Time," in a slightly different version, in *New Millennium.*
"This Year in Los Angeles" in *LA Weekly.*

"Atwater" won the Crossing Boundaries Award for experimental and innovative writing
and was published by *International Quarterly.*

"Interesting Times" incorporates material originally published in *LA Weekly.*
"A Note for Everything" incorporates material originally published, in different form, in
the *Los Angeles Reader.*

Visit our web site: www.citylights.com

CITY LIGHTS BOOKS are edited by Lawrence Ferlinghetti and Nancy J. Peters and
published at the City Lights Bookstore, 261 Columbus Avenue, San Francisco, CA 94133.

For Noah and Sophie, my two Angelenos . . .

"Los Angeles, give me some of you! Los Angeles come to me the way I came to you, my feet over your streets, you pretty town I loved you so much, you sad flower in the sand, you pretty town."

—John Fante

"What the world needs now
Are some true words of wisdom,
Like, la la la la la la la la la."

—David Lowery

ACKNOWLEDGMENTS

Over the past few years, certain people have contributed to my understanding of Southern California writing by sharing ideas and intuitions, or allowing me to write about the region in a way that helped me shape my thoughts. Bart Schneider, of the *Hungry Mind* (now *Ruminator*) *Review,* first encouraged me to consider the peculiar role of the writer in Los Angeles when he asked me to write an essay on the subject in the summer of 1997. Tom Christie and Sue Horton at *LA Weekly* enabled me to take this process several steps further by giving me the opportunity to construct a guide to the city's authors, a project that let me map out many of the corners of this diffuse literary world. In working on these pieces, I began to develop the central concept of this anthology—that, when it comes to L.A. and its literature, there is order in disorder, meaning in chaos, shape in shapelessness, and identity in cacophony, in the way we all press up against each other while refusing to coalesce. Such a notion is not only essential to how I came to think about the collection, but to my ongoing efforts to make sense of Los Angeles as physical and psychic terrain.

Particular thanks is due to Elaine Katzenberger, my friend and editor at City Lights, for her faith and enthusiasm throughout the compiling of this work. Kathy Kinney facilitated the project's completion by loaning me a computer when my monitor went down. I'd like to thank all thirty-six contributors, since without their talent and generosity, there would be no book at all. And of course, Bonnie Nadell, agent extraordinaire, has been a supportive listener and a tough-minded advocate, asking the hard questions and helping me to find my way to meaningful work.

In many ways, this book belongs to my wife, Rae Dubow, who, more than a decade ago, convinced me that our future lay not in New York but Los Angeles; as in so many cases, she was absolutely right. Ultimately, though, none of this would mean a thing without my children, Noah and Sophie, who make all else obsolete.

CONTENTS

Introduction xiii

Only Heaven 1
Marjorie Gellhorn Sa'adah

Interesting Times 5
Judith Lewis

Train 11
Ellyn Maybe

Minnie Riperton Saved My Life 13
Luis Alfaro

joseph speaks to gericault in the studio 19
michael datcher

The Exterminator 25
Rob Roberge

Maternity 31
Amy Gerstler

Bed and Brimstone 47
Bart Edelman

The Fecality of It All 49
Benjamin Weissman

Fried Chicken 55
Erik Himmelsbach

Magic Hour 65
Erika Schickel

Dear America 75
Jeffrey McDaniel

The Mutilated Man   77
    Sesshu Foster

Enter the Year of the Dragon, 2000   93
    Russell Charles Leong

Naked Chinese People   101
    Diane Lefer

before   115
    Amy Uyematsu

Cactus   117
    Tara Ison

Atwater   135
    Jacqueline De Angelis

Native to the Place   149
    Lynell George

When Mother Nature Visits Southern California   163
    David Hernandez

Job's Jobs   165
    Aimee Bender

Fascist Island   171
    Gerald Locklin

Los Angeles   173
    Richard Rayner

The Beach at Sunset   197
    Eloise Klein Healy

Bad Girl on the Curb   199
    Lisa Glatt

Day Time   203
    Bruce Bauman

Bieler's Broth   213
    Louise Steinman

Anagoge   217
     Aleida Rodríguez

A Note for Everything   219
     Samantha Dunn

Naked   227
     Susan McMullen

Inside Miss Los Angeles   229
     Jerry Stahl

Ezzie, Sweating   235
     Cindy Milwe

Trouble Man   237
     Jervey Tervalon

An Empty Classroom, Lincoln Heights   257
     William Archila

This Year in Los Angeles   259
     David L. Ulin

Good Wives Don't Drive   263
     Joan Jobe Smith

Lost   265
     Bia Lowe

INTRODUCTION

I N the late 1980s, a couple of years before I moved to Los Angeles, I began
to pitch a few editors I knew on a story about Southern California lit-
erature. The idea, as I recall, went something like this: Since L.A. was
known primarily through the filter of Hollywood, wouldn't it be interest-
ing to profile the writers there who weren't working on movies, and, in the
process, prove the city had some indigenous culture, after all? In retrospect,
this sounds more than a little patronizing, like the lip service of an arrogant
New Yorker, which, in fact, is what it was. But for all my condescension
(See? They have writers in Los Angeles. Just like a real city.), I also want to say
that my heart was more or less in the right place. At the time, I had just
begun contributing to the *Los Angeles Reader,* a small alternative weekly
where my friend Steve worked as book editor, and it was through his eyes
that I was discovering, from a three-thousand-mile distance, the outer edges
of the local literary scene. I started submitting poems to journals like *The
Moment,* and familiarized myself with seemingly exotic venues like Gorky's
and Beyond Baroque. When I came to visit, I went to readings and open
mike nights, and haunted independent bookstores for small press chap-
books and obscure 'zines. Still, although I was excited by the D.I.Y. quality
of these efforts — in New York, the past, with its accumulated load of lit-
erary history, made for an especially heavy weight — what pleased me more
was that the whole thing seemed so . . . manageable, a small and intimate
community of writers that I might easily encapsulate in one short maga-
zine or newspaper piece.

Manageable? Small and intimate? What was I thinking? All these years
later, my presumption — or perhaps, I should say, naïveté — makes me laugh.

Los Angeles, after all, is a city of writers (as I discovered once I came to live here), one whose literary culture has, over the last few decades, come into its own. Everywhere you look, you find writers writing, writers reading, writers desperate to communicate their experiences and tell us what they mean. Such a development is nearly seismic in proportion, since traditionally (if we can even use that word in connection with this city), L.A.'s literature has been one of exile, the work of expatriates who arrived grudgingly, lamenting lost histories, lost landscapes, dreaming of the past. What we see now, however, is increasingly a literature of belonging, written by people who have found a stake in Los Angeles on its own terms, whatever they might be. Many of these writers were born and raised in Southern California, yet even those who migrated from elsewhere seem less interested in distance than engagement, a way of setting roots down, of claiming this territory as their own. These days, in other words, the models for literary L.A. are no longer Thomas Mann and Bertolt Brecht, who sought political asylum, or William Faulkner and F. Scott Fitzgerald, drawn west, against their better judgment, by the voluptuous lure of Hollywood. Rather, we are in the presence of a whole new generation of writers, for whom Los Angeles is neither escape route nor meal ticket, but, in the most fundamental sense, home.

Unfortunately, like a lot of things in Southern California, all this writing can be difficult to see. Even today, literature here remains something of a stealth culture, existing below the radar, in little pockets of the creative landscape, an undertone to the ceaseless hum. Partly that's because, unlike Chicago or New York or San Francisco, words are not L.A.'s dominant form of expression; that role has long been occupied by movies, and, to a lesser extent, painting and sculpture — which is only fitting given the city's abidingly visual aesthetic, its insistence on looking for meaning in the surface of things. Equally significant is Los Angeles's residential nature, once described by Carey McWilliams as "rurban," a turn of phrase that, more than fifty years later, still reflects the city's inconsistencies and innovations, its strange mix of the suburban and the surreal. In "rurban" L.A., exteriors are placid, marked by light and lawn and single-family houses, which often makes it seem like nothing's going on. As a result, it's easy to get lost here, easy to be hidden, disregarded, overlooked. That, of course, has always been Los Angeles's affliction, to be not only misunderstood but marginalized, written off like a bottle blonde. Yet paradoxically, it could be this that gives the place its literary energy, since writers need quiet, need, in some essential fashion, to be forgotten, if they are to get their best work done.

It might be easier to talk about Los Angeles literature if, somewhere along the line, the city had inspired a big, iconic novel, a *Studs Lonigan* or a *Manhattan Transfer*, a *McTeague* or *The Adventures of Augie March*. Books like these provide a certain clarity, a way of saying, "This is who and what we are." The most representative Southern California writing, though, is small, particular, like snapshots of a moment in time. *The Big Sleep*, *The Day of the Locust*, and *Ask the Dust*—that first great trinity of literary Los Angeles—may together frame a vivid portrait of L.A. as quintessential existential city, all sun and celluloid, in which the residue of history collapses into the dreamscape of a neverending present, but on its own, each is a narrow story, constrained to a relative handful of characters and days. The same is true of later generations, whose signature writers seek definition in the little details, things seen and not seen, things observed. As to why this is . . . well, in the decade I've lived here, I've seen that question raised in countless articles and lectures, panel discussions and casual conversations, as we all, writers and readers, try to come to terms with what the literature of Los Angeles means. Yet for all the rhetoric, all the back and forth on L.A. writing, I have yet to find an answer that rings as true as this one, from Joan Didion's essay "Pacific Distances": "When I first moved to Los Angeles from New York, in 1964, I found [the] absence of narrative a deprivation. At the end of two years I realized (quite suddenly, alone one morning in the car) that I had come to find narrative sentimental."

When Didion calls narrative sentimental, she's not talking about personal narrative—that is, the stories we tell to make sense of our lives. What she means is narrative in the grand sense, a collective mythology under whose influence all our individual experiences may, in some strange way, cohere. She's right about that; when it comes to L.A., even to think about an all-encompassing narrative is to miss the point of the place, which sprawls and tumbles shapeless like a vast amoebic mass. There is, as Gertrude Stein once said of Oakland, no there there, or rather a hundred theres, a thousand, a million, all juxtaposed against each other like a succession of border towns. Take a quick drive through the city and you can see it, a random collection of communities, from the villas of Beverly Hills to the kitsch of the Farmers Market, from the old money of Hancock Park to the new money of Koreatown. There are African-American neighborhoods, Mexican neighborhoods, Salvadorean neighborhoods. There is the Valley, Silverlake, the South Bay. It's not this diversity that makes L.A. distinctive, for plenty of cities reflect a similar mix of cultures, races, points-of-view. Los Angeles, however, is not like those cities; it is another city, another kind of city, one with no single identity, no unifying *center,* but with many parallel centers instead. Once you recognize that, how could its literature be any different? No, it only makes sense that L.A. writing reflect the city's scattered energy: diffuse, defined by its own lack of definition, not the product of some homogenous aesthetic but of smaller, individual voices raised above the din.

Another City is an attempt to come to terms with that literary cacophony, albeit in highly subjective form. It brings together thirty-seven authors, operating in a variety of subjects and genres, whose work butts up against each other in a manner not dissimilar to the neighborhoods of Los Angeles itself. In these pages, you'll find writings about the city, writings about the desert, writings about how it was to come here, or what it was like to live here all along. You'll find essays and poems and pieces of fiction; arguments, reminiscences, imaginings, lies. If this sounds like the stuff of chaos, I'll admit that's part of the intention, although at the same time, it's my hope that all the fragmentation add up somehow, if not as a cohesive vision than with the intuitive logic of a collage. L.A., after all, is a collage city, a pastiche of time and place and attitude, and what I've aspired to do with this book is to compile a kind of literary atlas, a set of maps to the interior landscape, which we may use to navigate between imbalance and balance, discord and harmony, discovering, in the process, what E. M. Forster once called "the buzz of implication," the way writers can evoke the essence of their environment, of their *moment,* merely by recording the details of how they see the world.

There is another sense in which Forster's "buzz of implication" seems appropriate to *Another City,* for a book like this can't possibly do more than "imply" the breadth of its material, which, like virtually everything in the known universe, is too expansive, too complex, to be encompassed by a single work. Thirty-seven contributors is a ridiculously low number when you consider the range of Southern California writing, and any reader with even a rudimentary knowledge of the field will find omissions and oversights, some unintentional and others by design. I could take the easy way out and say this is simply in the nature of anthologies, which by necessity are reductive — sketchlike surveys no matter how "representative" they aspire to be. Yet while that may be the case, it's also true that I could have put this collection together in any number of ways, using different writers, different writings, and it would have felt equally representative and equally incomplete. Once I realized that it was impossible for me to be comprehensive, I felt free to operate from another set of criteria, to make *Another City,* first and foremost, a book I wanted to read. Every one of the pieces here fulfills that function, forming something of a reader's autobiography, a catalog of my concerns and interests — in short, my subjective experience of L.A. This, too, is only as it should be, for in ten years in Southern California, I have never been able to see the place as anything other than what you'll read here: a succession of glimpses, impressions, shuffled together and resonating, if at all, as a set of afterimages that linger in the heart, the mind, the eye.

Among the challenges in putting together an anthology like *Another City* is the need to give it some internal integrity, to have it function not simply as a sampler, but as an autonomous work of its own. To that end, I'd like to say a few things about the intentions, the standards, I used in bringing this book into being. Besides the obvious (literary quality, emotional honesty), I looked for material that hadn't previously appeared in book form, and, in fact, something like two-thirds of the writing here has never been published anywhere before. I also decided to leave aside excerpts in favor of complete shorter pieces, which would rise and fall and come to some resolution — pieces, that is, which would stand alone. Most important, I sought out writers who hadn't been overly anthologized, or even anthologized at all. One of the disheartening things about Los Angeles literature is that the same few writers get mentioned every time the subject comes up. From my (now) Angeleno's perspective, this reads like an uncomfortable form of tokenism, not dissimilar to the way I used to see it, more than a decade ago. I don't mean to disrespect these authors; almost uniformly, they deserve their attention, but they're not the only ones. In that sense, *Another City* is an attempt to open up the discourse, by turning the spotlight on other writers, and giving their work a forum, a context of which they can be a part.

In the end, this may be all any author can ask for, whether from Los Angeles or somewhere else. We want to be read, to be regarded, to be noticed — and, if possible, to be understood. It's hard to achieve that no matter where you are, but in Southern California, with its endless disconnection, its distances both real and metaphorical, its fluidity, its superficial reputation, those desires become more elusive still. What is the value of literature in a city that, even now, cannot quite recognize itself as a literary landscape? How do we begin to describe the experience of living in such a place, let alone account for what it means? These are questions every L.A. writer must continually ask him or herself, questions that have everything to do with why we're here. Ten years after my arrival, the answers seem less available than I would have thought, but like every contributor to these pages, I'd suggest, I find meaning in the asking even more.

David L. Ulin
Los Angeles, 2001

ANOTHER
CITY

ONLY HEAVEN

Marjorie Gellhorn Sa'adah

BETWEEN the old side of downtown and the new side of downtown, there's a bougainvillea-covered cracked retaining wall, one last vacant lot, a hill, an orange funicular, and, at the feet of two gleaming fifty-two-story office towers, a plaza.

Today, a Saturday, the plaza is quiet, and almost empty. I've read a third of my library book when a firefighter on break smiles at me in such a way that I want to drop a lit book of matches at my feet and look up.

When I leave, I walk around the fountain to the long staircase back down to Broadway. I pass behind the only others; they have been staring at the water the whole time. He has an iced tea bottle on the table in front of him, but she has the small medicinal can of a liquid nutritional supplement. They are young—forties—and I worry for them immediately.

Since they have been sitting there for such a while, staring at the water with great concentration, I figure her can is not because they are too hurried for a good meal. They are not quiet with the atrophied look of a married couple that no longer loves one another. It's something else, maybe something in a turn of their luck that is beyond them both.

If you stay here—I want to say—in the plaza, the chances are good that you will see a bride in satin, come to take her picture with this fountain as her train.

But if you come with me, you will see a hundred girls, on their way to try on a hundred shiny wedding dresses, and a hundred couples, leaning against each other, on their way to try two hundred golden wedding bands.

There will be little girls who are told not to drag their fingers against the walls as they look longingly at oversized books of stickers being hawked from the corners. Or, in storefronts smaller than your hallway closet, at toy trucks whose hoods and doors swing open, ready for a girl to really go somewhere. Down here on Broadway, it is hope on parade.

If you come with me to Broadway, you will hear a man singing "Supercalifragialisticexpialidotious" in a Lou Reed sort of voice, and a woman with a ukulele on her lap, plucking its only string. If she calls us over, she will wave at our wrists with an empty liter soda bottle that has a couple of coins at the bottom and ask, "Time, time, do you have the time?"

You may think that all of us this side of downtown have thin luck. But some days you couldn't be further from the truth. Some days we are all just here doing our shopping, or crossing the terrazzo into whatever we choose from the gleaming lines of food at Clifton's Cafeteria, or just sitting in our wheelchairs or leaning against a firehose hookup. Or we have spilled out here to ditch the landlord, to use the pay phone, or we are just watching nothing in the sun from a bench in Biddy Mason's backyard. We can't help but pick up our step to the one-man band who plays on overturned cat-food cans tacked to his belt, or to the storefront *banda* and *ranchera,* and the music lifts us whether or not it is what we play on our little radios in our S.R.O. hotel rooms or our one-bedroom apartments in buildings where you can always hear the noise from the street until one day you don't so much hear the noise from the street anymore. This weekend I can guarantee the sound of tambourines coming from the men washing apartment windows on the corner of Third.

Before I leave the plaza, I'm going to turn around. I'm going to go back to the couple and their troubles. I'm going to say, come, let's go. Come with me down to Broadway. If it's rest you need, we can sit on those red chairs in the Grand Central Market. They must have five coats of paint, those red chairs. We'll get something to cook. That will help. There are beautiful long red flat beans. And greens to simmer into some kind of gentle broth, with maybe a chile for bite. It doesn't matter that we don't know how to cook tomatillos. If we just stand by the men eating tacos at a steel counter, we will see a washtub-sized pot, blackened on the outside, shined copper on the inside, loaded with the little green tomatoes, boiling on top of four burners. I'll just hold one up, in its papery husk, and lift my eyebrows, and the Taiwanese vegetable man will say, "Peel," brushing the tomatillo with his thumb and slipping its sheer husk off. "Little water. Boil, maybe ten minutes. You can mix in your blender—you have a blender?—with chiles and cilantro. You—" pointing at me with the tomatillo "—you always buy so much cilantro." Shaking his head and laughing, he'll say, "You eat it like lettuce."

Come with me. I live here, right up there, above the market. We'll cook what we have in my little kitchen, and for dessert, we'll slice mangoes.

You know what? Another Saturday, a bird flew in my window. My window was open just two or three inches, and the bird landed next to me on my bed. I was sleeping, but I woke to the whirring of the bird's wings, and watched without moving as the gray-brown bird touched down on my feather comforter and then immediately traced its way back out the window.

And Monday, when I went to work and told the story, Alma said, "Is luck! Marjorie, is luck! A bird in your house!"

So I waited for luck to come to me.

Even the cat waited, sitting every day on the very edge of the bed, leaning toward the window with her ears forward. Even she hoped that luck would fly back in the window and present itself plainly.

One day a balloon floated by. One day a pigeon, so purposeful it resembled a swallow, flew by carrying an unfurled note on its ankle.

But there was no stunning exacta payoff. No good headlines the next morning. I didn't find my grandmother's ring that I lost six years ago. I didn't really expect any of this, and even a very small exacta payoff, say with the two favorite horses, would have surprised and sated me.

It was after luck didn't come back to me that in the market I saw the taco man tap the edge of a dime tip on the Roast To Go counter, like a blackjack dealer, and say, "Hey, and thank you very much." A man put down a crate he was carrying and pulled a folded paper from his pocket, on which was printed the names and quantities of his entire vegetable stand, and using his thumb to underline it, he said the word *verdulaga,* syllable by syllable. A man in a wheelchair waited less than a moment before the woman from Sun's Produce handed him an empty bag and said, "Whatever you would like to put in it, just tell me, or him, and we will help."

There is something lucky that day in seeing my father's wife, sitting on one of those red chairs in the market, finish every bit of a taco, licking her fingers, when it makes me want to take her thin face in my two hands and say, "I am so sorry I have never in nine years said happy anniversary to you."

And also something lucky in pouring salt in my coffee, but then after one swig, being distracted by a family carrying trays of lunch, who were so happy to find a round, not a rectangular, table, that one girl ran around it and even the teenager said "Round! This is perfect!" So as I go looking for a sugar dispenser from another table, pour sugar into the palm of my hand, and taste it, I think only of my family's round dinner tables, and of once being a trickster in diners.

This is why I ask you to come with me, down here, to Broadway. Because one way of luck is in what you see. You may have known this, looking into the plaza fountain. There is something to be said for every-direction-moving water when you are plotting for escape.

But if you come with me, this place will take you in. Whether you are missing legs, an eye, or someone in your family who you love. This place, it takes you in, and here, you'll find flinty glints of luck, bright things that change your mind about leaving and living. The plaza is nice. But come with me.

INTERESTING TIMES

Judith Lewis

I LIVE in Hollywood. It's a strange thing to me, this fact, as strange as if someone were to tell me that, twenty years from now, I will sit in on the French parliament. At the Mayfair supermarket a block from my house I spot celebrities: Lily Tomlin dresses up in a hat and sunglasses everyone recognizes as uniquely hers; Joanna Gleason walks the aisles with a look on her face that says *don't ask*. Up the street exactly eight-tenths of a mile, I exercise my dogs in a part of Griffith Park we call the "Bat Caves," not because they're home to so many bats, but because they served as the exterior shot of Batman's lair in the 1960s television series. On many mornings I have wandered through those caves in the silent company of so many movie people that I've been assumed to be one. A woman I know named Carol called me Jessica for years and I never thought to correct her, until one rainy day I let it slip that my last name was not Harper.

This, I think sometimes, is not the life for which I was destined. I did not expect to live among the moguls and demiurges of commercial entertainment; I harbored lust for neither beach culture nor the landmarks of noir fiction. And while I cannot pinpoint the moment I started bragging about my latest tumble in a robust wave, or when I took the first of many neighborhood walks to ogle Neutra homes, or stopped worrying about whether my doors were locked when I drove down Florence past Normandie, I know for certain when I survey my Self that I have become an Angeleno. I have grown into this scene; absorbed its perverse aesthetic by osmosis, along with its polluted air, impossible beauty standards, and bad driving habits. Cell phone caught between shoulder and chin, I drive wildly in the passing lane, dashing to appointments, always late, huffing about traffic as I breeze through the door. I jog, eat granola for breakfast, guzzle Chardonnay, practice yoga, attend premieres. I am a walking cliché.

On the other hand, I am not always sure this character is me. Like Estelle in Sartre's *No Exit,* I have the urge to pat my body to confirm my existence. When I catch myself wondering, as I stare at my furrowed brow, whether a little shot of botulism toxin, or "botox"—the cosmetic procedure that's all the rage in Beverly Hills—might be just the thing to smooth those lines out, I have to consider whether the crazy man I met nine years ago in Venice — the one who insisted I get a lead bracelet because aliens were about to bombard the West Coast with brainwashing radiation — might have been telling the truth. I didn't get like this without provocation. Something extraordinary must have happened.

I drove out from Minnesota to Los Angeles in 1991 carrying a copy of Mike Davis's *City of Quartz* and a bad attitude. I was emigrating for a job, not out of any particular infatuation with the city. I took Davis at his word: L.A., he argued, had been built on greed and was verging on apocalypse, and what emerged from his prose managed to dislodge any dim hope I had of fun in the sun and impending fame. In Pocatello, Idaho, I stopped in a cheap motel that had little but CNN to recommend it, turned on the TV for company, and happened upon a series of interviews with disgruntled Angelenos, all of them fixed on flight. The crime, the smog, the earthquakes, they complained — it's a wonder anyone settled here in the first place. My thoughts, as I crept toward the Pacific, turned from whether I should learn to surf to how to best dodge a gang shootout should I take the wrong exit off the freeway.

Like so many newcomers, I wanted a sprinkle of the city's faerie dust but none of its ashes, and as I wound my reluctant way west, dallying among the glorious red rocks of southern Utah and getting waylaid by blackjack in Las Vegas, ashes were all I could imagine. I would like to say that once I arrived the dread abated, but instead it lingered like a chronic illness exacerbated by a toxic environment. Within the first six months, my car — a nondescript foreign economy model in an apparently ill-fated red — was stolen twice, once from my driveway, again from outside my office in broad daylight. The second time it happened, Davis himself offered me a replacement, a VW Dasher he'd been planning to sell. He asked for no money right away; he insisted only that I register it quickly. I didn't. Instead, I drove the car for exactly nine days before it exploded in a rush of steam on the Glendale Freeway (an ending that seemed to me almost poetically Davisian). A series of other cars followed—a diesel Mercedes, an old Volvo station wagon, a ratty little Honda. Each of them at one time or another left me stranded mid-lane at night on some crowded freeway, and each of them, in the end, died painful, grisly deaths.

To be sure, those were difficult years for the whole city: On more evenings than I can now remember, I hunkered down in my nondescript Westside house watching some television station's Emergency Live Action Cam track bodies being swept down the Sepulveda Dam in a sudden rainstorm, or homes imploding in Malibu fires, or a fevered businessman on the roof of a La Brea Avenue stereo store defending his business from looters with a gun. In the five days following the verdict that acquitted the police officers accused of beating Rodney King, my neighbors and I sat on our lawns in the pink-hued air of dusk watching plumes of smoke rise to the south, wondering how it could be possible that, in this modern American city, we could be required by law to stay indoors after sundown.

But civil strife, like personal crises, has strange side effects. During those 1992 riots, I went to a wedding. It was held in a small church near the beach in Santa Monica; the reception was at a nearby hotel. After dinner, as expected, all of us who had attended were stuck in that hotel; to leave would have meant breaking the curfew. We were journalists, and could have traveled home with impunity by declaring ourselves on duty, but truth be told we all wanted an excuse to live life for a night as if during wartime. People broke off into small groups to secure rooms for the night and returned to party like the world was ending. Antisocial brooders drank too much champagne and told strangers their troubles; snobs gave up pretense to dance as flamboyantly as they would in their living rooms; ex-lovers made out in the corners, less for their own satisfaction than for the opportunity they had to create tedium-alleviating scandal. It was, at that time, the finest night of my life in Los Angeles; it remains one of my happiest memories. It was the night I learned that the saying "May you live in interesting times" is not entirely a curse.

It was then that my transformation began. At my neighborhood Vons supermarket — which was suddenly flooded with residents of Inglewood and South L.A. whose own grocery stores were closed, looted, or on fire — I would stare into the eyes of black women as bewildered as I was. We would shake our heads and roll our eyes like co-conspirators, as if we were assuring each other that this war was not between us. On the Venice boardwalk, I exchanged sympathetic glances with fellow joggers who had donned protective masks against the smoke — our faces half-covered, we still managed to telegraph camaraderie. As Parker Center's trees lit up with fire and Payless Shoes got ransacked, I felt myself increasingly ensconced in a community of reasonable people, black and white, who held in equal contempt then–police chief Daryl Gates's lawless hooligans, the exurban jury that exonerated them, and the opportunistic looters who rioted recklessly on blameless stores. Some new version of the city began to come into focus, some collective identity that had to do not with greed or artifice, but a tenacious insistence on remaining civilized even when bombarded by stupidity and turpitude. During those riots, I observed close up what riches adversity dredges up in people's spirits.

On the morning of January 18, 1994, I drove east on the 10 freeway, detouring with the masses around the segment near La Cienega Boulevard that had collapsed in the Northridge earthquake. Stunned and dizzy and guzzling coffee, I was struck by a comforting thought: Every driver on every side of me was in much the same shape. We were united by shock and sleep deprivation. A few nights later, over dinner at an Italian restaurant that had remained sturdy enough to stay open, I confessed to a friend that I would not for all the world have wanted to have been away when the quake hit. If this city were to be shaken down to rubble, I wanted to be here to feel it.

The belief that adversity gives depth to life, that we are better for having suffered together, sets the people I know in Los Angeles apart. What our counterparts in other American cities can only imagine, we have tasted and touched; we have proved to ourselves how intrepid we are, carried that knowledge with us into less eventful days. Angelenos get bad press—we are assumed to be shallow and apolitical; vain and fickle. When the British punk folksinger Billy Bragg visited the city during the combined strikes of the janitors, screen actors, and bus drivers in the year 2000, he expressed amazement that Los Angeles had become a hotbed of political action. But Bragg and others like him settle for surface appraisals—screenwriters, swimming pools, and movie stars; the infamous blond gargoyles of Bel Air, the followers of Fabio who crowd Gold's Gym, and those all-important People Who Don't Read. They miss the solidarity of small neighborhoods, the social activism television actors practice to compensate for work they fear is insipid, the steadfast friendships—even among Hollywood's elite—that survive widening gaps in income and notoriety, because even movie stars know that in a city so mercurial and sprawled, they run the risk of unbearable loneliness. Yes, Angelenos are isolated from one another. All the more reason, when you find one you like, to make yourself known as a true and trusted friend.

Los Angeles has always inspired ambivalence. But mixed feelings hold some allure. Bertolt Brecht derided this land of exile but wrote *Galileo* while living within its boundaries; Chester Himes wrote that the city's racism left him "shattered," but at the height of his distress, he began his startling novel *If He Hollers Let Him Go.* People who say they hate New York City generally avoid New York City, but people who say they hate Los Angeles take up defiant residence in its hardest neighborhoods to chronicle their resistance to its empty and awful culture, and sometimes, for their pains, find themselves honored with grant money. Ambivalence is not an incidental feature of this city's citizens. We do not stay here in spite of our mixed feelings. We stay here because of them. Ambivalence defines us.

Long after I had acclimated to the pitch and yaw of Los Angeles life, after I had learned to swim in the big waves (both literally and figuratively), feared no freeway exit, and accepted the inevitability of collapsing book-shelves and broken dishes once in a while, I reflected, as the helicopters circled over O. J.'s house, that all this artifice outsiders insist on associating with Los Angeles serves merely to distract them from the city's true cultural muscle. Los Angeles is where life is being lived most vigorously in this country, be it over movie-deal lunches, or on crowded Saturday sidewalks in Koreatown, or at the beach in Malibu. Life here is not simple, and many of this city's rewards have emerged from events that initially seemed like doom. But after a decade, I have finally come to realize that Los Angeles has treated me well — not by allowing me an undramatic, luxurious existence, but by giving me a world to battle as much as I revel in it. It has given me a life in interesting times.

TRAIN

Ellyn Maybe

It's like when a train is making a stop at a city that's never had
    a train before.
Sometimes you ride with the baggage.

It's like dreaming night after night of *An American in Paris,*
    and not knowing if you are Gene Kelly, Leslie Caron,
    Nina Foch, or Oscar Levant. Or a medley no one will
    ever score.
It's like being made of apples and finding you're forbidden.

It's like the episode of *The Twilight Zone* where the bandages
    are removed and you're still appalling.
It's like finding the perfect Mont Blanc pen and as soon as you
    put it in your pocket, the world changes to invisible ink.

It's like someone said come out of the cave decorated with rare
    L.P.s and canaries who rebel against the coal miner's
    broken throat — you feel the avalanche in the bone of the
    land itching like the first day of junior high.

It's like someone yodeled to you and when you yodeled back,
    they set fire to your Nelson Eddy and Jeanette McDonald
    records.

It's like wearing 3-D glasses and saying "let's be silly together"
    and the other person saying "G-d, you're ugly."

I trusted you.
I've worn glasses since I was two.

MINNIE RIPERTON SAVED MY LIFE

Luis Alfaro

THE summer that we graduated from Berendo Junior High School was the year that Minnie Riperton saved my life.

My brother and I were supposed to go to Belmont High School in our Pico-Union neighborhood, but because of overcrowding, we were told we were going to be bused. Almost all the poor Mexican kids in our downtown barrio who were bused were sent to Grant High School in the Valley.

The Valley? Well, there's a valley that we come from, with grapes and peaches and cherries to pick and sell. But this one was very different. This valley is where the rich kids live. The kids who have staircases inside their houses. Staircases that lead to lots of bedrooms without bunk beds that you have to share with your little brother. Houses with manicured lawns that don't have my dad's Orange Monte Carlo sitting on cinder blocks waiting for someone to change the rims, the muffler, the whatever.

Busing? We protested, but my parents thought it might be a good idea for us to meet other kinds of people. Other kinds of people? What other kinds of people can there be in the world? There's the rich and the poor, huh? One time we went to my dad's boss's house in Beverly Hills because he let us pick avocados off his tree. My mom and my sister waited in the car, while my dad, my brother, and I climbed the big trees in the front yard on a street called Camden. I'll never forget how sad and poor and dark we looked next to the boss and his wife. But my dad didn't care, we got some free avocados.

My mom and dad are farm workers. Well, not anymore, but always, if you know what I mean. Even after they moved to downtown L.A. from the

Central Valley, my Dad would still pull over the station wagon at the sight of a cherry grove, a grape field, or an avocado tree. That's the way they used to live before they came here from Mexico.

But not us. My dad embarrasses us. We got too many Marvin Gaye albums inside us. We've started talking *Soul Train* dialects, and my brother is already walking like Antonio Fargas on *Toma*.

We were really scared about busing. We had never been around people who were not like us. You know, people like us. People who shopped at the open-air mall on Crenshaw near Stocker. People who bought Simplicity patterns from the Newberry's at Pico and Western. People who bought small bags of popcorn from the Midtown Sears and later went roller-skating at the rink across the street. People who bought Spicy Cajun from the first Church's Fried Chicken in Inglewood on the way home from the race track. People who brought home live pigs from the Farmer John's factory in Vernon for victorious post-soccer parties. You know, people like us.

That summer we went downtown and bought Superfly outfits for the first day of high school and first impressions. With both our parents working, we spent our weekends cashing in Coke bottles and watching triple features at the Tower, the State, and the Orpheum theaters downtown. Raised on *Superfly, Shaft,* and a diet of Bruce Lee movies, I was hooked on ultraviolent, sexy Pam Grier/Tamara Dobson spectaculars like *Cleopatra Jones* and *Coffy*. These were the people I knew. At Berendo Junior High we were a minority. Surrounded by African-American neighborhoods on all sides, we took the number twenty-six bus down Pico to Vermont.

My brother joined the 18th Street Gang just so he could talk back and show everyone that we couldn't be pushed around. I studied and concentrated on winning Highlander workbooks with my conformity. I joined the gifted programs, and my best friend was a six-foot-five seventh-grader named Clarence who later became the drag queen Vaginal Creme Davis, lead singer of a Menudo-type singing group called Cholita. People sometimes pushed around Clarence and me and our other friend, Paul Lee, for being smart, but mostly they left us nonthreatening kids alone.

At lunchtime, we had noon dances in the gym. This was the greatest moment of junior high school for me. The only time in the day when I got lost in the magic of being American. Being far away from my father's soccer cleats, domino games in the backyard, and that *Espanol* we had to speak in the house. *Afuera de la casa,* we spoke a kind of English that belonged only to us. And that's when I heard it. At the noon dances. A song. One of those songs that stays inside you and wraps itself around your soul. Later, after school we'd go to the factory and make carburetors for extra money to feed our family, but I remembered the cover of that album. A woman, beautiful with *piel de canela,* sitting next to a lion that's reclining. She's got on an angelic white dress and baby's breath in her hair. A big puffy afro sits on top of her head like a dangerous storm cloud.

And her name, Minnie. Like something sweet. Something American. And she's singing about coming inside her love. And I don't get it really, because I'm just a seventh-grader, who wishes he could play tetherball on the playground. But I hear her hold that note. A long high birdsong that reaches to the clouds. *Come inside my love.* I understand that note like I understand how to roller-skate without trying, like how to float in the deep section of the Red Shield pool without drowning.

Late on Sunday nights, there's a show that I listen to on K-Day from the small portable radio that I sleep with on the upper bunk. A woman named Nancy Wilson sings a song and she also holds one of those notes, and a connection starts for me. That note sounds like a wail that Lola Beltran or Lucha Villa or even Edie Gorme on the Blue album of Mexican standards would moan. A song about missing a home, a piece of land, a man. They call it The Blues on K-Day, but in my neighborhood we call them *Rancheras* or *Corridos.* Songs about love and loss, working the land and missing home. How come I know that feeling and I ain't even lived yet? I mean really lived. Fallen in love or kissed someone on the lips or gotten dumped or had the government repossess something of mine. How can you know the soul of soul music, Mr. Al Green asks, even before he became a preacher? And when Miss Nancy Wilson asks me to Guess Who She Saw Today, I think about Lydia Mendoza asking me to Jurame, to swear it. That love, that land, that feeling.

The very next day I join the Columbia House Record Club without my *Ama's* permission, and I order twelve new albums, all for one penny! Plus, I get to sample a new record every month. It sounds so good. I get Mr. Barry White, who can't get enough of my love; the Three Degrees, who wonder when they will see me again; Shirley Brown, who gives me the 411, Woman to Woman; Harold Melvin and the Blue Notes, who tell me all about their Bad Luck; and even Love Unlimited, who say they belong to me. I get hit by my *Apa,* and good, for joining the Columbia House Record Club and forging his signature, but it's worth it. Thanks to all those records, every day that I get ready for high school, I feel like I know who I am, more and more.

When the busing letter finally came, my *Ama* and my *Apa* were really mad. My brother and I were not going to the Valley after all. We were going to go to Wilson High School in El Sereno, in the northeast part of Los Angeles. *Cabrones,* my father shouted. How could they send us to a Mexican school in East L.A.? What was the point of busing anyway?

My brother and I were excited. We never really went to school with a bunch of Mexicans. We joined gangs just to get noticed. Now all we would had to do was be ourselves. The first day of school, we got off the bus and a sea of brown swept over us. In our silk shirts and platform shoes, we looked like two pimps on our way to urban training camp. This was east L.A. Kids in corduroy pants from Miller's Outpost and Wallabee shoes from Kenny's. We bought our duds from Main Street and Broadway in downtown. The kids laughed at us, and we spent the first week hanging out under the bleachers on the football field till we could get to the mall and dress like everybody else.

I met my first friend in gym class. He liked Donna Summer's *Four Seasons of Love.* I thought it was just okay. Every heard of Millie Jackson, I asked?

Nah, do you like Aerosmith?

Arrow-what?

After that, the only way to make friends at Wilson was to keep soul music inside my soul. Instead, I had to listen to the Eagles and Queen and

Alice Cooper and Boston. The closest we got to soul music was Joni Mitchell's *Blue* album, which I played religiously because it sounded like something Minnie Riperton would have recorded had she not died.

Minnie Riperton died, and I started to grow up.

My *Ama* and my *Apa* were worried about how come I liked the blues so much. They didn't let me listen to the blues in the house, but they let me go to gospel concerts. Gospel was God's blues. I went to see the Clark Sisters and Shirley Caesar, and later my mom dropped me off at a church on Adams so that I could see Sweet Honey in the Rock. Shouters, all of them, who spoke about hard times, but this time they spoke it to the Lord.

The same week that Minnie Riperton died, Pee Wee Crayton was in a car accident. Pee Wee was one of those old-time blue singers. A shouter.

One Saturday I told my *Ama* I was going to the movies with my friend from South Central and she drove me to the bus stop on Vermont and Venice. I took that bus to a place called the New Mint Saloon on Vermont and 89th. My brother lent me his fake ID, and I dressed older in a velvet blazer à la Richard Roundtree. It was a benefit for Pee Wee Crayton. A lineup of some of the best of the old school. Blues singers I had just heard of, but couldn't even find their records.

I had never been in a bar before. The smoke and the smell of the liquor made me feel like I was going to some place dangerous and adult. I was in the world of knowing. I drank a tonic on the rocks that tasted like bad water with bubbles, but I didn't care, I was in the middle of someplace powerful and important.

I sat next to a couple at a little table with a red round candle in the middle. They looked at me funny, but I didn't care. I could feel the soul inside of my soul coming out, just like Mr. Al Green said. I was the only Mexican in there, in fact I was the whitest person, but nobody said anything. I was where I needed to be.

As the night went on, I heard the best of the best. An amazing soulful man named Eddie "Cleanhead" Vinson blew his horn. Harmonica Fats blew his, too. Barbara Lynn played a slide guitar, I had never seen a woman do that, and sang her biggest hit, "You'll Lose A Good Thing." Linda Hopkins shouted through "All of Me" and then everything went quiet. It was almost like one of those important moments at church right before you pray.

From the back of the bar, a big, heavy, heavy man made his way through the audience. He was on crutches and he was helped along by two older men in sharp pinstripe suits. When he finally made his way to the stage and sat on a chair, he clutched his harmonica and the microphone like those Sunday morning preachers on local TV. His name was Big Joe Turner, and he made everybody Flip, Flop, and Fly. You couldn't do anything but stand and do the *Soul Train* lineup in the little space in front of you. He shouted pure joy, pure soul, pure blues, and the New Mint Saloon was blown away by his tornado. I was taken to someplace beyond Vermont Boulevard. I was back in the Central Valley with my Grandma picking grapes off the vine. I was in Tijuana feeding the pigs in the backyard. I was watching my dad play soccer. I was watching my mom curling her hair like Elizabeth Taylor in *Butterfield 8*. I was in the world of my people. A world of simple pleasure, of being poor, of downtown streetcorners. Buying pizza slices from the counter at Woolworth's on Broadway. I was sitting in the last row of the number twenty-six bus running down Pico. I was free. I was a queer Mexican boy from the barrio, but I was also one of the *Soul Train* dancers. I was one of the Three Degrees. I was one of Harold Melvin's Bluenotes. I was the guy in Bloodstone who sang the falsetto in "Natural High." I was one of the Stylistics. I was one of Freda Payne's backup singers on "Band of Gold." I was Minnie Riperton's Perfect Angel. I reached in and pulled that note on *Loving you is easy because you're beautiful*. And I held it as long as I could. Until I grew up.

Minnie Riperton saved my life.

JOSEPH SPEAKS TO GERICAULT IN THE STUDIO
(AFTER THEODORE GERICAULT'S *PORTRAIT STUDY*)

michael datcher

search the length of your eyes
to find how you judge me. crucified
up
side
down
on your iris. inverted hologram
captured in your acrylic
embrace.

this is how you like me.
still
as the hangman's poplar tree
when the kicking has ceased.
    silent.
a mute victim of french
imagination. i make the fatal
segue from subject to object.

you know me not.

i am more than santo domingo
mythologies
    exoticized in oil.

the things you sketch into my eyes. bequeath
the borrowed blues

of others, their minor chord pupils.
my sockets are pall bearers
                    wailing eulogies
for the dead dreams they carry.

someone else's pain is
buried in the sarcophagus
of my face. the life sentence of salon sight.
penalty served
in number of hard stares.
a man is not meant to have
such a close reading of his face.

under the festering
gaze of museum patrons
i become an abject thermometer.
mercury as curiosity. peppery skin tingling
nostrils raw.
scalding is my name.

wear my eyes and see
if you can bear the heat
of revulsion
in the casual glance of pedestrians.
the heat of terror in a child's
shudder
        at your smile.
the gravity of not being able to find
beauty
in a mirror.

no you can't touch my hair. its natty
roots will not lead you

to the primitive
innocence
you assume I possess. you cannot access
your past through me
only your uncouth shame.

i am steps removed from being a friend. you paint
my naked body
but I know none of your secrets.

fabricated amnesia:
france has not forgotten
    storming the bastille
      declaring the rights of man.
she has forgotten
that nappy heads hold souls
that pine for justice too.
beloved homeland hispaniola.
    colonial whore.
        bedwarmer for the city of lights.
you ravish our sugar
cane, tobacco leaves
and young girls.
make them come
    in the name of napoleon.
i can still hear the sweet
resistance
of their guilty moans.

i seek retribution
in the wombs of french
women. burn inside
their solvent fascination.

an acrobat's torment
cannot be captured in water
colors. it leaks out the frame
into a ring of fire. the viscous twists of his life
require a medium
with more texture. something you can rub
between your fingers, squeeze into your mouth.

what is the degree of difficulty
to double somersault
a soul
          inside out?

the pernicious whispers i have heard
meditating on museum walls
could shake a nun's faith.
niggers hang in the permanent collection
because we have practice on tree limbs.

a sacred text
rescued me from the raft
of the medusa:
the holy book of strategies for surviving oil-based quicksand
can be found
on the papyrus of osiris.
i read it by candle light.
it recites itself
as i sit still for a living.

a man should narrate
his own psalm. that way nothing
gets lost in the translation
          between self & easel.

i sell my soul, my body. i cannot
get them back. they are dried
on the edges of brushes.
        joseph is my name.
        i am a man
                no matter how much oil
        you spill in my eyes.

THE EXTERMINATOR

Rob Roberge

THE exterminator drives a canary-yellow company van with enormous mouse ears on top and a fake mouse nose painted on the spare tire mounted on the grille. Across the side of the van is the company phone number and the logo, "We're The Critter Ridders."

He comes to a white farmhouse with an old amateur stone wall bordering the road and driveway. The house is on the crest of a hill and it has a crumbling Norman Rockwell porch. The porch is in a terrible state of neglect, tilted and falling into the earth on the side facing the driveway. It looks like a wheelchair ramp with a love seat, grown over with weeds.

The exterminator walks to the door. A couple in their mid-twenties, about his age, meet him.

"We've got a rat trapped in the bathroom," the man says.

"Yeach," the exterminator says. "I hate rats."

"You hate rats?" the man says. He looks at the exterminator, then at the woman, wide-eyed in disbelief.

The exterminator shrugs. "It's a job, right?" He walks past where they are in the entrance of the kitchen. "Bathroom?" he says.

They lead him out of the kitchen, into a room full of heavy-looking Victorian furniture and into a living area. The man points to a closed door.

"He's in there?" the exterminator says.

"It's in there," the man says.

The exterminator puts his ear to the door. "Male," he says.

"How can you tell?" the man says.

"Females never get trapped. Too smart."

"Really?" the woman says.

"Really," the exterminator says, although he actually has no clue to the sex of the vermin. The exterminator makes things up. He's told clients that roaches, as far as entomology can determine, have sex for fun as well as procreation, that fleas mate for life — albeit a short life. That mice bite their finger and toenails to keep them sharp.

He has no idea whether any of this is true.

The exterminator walks away from the bathroom. His boots clump on the hardwood floor. He tells the couple he'll be back in a moment with the tools he'll need.

More snow is falling. The exterminator feels as if time were standing still. He will open the back of the company van in a moment. He's in the company-issue uniform; thick steel-toed boots and a canary-yellow jumpsuit with a beeper hooked into the belt.

The exterminator:

Bites his nails.

Suffers from insomnia.

Hates driving a van that's made to look like a giant rodent.

Has not always been an exterminator.

Has a daughter he's never seen.

Can't stand to be alone.

Is not fond of others.

Has a Beagle named Fausto.

Smokes two packs of cigarettes a day.

Goes to AA meetings sometimes.

Knows a man who glazes hams for a living; a man he used to drink with.

Misses drinking more than the daughter.

Is not bothered by not seeing his daughter.

Is bothered that it doesn't bother him.

Is standing in snowfall.

He opens the back of the van and the overhead light comes on. He takes out four long boxes and leans them on the bumper. He thinks of using traps and quickly decides against them.

The last time he used traps, he splattered the walls of a house with blood and had to stay behind, off the clock, to clean.

He takes a rubber mallet from the van, gathers the four boxes and kicks the door closed. It doesn't close properly and the light is left on. He walks back to the house.

At the door to the bathroom, the exterminator bends down and opens the first of the four boxes, which are about a yard long. He handles the glue sticks with gloves, peeling back the protective layer.

The glue sticks look like ordinary baseboard but, once peeled, are incredibly sticky. Guaranteed to hold a twenty-pound rodent helpless. The exterminator hopes never to test this promise. He looks up at the man.

"You got a big shovel?"

"A shovel?"

The exterminator nods. "A big one."

"Why?"

"Because I'm going to try and trap him with glue sticks, but he might get away. I need to open the door so he thinks he can escape. That's when — if he's not stuck — you lower the shovel on him."

"What are we paying you for?" the woman says.

The exterminator gets out of his catcher's stance and stands up. "Look," he says. "I can cover the walls in there so ugly that you'll spend the next six months finding little rat parts on everything. This way is much neater."

The exterminator feels guilty for snapping at the woman, as he always does when he says what he's really thinking. He smiles an apologetic smile. "I'm sorry," he says. "Trust me."

"Fine," she says. "Just get it out of here."

"I've got a snow shovel," the man says.

"Good," the exterminator says. The man starts out of the room. "And put on some boots if you've got 'em."

"Boots?" The man looks worried.

"Boots. Thick." He finishes opening the boxes of glue strips.

The man comes down the stairs, wearing boots, carting a shovel, a tennis racket and another pair of boots. "Here," he says to the woman, handing her the boots and tennis racket.

"In case he gets by me," the man says.

"He probably won't even get out of the bathroom," the exterminator says.

"Just in case," the man says. The woman puts on the boots and stands behind the man, holding the tennis racket.

"I'm going in," the exterminator says. "You ready?"

The man nods and the exterminator realizes that he's actually getting into this. "Ready," he says.

The exterminator opens the door and immediately sees the rat run under the large claw-foot bathtub. He lays the glue strips, one on each wall in front of the floorboards. The side with less adhesive sits toward the wall. The other, much stickier side, faces out to trap the rodent.

He gets in the tub, mallet in hand, and starts jumping up and down, trying to scare the rat out of hiding.

"Okay. Open the door," he says.

On the third jump, he catches his reflection in the mirror; a great yellow flash going up and down. His boots are dirtying the tub.

The exterminator senses the couple beginning to doubt him.

"Done it a thousand times," he lies. "Best method."

On the tenth or eleventh jump, the rat runs to the middle of the room. It looks one way then another. The man moves the shovel and the rat runs away from it, straight into a glue stick. Its two right legs are stuck to the board, the other two scrape against the black-and-white tiled floor making a high-pitched noise.

The exterminator gets out of the tub. "You might want to close the door now," he says. The man leaves the door open.

The exterminator brings the mallet down on the rat's skull. It makes the same crunching noise his boots made on the frozen ground. The rat rolls away from the blow and is now stuck full on its back. It lets out a moan that sounds almost human. A noise too big for such a small creature. The second hit ends it. Dark blood, the color of aged mahogany, trickles onto the glue strip.

The exterminator puts on gloves and takes the rat out to the van. He scrapes it, using the mallet, into a destruction box that he will take to the office destruction wing. The used glue strip is now garbage, the others he re-boxes and marks them with a check so anyone who uses them will know the protective layer has already been peeled.

He closes the van door and then opens it again. The light is dull, nearly out.

"Shit," he says.

In the house, the exterminator cleans what little mess there is out of the bathroom. He walks to the kitchen, where the couple sits at a modern table that seems out of place in a house full of old furniture.

"Coffee?" the woman says.

"I should get back to the office," the exterminator says. "Thanks, though."

She has the checkbook out. "What do we owe you?"

"No need to worry about that now," he says. "Billing handles all the money. It's fifty for the visit, plus the rate for whatever was killed. You do get a 5 percent discount, though."

"Why?" the man says.

"January," the exterminator says. "Rat is the pest of the month." Which is true. Every month, on the billboard outside the office, there is a five-foot by ten-foot poster of the pest of the month.

The exterminator once had a dream where he drove to work, saw himself on the billboard, and was gassed by fellow employees.

"That's . . ." The woman pauses. "Nice, I guess."

The couple thanks the exterminator as he leaves. He gives a little wave and walks to the van. More snow has fallen, is falling, and he stands again for a moment in the quiet motion.

He gets in the van and turns the key. The engine hints at turning over and then abandons itself. The exterminator turns the key again. The engine turns a little less. By the third turn of the key, the sound is reduced to a click. The exterminator surprises himself by not being angered at this. He steps out of the van and stands again in the snow.

The exterminator will:

In a moment, go inside and ask for a jump.

Go to the office.

Dump the rat and glue strip off to be cremated.

Log his hours.

Go home.

Feed Fausto.

Drink coffee.

Take a shower.

Watch TV.

Wait for his phone to ring.

Want a drink.

Read.

Listen to the clock tick beside his bed.

Try to sleep.

Read.

Listen to his heartbeat.

End up back at work tomorrow, killing things to pay the rent, driving around in a giant rat.

He will do all of these things, he is sure. But for now, the exterminator stands motionless in the swirling whiteness, unsure of his next step, looking up toward the source of the storm.

MATERNITY

Amy Gerstler

M Y sister squinched up her mouth into a mock pout. "When's the bliss going to kick in?" This was her refrain throughout her pregnancy. Other women we knew, first-time mothers, or those who'd produced fleets of kids, or authors of books on childbearing, all spoke of pregnancy's hormone-induced "highs": waves of euphoria, energy surges, peaks of libido. It seemed reasonable to expect that Tina, in her late thirties and pregnant with her first child, could look forward to some of these promised perks. Hopefully, all of them. But to our mutual regret, she detected no flashes of nirvana. Tina was seriously nauseated and mildly to deeply annoyed the entire nine months. She complained comically and a bit desperately about not being able to knock back cocktails just when she most needed a dose of chemical transcendence to dull the discomforts of carrying the growing load in her womb. During her sixth month, we were chatting when she abruptly dropped the phone. She was in Colorado, I was in California, and thanks to Alexander Graham Bell, I could hear my little sister retching and vomiting several states away. When she returned, she said raggedly, "Well, that was fun."

I don't think Tina enjoyed any aspect of being pregnant. The smell of percolating coffee, formerly a morning pleasure, made her ill. Her normally robust appetite deserted her, just when, for the first time in her life, everyone was urging her to EAT. Meals became a horrid chore. It was impossible to find a comfortable position to sleep in. Tina fought her obstetrician about drinking milk, a liquid she has always found repulsive, though low calcium caused her leg cramps. The prenatal vitamins she'd been instructed to take on an empty stomach made her puke. Her feet swelled. Like the majority of pregnant women I've known, she loathed maternity clothes, most of which look designed with a prissy, oversized toddler in mind.

Tina has never been one to hide her feelings. She complained loudly and often hilariously as her growing baby began elbowing and kicking her internal organs out of its way. I'd watched some of the most acidic and cynical of my friends go all gushy and earth goddess-ish when pregnant, and while I was of course happy for them, the major outlook shift made me feel like I didn't know them anymore. I preferred Tina's more curmudgeonly approach. It was consistent with her nonpregnant personality. I was relieved to hear my sister grumble and curse her way through the trimesters in an endearingly familiar manner. This was partly because it seemed healthy for her to vent, and partly because as she became more and more physically changed by pregnancy, her manic sense of humor told me in no uncertain terms that it was still feisty Tina in there, behind that mysterious, swelling watermelon belly.

A dancer/choreographer, my sister's been under pressure, from too young an age, to keep her weight unrealistically low. When she was eight or nine, the ballet troupe she was a member of began weighing each dancer weekly, in front of the whole company. A gained half-pound was cause for public humiliation. So Tina had an especially hard time with the girth of impending motherhood. "I look like a huge cow," she grumbled, sitting at my dining room table, glaring at a sweating can of ginger ale she'd requested but didn't drink. "You look sooo skinny. I'm not a person anymore. I'm just a blimp." She had on a short, sheer tent dress printed with giant daisies. Tina told me that a week ago, back home in Denver, she'd run into a woman she hadn't seen for years at a party. Tina was five months along, quite obviously pregnant. The woman kissed her on both cheeks, made small talk for a few minutes, and then flounced off to get a drink. Toward the end of the party, the woman returned and said, "Oh congratulations. I had no *idea* you were going to have a baby." Tina was livid and let the woman have it. "Oh, you just thought I turned into a tub of lard since we last saw each other?" she inquired, making no attempt to hide her fury. I kept telling Tina she looked beautiful pregnant, which was true. "Pregnant women look all ripe and sexy," I declared. "Is this another one of your harsh self-judgments? Do you think *you* look bad pregnant, but other women don't?" "No, all pregnant women look grotesque," she insisted, in tears. We'd come to a parting of the ways. I could do nothing for her. A pregnant woman, although she contains another human being, is freakishly alone. Over the years, I've become very accustomed to trying to cajole Tina out of attitudes I think should be edited from her belief system. My rights to lobby for her to think differently, to ease up on herself, to calm down, are outlined in the fine print of my older sister job description. Though I like to think I have a moderately successful track record when it comes to nudging Tina to alter her views, I could tell by the look on her face this time that she wouldn't budge. My position in her life and hers in mine were shifting even as we spoke. Our relationship was being eclipsed by a rapidly developing, higher priority allegiance. She was becoming someone's mother.

Luckily, there were a few moments when Tina seemed more relaxed about her temporary largeness — like the night she was at my house while a friend was visiting from New York. The three of us were joking around, drinking mineral water in my living room. Eight months along by this point, Tina kept flipping up the front of her dress and directing David to touch her tight, distended belly. Finally I said, in partial jest, as she became more insistent, thrusting her big gut at him for the third time, "Stop it, Tina, you're scaring David." She laughed and said, "I'm not frightening you, am I?" David smiled a little crookedly. "Tina, I'm a homosexual man and I'm not that comfortable with women's bodies. I don't *want* to touch your stomach. Is that okay?" She laughed and politely dropped her skirt.

Tina asked me to be present at the birth of her baby. It was a forceful invitation, issued repeatedly. I was flattered and moved that she wanted me there. I was also worried about my ability to do a "good job" of assisting her. I've never given birth and know next to nothing about labor or babies. I berated myself for my lack of medical knowledge and practical life experience. Why didn't I know how to do anything *real* or *useful?* When the time came, would I faint? Barf? Run out of the room? My guidebook, *The Birth Partner*, which I began studying, highlighter in hand, as though I were back in college with a physiology test in my immediate future, warned that newborns are incredibly slippery. So if the baby comes too soon, say, on the car ride to the hospital, the book said you should remove your shirt and catch the infant in that. I pictured myself standing around in my bra, holding a bloody squalling bundle wrapped in my favorite gray cashmere sweater, thinking, "okay, now what???" Tina's husband looked on admiringly and my sister reclined in the backseat of their car, pale and spent but smiling. I stood there trying to look heroic, blushing at my state of semiundress, and praying I wouldn't drop the squirmy little thing.

The fact that I was not the star of this show by a long shot didn't stop my obsessive fretting as Tina's due date, October 17, approached. How would I get from Los Angeles, where I live, to Oakland, where Tina and her husband had moved, in time to be there during the birth? Would the baby give us enough warning? I mentally addressed Tina's in utero daughter via long-distance ESP every day. *When you're ready to be born, wait for me to get there, Sidney. Please.* As Tina's due date drew closer I packed a small canvas bag with underwear, pajamas, a couple of books, toiletries, and a few rattling bottles from my extensive collection of vitamins and Chinese medicines. The agreement was that Tina's husband Jose would phone me when her contractions were an hour apart. Their obstetrician felt that should constitute enough advance notice to give me time to hop a plane and get to Oakland before the blessed event. Convinced I wouldn't make it there quick enough to beat the baby, I didn't know whether to mourn or be relieved about the possibility of missing the birth. My dreams began to feature various slapstick fuckups performed by me in the delivery room. I knocked the doctor over. I was somehow responsible for marching all sorts of unsanitary zoo animals in as Tina was giving birth. I found myself having a baby too, which I immediately misplaced. The rest of that dream was devoted to frantic searching for the lost child in a series of foggy, unfamiliar settings.

Since Tina's husband Jose was at first unsure whether he wanted to be in the delivery room when she gave birth to their daughter, I felt my presence was even more essential. Later, after he decided he'd brave watching his child enter the world, and after Tina had extracted promises from my parents that'd they'd try to race up from San Diego to attend the birth too, Tina told me she still wanted me there. "I'm going to need all the support I can get," she said. "And since you're never going to do this, it's your chance to see what it's like." I felt a pang hearing this. At forty-one, the possibility that I might ever have a child had pretty much evaporated. Though I'd never really wanted children, it was harder than I'd thought to reconcile myself to the fact that now it wasn't up to me. I *couldn't* procreate, even if I wanted to. I tried not to let my sister's remark make me feel old, washed up. For a day or so, which was as long as the funk lasted, I wondered if I was harboring the unfeminist misapprehension that by giving up the possibility of motherhood I had also relinquished my claim to full womanhood, whatever that might mean. Certainly, I didn't think my childless female friends were diminished or unwomanly. Was I worried that other women who were mothers, like my sister, would shun me a little, judge me as lacking, view me as some species of pitiful babyless creature, a bit freakish in her refusal to be fruitful in this basic way? *If I was a man*, I thought, *I could knock chicks up till I was well into my fifties or sixties, or longer. Look at Sam, Saul, Jim, Peter* . . . and I ran through the names of all the men I knew or had heard of who'd become midlife dads. Though I'd never planned to make use of it, I found to my surprise that I resented the idea of a time limit on my fertility. I didn't want outside forces to determine what was or wasn't within my power. It was hard to tell how much of the ache I felt at Tina's remark had to do with unrequited baby-longing (I had made up my mind long ago not to succumb to this urge but am certainly not immune to it), and how much was the result of the shocking realization that, like everyone else who has ever been born, I too am aging, and therefore all possibilities won't remain endlessly open to me.

Tina had intermittent contractions on a daily basis during the last, long month of her pregnancy. On Thursday afternoon, October 8, her contractions began occurring one hour apart. Jose called me with this information at about three P.M. I burst into tears, grabbed my overnight bag, shakily hugged my husband, and reserved a seat on the next available flight to Oakland, which was not till seven P.M. I drove to the airport two hours early, clutching my copy of *The Birth Partner,* in a state of great anxiety. I sat at my departure gate and ate a tasteless bean and cheese burrito that resembled a soggy white wallet, positive that by the time I got to Oakland, the baby would have arrived. During the flight, which was packed — the last commuter plane of the day — I stared out the window at acres of clouds and thought about how I was letting my sister down by getting to Oakland so slowly.

I was shocked when Jose and a still-pregnant Tina picked me up at the airport. My sister seemed the most jovial she'd been during her entire pregnancy. The end was in sight. If she was in labor now and could waddle around the airport making chipper conversation with me, then maybe this giving birth thing wasn't going to be as wrenching as I'd dreaded. Maybe it was going to be no big deal. Tina informed me that our parents would arrive in a few hours. It suddenly seemed an act of vast generosity for her to invite my parents and I to witness her daughter's birth. I made it, I thought, with a shiver of relief, dampened by the cold sweat of apprehension. I looked at my sister, and thought, *what on earth is about to happen to you, who are so dear to me?*

Later in the evening, our parents arrived, carrying raincoats, a transistor radio so my mother wouldn't miss any important sporting events, and a substantial amount of luggage. My mother was almost finished knitting a sort of Halloween costume for the baby — a pumpkin colored wool hat, with green knitted leaves instead of a tassel. We were all staying at Tina and Jose's house, with their three dogs and two cats. Everyone was keyed up, giddy, at a loss. The doctor had said not to go to the hospital until the contractions were five minutes apart, because we'd just be sent home. Tina's contractions slowed, and began ranging from between one-to-two hours apart. She'd go cross-eyed when she had one, or close one eye for the duration. We labeled these latter, one-eyed spasms "pirate contractions." She'd cradle her belly, or press a hand to her lower back, frown deeply, and gasp. The rest of us — our parents, her husband, and I — couldn't do much for her. We held our collective breath. When the contractions started getting closer together, thirty to forty minutes apart, I'd keep track of them on paper, as *The Birth Partner* advised, feeling excited and efficient, only to abandon my notetaking as the pains drifted farther apart again. While we waited for Tina to go into more active labor, she got tenser and tenser. She began to feel like she was letting everyone down by not having the baby right away. "I've gotten you all up here on false pretenses," she said repeatedly to my parents and me. Though we were tripping over each other to reassure her that we weren't impatient, that she'd have the baby soon enough, that we loved her, that we just wanted her to relax and to assist her in any way we could, the suspense was, as a Bronx-born friend of mine likes to say, *working our nerves.*

Tina swung back and forth between depression and fury. Two days ticked by. Everyone's awkward efforts to help her began backfiring. One night at dinner she got angry because she claimed I hadn't pricked the potatoes thoroughly enough before baking, causing some of them to split in the oven. After the meal, as I was cleaning up the kitchen, she yelled at me because I covered a dish of food with tin foil and put it into the refrigerator. These were things Tina wouldn't have noticed if she hadn't been wracked by contractions and strung out waiting for full-on labor to begin. "Tin foil is expensive!" she chided. "You use tin foil for *cooking* and *Saran Wrap* for storing food. What's the matter with you?" The same thing that was the matter with all of us, I suppose, including the dogs and cats. One cat wisely retreated to the top of a closet for the duration. We were all in an agony of fearful anticipation about the seemingly never arriving but inevitable birth.

Another day dragged by. Tension turned Tina into a kitchen dictator. Things had to be done just so or she went ballistic. If my mother was unloading the dishwasher and she put the coffee mugs away in the wrong closet, Tina was genuinely offended. If I put food back on the incorrect shelf in the refrigerator, or put flowers she'd received into the wrong vase, meaning not the vase Tina would have chosen, she took it personally and seemed pained, which made me feel terrible, as she was in enough pain already. At one point, I found her sprawled on the kitchen floor, a filthy dishtowel in her hand, unable to get up. She'd been cleaning underneath the stove. She wasn't hurt, just too heavy to get up off the linoleum without assistance. "Can't that job wait till after you have the baby, or maybe forever?" I tried to joke as I hauled her to her feet. "I try to keep my house clean, no matter what," she sniffed, implying that I don't, which is unfortunately quite true. I'm not brave enough to even peek under my stove.

My father hated to see his wife and two daughters drawing battle lines in that traditional female war zone, the kitchen. His lower lip began to protrude a little. He lapsed into silences that lasted for big chunks of the day. He badly wanted to take care of Tina, to erase her pain. Since he couldn't do that, he decided, consciously or unconsciously, to try to take care of me, as a sort of proxy. With gentlemanly concern, hands jammed deep into his pants pockets, he ordered me several times a day to *sit down for god's sake* if I was drinking a cup of coffee, *or you'll ruin your digestion!* He told me to put on a jacket every time I went outside, even if it was only to fetch the mail, even if it was eighty degrees out. He asked me if I was hungry or cold at least nine times a day and looked like he didn't believe me when I said no. He pointed out the exact spot on the bridge of my nose where I must perch my reading glasses for optimum vision. He tried to compel me to eat breakfast, a doomed endeavor if ever there was one. I tried hard not to slide into some old parent/child power struggle with him, but I was getting irritated enough to need to bite the inside of my cheek so I didn't snap: *I'll drink this coffee standing on my head if I like. I'm an adult now, in case you hadn't noticed.* I reminded myself: Here is the sweet man who sired you, flummoxed because this is one situation he can't resolve by paternal edict or aid. Tina's response to my father's ministrations, when he made the mistake of aiming them at her was a tart, "Who asked you?" her new favorite expression. He quickly retreated and went back to trying to daddy me.

At ten P.M. that night, Sunday, October 11, I was tapping out a complaining e-mail to my husband. My family's patience with me and mine with them was wearing thin. Jose stuck his head into the downstairs family room where I was typing and quietly announced that Tina's contractions were now ten minutes apart. He'd phoned the hospital. They'd said to bring her in to see if her labor had progressed enough so that she could stay there and give birth tonight or tomorrow. I'd just taken a sleeping pill in an attempt to rest better than I had the previous three nights, when I'd slept in my clothes like a fireman, thinking I'd have to leap up in the middle of the night to rush to the hospital. Now I was worried I'd fall asleep during the important hours ahead. But that didn't happen. Not even close. Adrenaline must have chemically counteracted the pill completely.

We arrived at the hospital and proceeded to the "birthing center," a new name for the maternity ward. Tina and Jose were whisked into "triage," an area with many curtained exam cubicles, where she was given the first of what seemed like hundreds of pelvic exams that night. This one was to determine whether she'd be allowed to remain, or get sent home. Four centimeters dilated (a woman's cervix is ten centimeters when the baby is born) was the verdict. Tina was told she could stay. We were shown to a private labor and delivery room that had a big bed in it for Tina and a couch at one end under a large window. There was a plastic hooded warming table near the door, covered by a flannel receiving blanket printed with rattles and diaper pins, which the baby would be placed on. Our parents sat on the couch pretty consistently from the time Tina was admitted till the baby appeared, like two watchful owls perched on the same branch. Our mother kept remarking how much hospital childbirth had changed since her day. "When are they going to shave her?" she asked at some point. "Aren't they going to give her an enema?" Tina and I explained that those things aren't done routinely anymore. My mother was particularly fascinated by the two monitors seatbelted to Tina's belly during most of the proceedings. The first graphed her contractions as a bright green jagged line on a small screen. The second was an audio monitor of the baby's heartbeat, which, when the volume was turned up periodically by the nurses, sounded like hoofbeats, or some staticky Morse code from a remote galaxy.

From what I've observed, there's a sort of competitive fem-machismo among women in some circles about giving birth without narcotics. All the women I know who've had children asked me, "Did she have drugs?" within the first two questions when inquiring how Tina's birth experience went. Tina and Jose were both adamantly pro-drug from the beginning. Their obstetrician approved. Jose felt so strongly he was moved to stand up at their third birthing class and declare to the group of expectant mothers, fathers, and the two instructors that in his opinion any woman who'd have a baby without pain-mitigating drugs was stupid, a masochist, or both. Needless to say, he was the focus of many attendees' indignation. Luckily, Tina gave birth before the next class session took place, so that was Jose's last speech to such an unreceptive audience. At one end of the debate, there's the antidrug camp that believes women should bear any and all labor pain so the newborn doesn't get pumped full of drugs during birth. I had always considered myself an informal member of this group. After seeing my niece born, I honestly don't know what to think. Clearly, both approaches have merits. At the other pole are lots of women, doctors, etc., who, like Jose, are militant about the mother *taking* drugs for the intense and protracted pain of childbirth. Obviously, there's a lot of territory between these two positions. One editor I spoke to, a peppy mother of three who'd had babies both drugged and undrugged, said, "I have one word of advice for your sister: *epidural.*"

Tina ended up having the unusual and dubious distinction of having *two* epidurals, because the first one "slipped" at some point, as her labor grew more intense. This meant that painkilling drugs being dripped into her system by a thin tube inserted into her back had somehow gone from being effectively delivered to the correct area, to getting misdispensed into some anatomical no-man's-land where they gave her no relief at all. They might as well have been dribbling into the spanking clean industrial sink across the room. You have to hold as still as you possibly can when an anesthesiologist administers an epidural, because squirming could cause a misplaced jab that might damage your spinal cord. Toward the end of Tina's labor, when the epidural had to be reinserted, she was instructed to remain absolutely still for several minutes, sitting on the bed, legs crossed, completely hunched over into a ball, so the anesthesiologist could get optimum access to the targeted part of her back. She was supposed to do this even though she was being racked by towering contractions every thirty seconds or so. I know the contractions were towering because I watched them on the monitor. They had gone from looking like little anthills to resembling tracings of great mountain ranges. The most difficult part about seeing my niece born was watching my sister in abject agony during parts of labor, most notably during the period of time between when her epidural went awry and when the hospital staff figured out what had gone wrong and readministered it. Even though they responded fairly quickly, I had to restrain myself from yelling at them to HURRY. I had seen Tina in pain before, from dance injuries or childhood accidents — like the time she got her fingers slammed in our neighbor's car trunk, which automatically locked, and then no one could find the keys for a while while Tina screamed and screamed. But this labor pain was way off the charts, beyond comparison.

After the second epidural finally began to take effect, Tina seemed less tortured. By this time, it was morning. Standing between Tina's legs (o honored position!) during this last stage of her labor, I found myself with the sole of one of Tina's feet rammed against my chest, just below the shoulder, as she lay on her back and worked to push her daughter out. A nurse's aide was holding Tina's other leg in a similar position. I had a lot of affection for the banged-up dancer's foot I was now getting to contemplate at such close range. I'd often seen it in pink satin toe shoes, and watched it pound the hard wooden floors of modern dance rehearsal spaces, unshod. Then, most of the toes were bandaged with white surgical tape. But my attention was drawn from the foot firmly planted below my collarbone to other, pinker regions of Tina's anatomy.

My main surprise about seeing a birth, and this is so simplistic it's embarrassing, was that I'd never properly appreciated the enormous physical effort involved in pushing a baby out, at the very end, when it's actually emerging from the woman's body. Of course, I knew you had to push to give birth, and hard. I'd seen Westerns where a woman has to stop the wagon train to have a baby. She pants. Her forehead gets a little sweaty. As we were growing up, our mother would repeatedly tell us that childbirth was just like taking a difficult shit. I've since heard others repeat versions of this earthy truism. I can only say that as I watched my sister bear down with every fiber, grunting and yelling and yes, defecating a little ochre ribbon, I thought that if she were a cartoon character her eyeballs would have popped out and rolled crazily across the linoleum. Tina's face was purple. Her neck veins stood out and her neck contracted into her shoulders when she pushed, as though she were a turtle pulling into its shell. In the throes of a big push, I hardly recognized her. I thought her cranium was going to explode and her brains come spewing out of her ears. The maternity nurses, who were some of the most admirable women I've ever met, were nodding sagely and SMILING encouragingly, as if pleasing progress was being made, as if it were perfectly fine that my sister was eggplant colored and was about to blow all her organs out of her body in some awful visceral geyser. Nurses were telling Tina to push harder, as if that were humanly possible, or to wait for the next contraction, or to push from "lower down in her pelvis," whatever the hell that might mean. Tina seemed to understand. A greenish fluid came sluicing out shortly before the baby did, flecked with what looked like bits of drenched cotton. The liquid smelled like hot, melted wax and sourish seawater — some long-simmered, inside-of-the-body smell. Since the morning I saw my niece born, I could swear I've gotten whiffs of that odor several times when I've been in unwashed crowds — in the lobby of a bank, waiting on a long line at the post office. It must be the scent of some primary human ingredient.

I've seen my sister naked plenty of times over the years, both as a child and an adult. Tina's utterly unselfconscious about nudity, so the sight of her cheerful brown pubic fluff did not surprise me. But I certainly wasn't used to squinting down her vagina as though it was a lane in a bowling alley involved in a big game I was following closely. By the time she had her baby, though, the inside of her rosy canal seemed more familiar than the street I live on. Just about EVERYONE in the hospital had been rummaging around in there, hands buried to the wrist in her tissue, giving their (often conflicting) opinions about how dilated she was, and about how soon she would go from being a woman in labor to an actual mother. Tina was perfectly comfortable with both my parents and half the hospital staff staring at various times into the tunnel of her sex organ. This is another of the many differences between us, I thought, as I watched her escalating contractions sketch themselves on the monitor. I don't know how well I'd handle being the subject of this complete a suspension of modesty. I don't even like being seen in a bathing suit.

During this late, intense stage of labor, with my sister's foot pushing against my breastbone, the most expert of the nurses kept plunging her gloved hands into Tina and holding the upper reaches of her vagina open to reveal what looked like a round rock—a piece of streaked granite a little smaller than a baseball. Blood had been slopping out of Tina for a while now, some liquid, some jellyish, spattering the floor, the bed, my shirt. The nurse was trying to help ease the rock, which was supposedly a baby's head, down the birth canal. When Tina pushed, the rock/head would move a little farther down, toward us, toward being born, and then it would recede again, swallowed back up by the crimson wadding inside Tina's body. It seemed like the nurse was trying to haul a small but immensely heavy stone up out of a well of red sucking mud, and the mud was winning. The petite round rock was crisscrossed with broken, gloppy strands of blood, and for a second I stupidly thought, *oh no, the baby's head is bleeding,* because my mental processes had gone into some sleep-deprived wipeout. Then the nurse wiped the strings of blood away with a rubber-clad finger during one push when the top of the head appeared again, like a shy planet, way up inside my sister. Blood was soaking through paper drapes, which were continually being placed under Tina's hips and changed every few minutes. There was enough blood on the floor that when new nurses came into the room they had to be warned not to slip in it.

The nurse in charge dumped what seemed like half a bottle of mineral

oil into Tina's vagina to help lube the baby out. The black streaks on the
rock that had made it look like granite became readable as matted, wet hair.
How far does this poor baby have to travel now? I wondered. It can't be
more than ten inches or so, but it seems like the world's most arduous jour-
ney. I'm sure this is a thought everyone who's witnessed a birth has had. My
sister was bearing down with all her might, her face violet-red and bal-
looning, doing three or four ten-second pushes during each contraction
while we all counted off the seconds and tried to cheer her on. The rock,
which I knew but didn't believe was a baby's head, was getting closer.
Eventually, it began to verge on showing, without the nurse having to part
Tina's flesh. You could see a little slice of the top of the cranium starting to
peek out. In a gentle voice, the tall expert nurse asked my sister if she
wanted to reach down between her legs and touch her baby's head. My sis-
ter screamed at the tops of her lungs, in a way that was both dire and hilar-
ious, NO! I DON'T WANT TO TOUCH THE HEAD! I WANT THIS
BABY OUT OF THERE, NOW!! Then things began happening fast for
the first time in a week. It seemed Tina was going to split. Her face turned
dark purple. She yelled a yell that made Tarzan sound soft-spoken. In
another minute the alleged baby's head was out. I could only see the back
of it, which still looked like a mossy stone. Then the rock swiveled toward
me about ninety degrees and I could see, being less than a foot away, that
the rock had a very particular individual face on it. A face that was mov-
ing. I don't know when I've beheld anything eerier. I went wild. I started
yelling like a psychotic, "Tina, push, push, it really is a baby, come on, come
on, it's almost out, it has black hair, it has lips, PUSH PUSH!!!!!" The rest
of the baby seemed to slither out almost on her own in the next few prodi-
gious pushes. The baby's labia were big and inflamed, which I have since
learned is normal. They looked like a fuschia-hued caricature of female
genitals. Then there was the umbilical cord, like some rubbery rope made
of superthick purple pasta, kinked like old-fashioned telephone cords are.
The placenta burbled out, resembling a gelatinous conglomeration of a
year's worth of menstrual fluid. It was dumped into a giant silver cup that
looked quite pagan for a hospital receptacle, or like a bowling trophy. The

baby's official birth time was six minutes after noon on October 12, 1998. Healthy and slim-bodied, she was lilac-colored for the first few minutes of her life — a pale dusky purple that reminded me of a shade of powdered eye shadow popular when I was in junior high.

The Birth Partner made a big point of saying that right after the baby is born, one of the most useful things you can do is talk to the infant, let her know how happy you are to see her, reassure her that she's slithered into a friendly environment. That way, hopefully, the baby feels comforted and soothed rather than violated and distressed while nurses' gloved hands briskly perform routine postpartum hospital procedures upon her — cleaning, inspecting, measuring, suctioning, swabbing, etc. I had spent the last fourteen hours, make that the last few weeks, make that the last nine months, aching to find ways to aid and abet my sister in her amazing maternal endeavor, and feeling mostly useless and ineffectual. So I cooed at her baby with great dedication. Drunk with emotion, I repeated the baby's newly applied name to her over and over again, as though that would help it adhere like some kind of protective bandage. I kept saying her name like it was the only word I knew. Then I managed to add the word, "Hi." I spoke in the most welcoming tones I could muster, and watched her wiggle her feet and pinch her fingers experimentally together. Her skin quickly pinkened. I expected my one-sided tête-à-tête with the newborn to be like talking to a zombie or a sleeping person, but unnervingly, the baby appeared to be staring right at me as I babbled creaturely greetings.

Tina was getting sewn up. She hadn't had an episiotomy, but there were still a few small tears in her vagina that needed mending. Two efficient neonatal nurses, whispering to each other, were evaluating her daughter on the warming table, ticking off numbered items on a list. My sister turned her head toward me and said, "You have blood on your face, you have blobs of blood in your hair. Go get cleaned up." I could tell by the look on her face that she thought I looked somewhat amusing, but also gross. I was going to sass her back and say, "If you think I'm a mess, you should see what you look like from the waist down," but instead I just did what I was told, though I was a little reluctant to wash Tina's blood off.

BED AND BRIMSTONE

Bart Edelman

The tussle of love
Knuckles between us;
Red sheets askew
Before a blue fire
Burns the bed black.
By the next morning
Only powdered ash remains
And the white heat that hovers
Above our prickly pink skin.
Now we know how easily
Desire consumes the souls
We were saving for God,
Long before it became time
To find an acre of Paradise
In the only garden
Worthy of being named Eden.
Here is where we return,
Again and again to learn
The apocryphal lesson
Lust has in mind for us
When it slithers through the grass
On its empty belly.
Yet, for the moment,
Our only worry is simply
The replacement of the bed
And the sheer cost involved

To clean up the residue,
Ridding the room of smoke
And the smell of brimstone —
We seem unable to escape.

THE FECALITY OF IT ALL

Benjamin Weissman

*Reader beware, this is not a pee story in the true sense of Number One, it is with-
out question a Two; but peeing does take place, and without the expulsion of urine
none of this would be worth telling. What happened yesterday could only happen to
me. The sad events narrated herein speak to the core of who I am. Why this is the
case I do not know. By sharing this story with others I will not learn more about
myself, but I do it anyway because that's all I really have: accidents and memories
and then a little theatrical show and tell for a select audience to whom I can hold
my head high in shame.*

THE morning started like any other: I staggered out of bed, shuffled
down the hall, dog and cat in tow. George, the cat with black and white
tuxedo paws, wanted out. He's never grown up. He's small and has remained
a kitten. Gina, the dog, craved breakfast. I filled the kettle with Arrowhead,
turned on the gas flame, fed Gina lamb-rice pellets in warm water, and
brewed coffee. Then I entered the bathroom, not to j.o., just poo. The smell
of coffee triggers the *movement*. I have always been as regular as the sunrise.
Thank you very much, but it's not a talent, it's a court order. I picked up a
catalog of children's toys (nephew's birthday approaching), and let loose a
gargantuan log. I screamed as it came out. From the bedroom, my sleeping
Bride asked if it was a boy or a girl? Both, I shouted back. Still clothed in
T-shirt, pajamas, and white socks, I gulped some coffee, read the morning
paper (the new prime minister of Israel was once a military assassin who
dressed up as a woman and killed three members of the PLO). In one quick

motion the Bride is out of bed, in and out of the shower, driving across
town to get her hair cut — all this without a sip of coffee or a single scrap
of food. I hunker down in front of the TV and resume the arduous task of
dubbing rented porn tapes (three a day, just the good parts). I title the tape,
"Rhymes with Corn." During each edit I drink deep from a 64-ounce
Nalgene bottle of water. After thirty minutes I refill the jug and drink more.
Dubbing porn dehydrates me. In forty-five minutes I've drank 128 ounces
of fresh, mountain spring water. (Many a fool has been attacked in a bath-
room after a predator, lying in wait, patiently observes his subject guzzling
beer, usually at a neighborhood bar, pool hall, or bowling alley, it can hap-
pen anywhere — the bladder fills, the cheerful unsuspecting drinker stum-
bles into the men's room whistling dixie, faces the urinal, unzips trou; while
the subject releases his full bladder the perpetrator of pain strolls in and finds
his vulnerable, stiff-legged victim, looking down or straight ahead, it doesn't
matter, nothing in the world would make his face turn and look, unless he
was under five foot eight, short guys need to be on the defensive, it's a full-
time job; if the abovementioned thug called out the urinator's name he'd
continue to stare at the round rubber thing with holes in it that prevents
splashing and encourages American males not to use drugs; during this pro-
tracted sixty seconds the attacker, who never had it so easy, strikes the blad-
der releaser on the back of the head, and out he goes.) Soon I must urinate.
I go to the bathroom and find the aforementioned big poop from an hour
earlier still in the pot. Not in its natural configuration, but roughed up by
the previous flushing. I pee on top of it, and then flush. Here is where our
story begins: The XXL doesn't go down. It chooses a different direction. It
resists gravity and pipes, the common sewer system journey, and travels
upward, toward heaven. As the water rises to the rim of the toilet I'm think-
ing the usual, this isn't possible, not here, not on this street, in this town. But
yes, it will happen — your secret, morbid life erupts, the toilet overflows
with your soft sculpture. The "mirror phase" and the "potty period" and all
the other psychological stages that you never quite made it through come
to mind because you are not a mature person. Adult in age, not by action
or thought. I was calm, enveloped in self-reflection as fecal water poured

onto the tile floor. As murky water approached my feet I hopped onto the counter, took off my socks, rolled up my blue-and-white-striped pajamas, and waited for it to end. A very familiar grape leaf floated by. Just a fragment. Everything up to this point could not have been avoided. Here I made my first mistake. I scooted off the counter, stepped barefoot into the mire, and flushed the toilet a second time (in all fairness to myself, the genius, the plunger was downstairs in my playpen, my office, I had been drawing pictures of it). Several more gallons of water flooded out into the bathroom, down the hall, and into the Bride's work cubicle. It was time to move into action: Green light on rescue operation. A tornado of shit halts your melancholic, porno-dubbing life and slams it to the ground. You grab a bucket and a dry, aging, sponge mop that practically says, *who me? I can't do anything,* and go at it. You start in the bathroom, where the tragedy began, and work your way out. After two useless minutes the sponge peels off the frame of the mop so you grab the oldest, least attractive beach towels in the closet and commit them to biohazard. A ninety-minute job which included a final rinse of Pine Sol. When the woman you refer to as "The Bride" returns, you are in the kitchen, in a room that has not been damaged, but you are so obsessed with cleaning, with turning around the malicious direction of your life that you can't stop yourself. Just by rubbing you can make a stain vanish from the earth. That's a powerful act. The Bride looks even more beautiful than when she left, especially from the floor, which is where you are, on hands and knees, mouth open, a broken-off piece of sponge in one hand. You are fond of this hapless sponge. It pitched in. It did what it could and stayed with you to the end. Not many sponges would do that. You'd kiss it if you were alone with it.

"You got inspired to clean," the Bride says. "How nice of you."

"I wish I could take credit for such a noble gesture, but I can't," you say, sounding strange. "That's not what happened."

"What happened?" she says, removing her leather jacket, dropping her beautiful black purse on the table.

"Something terrible happened," you say, and then you retell the story. A big shit, massive overflow, no plunger, a second flushing, water everywhere.

"Poor you," she says, "that's awful."

And then, like always, you go too far with your descriptions. "Yeah, I even saw the grape leaves I ate yesterday."

"Yuck," she says. "Now I'm going to barf."

Why would you tell her something like that? You look down and see another spot on the floor and rub it out, then another. Soon the Bride, who frequently takes on the role of nurse with you, tries to lift the pitiful patient off the floor but he weighs too much. She tells him to stop cleaning.

"It's over," she says and kneels down, kisses your sweaty forehead. She is infinitely kind. "I'm going to make myself a fruit drink, do you want some?"

"Can you smell it?" you ask.

She tilts her ballet dancer face back, and sniffs. "Well . . ." she says, and closes her eyes for fine tuning. "Sort of."

You stand, a little lightheaded (ah, the elephant rises). Suddenly there's nothing to do. The job's done but you won't let go of the sponge.

The Bride walks into the bathroom and lights a tiny pyramid of incense. You go down to your playpen in the basement thinking this would make a good story. In a way, you enjoyed the experience.

Sometimes you leave your laptop computer on all night and that's what you did last night. When you approach your desk you see water everywhere, books, papers, and drawings soaked, and a smell even worse than your previous upstairs encounter. First you were ankle-deep in goop. Now you are under it, a thin layer of feces above you. You look up and see a big coffee colored drip.

Say it, "I defecated on my computer."

You just clean and clean, that's what you were put on earth to do. You mess yourself, you wipe, you crawl around, and then you clean some more. You pick up all the sopping wet papers, smeared and stained, and throw them in the trash — don't even think about what you've ruined, just dump it all in the basket. Oh look, all your plunger drawings. You hang them out to dry on the clothesline, thirty of them, reeking and streaked with brown. Since you're one of the infirmed it makes sense that you live and work in your pajamas. Now scamper upstairs like a nice boy and tell the pretty lady what else has happened. The whole process is second nature to you. You take all the dung-infested books outside and stand them upright with the pages fanned out. Maybe they'll dry without sticking to each other. But is it really possible to read Emily Dickinson when you know that every page has been simmering in your own excrement?

How do you get something like this repaired? If you send feces in the mail the government will prosecute you. It is indecent and against the law. Even though you're a person with a short fuse none of this has caused a serious tantrum. In fact, you have not reacted. You're numb and at peace. Your breath is steady, and that terrible smell is fading, or so you'd like to believe.

O please, dear reader, drop that stone. Do not judge me, for I am an unfortunate person, a silly man, who doesn't know up from down. Open your heart, diaper me. Lay me down in my crib. Press a cold compress to my brow. Let me rest. My world has caved in and I am weary. If there's a lesson to be learned maybe it's this: If you feel a giant number two coming on flush it down in installments, not all at once; and if your plunger moonlights as a model for figure drawing, make sure you acquire a second plunger that is young and full of appropriate suction. Humble is the man who is backed against the wall by his own bowel movement. Lest we need to be reminded, the rear end is the devil's public address system, it points in the opposite direction for a reason, to contradict all the good the face and eyes create, and it will always steer us into hell.

FRIED CHICKEN

Erik Himmelsbach

SHANE Goldberg had the best tits in the seventh grade. They were fucking huge — at least a C-cup, I shit you not — and you could actually see the nipples (big, round, Crayola pink) under his clingy, tight-ass rugby shirts. Not that I spent a lot of time looking at them. Not really. You just couldn't help it — they bounced and bobbled when he moved, even if he was just squeezing out of his desk to sharpen his pencil — and, unfortunately, you could hardly expect as much from most of the girls at Sepulveda Junior High School.

Sure, some of the ladies-to-be wore tube tops, but it was wishful thinking more than anything else; the formless fabric wrapped around their yet-to-develop bodies like large, colorful rubberbands. But at least those few girls whose boobs were beginning to sprout stood reasonably at attention. By contrast, Shane's were hardly of the perky variety. He was clearly a future sagster, a prime candidate for liposuction with a Prozac chaser down the road.

Basically, Shane could've used a bra. Which was something he was constantly reminded of. When you're a fat kid with tits, you sit with an anchor around your ankle at the bottom of the foodchain. You avoid certain people in the halls. You learn alternate routes home. It messes with your head.

Poor Shane. He just made it so damn easy for any asshole with an attitude; he might as well have had a target on his back. Shooting fish in a barrel, it was: He was a freckled, gelatinous, curly redhead who walked without ever seeming to lift his feet, in a sort of shuffle-wobble. Wearing his bumblebee-colored shirts, Toughskin floods, and yellow canvas Adidas with blue stripes, he looked for all the world like Bobo the Clown wrapped in flesh. Given the chance (meaning whenever he was with people even more pathetic than himself), he bragged about his stylin' dad, a man whose American Dream had come true: He owned a Pioneer Fried Chicken franchise somewhere out in Simi Valley. Woo fucking hoo.

To most of us, Simi Valley was in another universe, yet it was only separated from the San Fernando Valley by about ten miles of mountain range. It was just like us, only cleaner, newer, and whiter, like our Valley had probably been twenty years earlier, when post–WWII prosperity flowed like flooded storm drains on Nordhoff and Woodley during a heavy rain.

Simi was a brand spanking new suburb, or at least that's what they told us. We couldn't drive yet, and even if we could, how the hell would we get there? The 118 freeway wasn't finished; it was a stretch of only a few miles, stopping suddenly in Granada Hills, dumping you on Balboa in the north central Valley, where orange trees still grew and the neighborhood streets were bereft of sidewalks. To get to Simi, you had to venture through the winding hills of the Santa Susana Pass, past Chatsworth, past the Friday night hang Stoney Point (or Stoner's Den, depending on whether you were a hiker or a toker), past the Manson family's Spahn Ranch, whose stench of death had only just begun to fade.

Simi may have been where Shane and his family found peace, prosperity, and lots of white people, but things were a lot more treacherous at school. Am I being too hard on the guy? I don't think so. I mean, that jokey Yiddish stuff you share with your family may be a hoot when you're leaning against the shiny industrial fridge in the kitchen at Pioneer Chicken headquarters, as the El Salvadorean illegals clean dishes wearing yellow gloves that go up to their elbows. But when you use the word *meshugina* as a punch line at P. E., brag that Morey Amsterdam — a family friend — will be at your Bar Mitzvah, or proudly serve up *kreplach* at ethnic food day in history class when everyone else brings lasagna and tacos, you're in deep shit. The cross-burning fantasies begin dancing in the heads of those second-generation inbred sons of Okies — those whose lives, we liked to say, would peak in ninth grade. You could almost see the thought balloons materialize as their minds revved up to sixteen rpm and they smacked their lips, real slow like: "Hmmm, where does Dad keep them white hoods?"

Those of us who got it, who were quietly dealing with our own Jewishness — fellow tribe members with surnames like Moss, Rosen, and Klein — kept our heads down and stayed out of it. We pretended that we, too, had no idea what he was saying, muttering, "What a dick," under our breath. C'mon, only a moron knew not to leave it at home. Besides, very few of us had a burning desire to mimic the bad jokes cousin Saul told at the Seder.

Yet in spite of all this, I became Shane's friend, at least for a while. What the hell. I met him on the first day of summer school, when it's all a crapshoot anyway. You have no idea who's cool, so you chat away and deal with the fallout later on. I always figured it better to small talk the loser than sit alone at my desk, surrounded by kids who had no interest in talking to me. Validation is validation, right? I hated to have to pretend to be busy, even if it was just to draw the Kiss logo on a Pee-Chee folder, using each of the four colors on that big blue Bic pen. And I didn't even like Kiss.

Truth was, in my head, Shane and I weren't too far apart. Except that I didn't have the neighborhood, the married parents, or the chicken franchise. I was a latchkey kid living in a shabby two-bedroom apartment on rundown Langdon Avenue with my mom and whoever she happened to be sleeping with that night. Mom and her friend Bunny, who lived across the courtyard, spent most of their evenings at Randy Pasqual's Gold Rush, a saloon down in an industrial part of Roscoe across the street from the Van Nuys Airport, where the clientele, I imagined, were guys with droopy mustaches, pointed boots, and big belt buckles. Their pores oozed with the rank scent of stale Budweiser. I think Mom got beat up sometimes by these guys. That's probably why our apartment manager's kid brother spent the night a few times. At least he didn't hit her. It was weird — he'd slink in after I'd fallen asleep and would just leave and not talk to me as he sped out in the morning, pulling on his shirt and zipping up his fly. I barely had time to look up from my Count Chocula. It made me depressed and sad, and I began to think my Mom was cheap and sad. Mothers just didn't act this way. Not my friends' mothers, anyway. This is why my friends never came over. That, and the leaky roof, and the shag carpet, and the black-and-white TV.

The sketchiness I confronted at home bled into my life at school. My M.O. was to bob and weave, never reveal too much, leave only a shadow in their memory. I didn't want to seem like one of those messed-up kids, and I could always spot them. You'd hear the last names of their parents and they'd be different, and they were never smart or cool. I wasn't sure where I fell in the pecking order, so I straddled many fences before I settled somewhere I felt comfortable. It was all very strategic, figuring out who would have me as their friend. I was like a dog sniffing another dog's butt, making sure I could deal with the odor, and wouldn't be rejected because I stunk too much. I guess you could say I had my nose in Shane's butt for a little while.

He was happy, ecstatic to have me as a friend. After all, I worked so hard at my own façade that I sometimes began to believe my own hype (at least until I got home). That made this a safe little power thing, because it was clear who had control. I got to choose the activities, the movies, the fast food. And admittedly, I was silently intrigued by the Jewish thing, since I was in Hebrew school and was on the Bar Mitzvah track.

Besides, it was summer. And summer was more flexible than the school year. It never really counted, not like those two twenty-week semesters. You'd sign yearbooks with "K.I.T." and scrawl your phone number. But you'd only even see your best friends a few times in those three months, maybe a trip to the beach with your boogie board via the RTD bus, taking the 88 from Plummer and Balboa to the 83 at Wilshire and Westwood, right in front of Ships, which took you straight to Santa Monica. Mostly, it was as if everyone had vaporized when the weather turned warm.

So Shane and I went to movies, played tennis, and I even spent the night at his house once. It was easy, insta-company, a diversion from my usual solitary amusement, playing a game of my own concocting that involved a deck of playing cards and baseball cards. Then summer ended, and it was over. The exhibition season had concluded and he didn't make the cut. I dumped him cold, pretending he didn't exist. First day of school. New clothes, new notebooks, new people. All these people!

Shane found me on Day One, before fifth period, putting books in my locker. I never looked up, fixing my gaze on the combination lock in front of me. I was a block of ice.

"Hello there," he said in that annoying, sing-songy, borscht-belt way. "Did you get Mr. Bell for science?"

"Yup."

"Great. Maybe we can sit next to each other. You know," he said, lowering his head and voice. "I hear he's a flamer. He wears pink shirts and key lime–colored shoes. And he talkth jutht like thith." Shane flipped a limp wrist downward, attempting the universal fag symbol.

Silence. I remained hunched down, knees bent, pulling out some books. I wasn't playing along, and he knew it. Shane stood over me, his weight nervously shifting from left to right. No explanations were needed; he knew the score. Time's up.

For me, sacrificing this giant kosher turkey meant I could make the next three school years more tolerable. I knew that walking the halls on the first day of school. I looked around and saw the possibilities, and they all led back to a place I didn't feel like going: inside my own life. The bottom line was I could do better. My friend Richard Espinoza once gave me sage advice: Women are like cars. You have to trade up. Maybe it was like this with friends, too.

I was long over Shane when I received the thick envelope in the mail, addressed to me with what looked like gold–leaf calligraphy. Inside was an invitation, an RSVP card, and a smaller envelope, already stamped. All of the paper was strangely textured, like they used designer trees to make the pulp. "It would be our pleasure to have you worship with us at the Bar Mitzvah of our son, Shane Laurence, at the Ventura Club in Studio City," the invitation read.

Oh, man. I knew Bar Mitzvah season was upon us, since I, too, was a Bar Mitzvah boy. And where you held your reception meant everything. It was class, stature, and coolness all wrapped up into one. The pantheon, from a kid's perspective, was the Odyssey, a yarmulke-shaped restaurant. Carved into the Mission Hills, its sign sat majestically in view of commuters on the 405 north toward Sylmar. It was like the Hollywood sign to a twelve-year-old Jewboy from Northridge, who would no doubt make a serious pact with God to memorize his Torah portion really well in order to experience manhood there.

But to the old-school Encino Jews with money — the ones who'd moved to the Valley from New York twenty years earlier — the two holy grails were the Sportsman's Lodge and the Ventura Club. Adorned with dark woods and red velvet curtains, they reeked of eastern respectability, the kind that big fat guys who looked like bullfrogs could appreciate. These were the domain of the gray and hairy-chested men who began playing tennis in the mid-seventies, and thought backgammon was the shit. They'd hit the motherlode in retail at one of the new malls but they still played cards every Tuesday night with Morty and Meyer and Sammy from high school. All of them had bought ranch homes in Woodland Hills and went to temple on the high holidays to remind themselves that they were Jews.

Two horrific thoughts entered my head when I received Shane's invitation. One, of course, was the prospect of actually going. I hadn't so much as spoken with him for months, yet I would be expected to attend and pretend like nothing had ever happened. The other problem was protocol. Here's where I was really fucked — I was now obliged to invite Shane to my own Bar Mitzvah. It was scheduled to be held a few months later at the Denny's of banquet halls — Nob Hill, a low-budget alternative for single moms who ask their older, financially successful brothers to flip the bill. It sat cheesily on Van Nuys Boulevard in Panorama City, across the street from the Big Boy and Arcade U.S.A., where I often went to inhale smoke and play Fireball while the older, more bitchen kids shot pool. The faded, second-rate Nob Hill told too much of the story of my life, a tale I'd skillfully kept from all those I wanted to invite and sit with me at the table of honor. And now I had to ask Shane, as well.

Shane was probably allotted ten guests who weren't relatives or his parents' friends. This usually meant five kids from Hebrew school who had even fewer social skills than he did (they wore polyester slacks when everyone wore denim; they wore yarmulkes in public when they didn't have to), some hideous yenta girl Shane had a "secret" crush on, and whoever he could round up from school, meaning anyone who hadn't pulled his pants down, thrown him into a trash can, or tossed him up against a wall of lockers.

As his Bar Mitzvah buzz built, Shane went berserk. With the invitations out, he was an unsubtle little SuperJew, barely containing his glee. He actually began making Bar Mitzvah small talk to anyone who would listen. The boy had no shame. In fact, he talked up damn near every ugly girl in school to get them to attend.

"So, [insert name here]," Shane would say, in his best I-can-meet-anyone's-prices shtick. "I'm gonna be a man real soon. I'm having my Bar Mitzvah at the Ventura Club."

"Yes, Shane," [insert name here] would respond in a snarky monotone. "I can't imagine anything I'd enjoy more. Actually, I'd rather eat cafeteria food." And on it went. I swear, he did this for weeks.

Of course, he finally tracked me down. It was nutrition time on a sticky hot late morning where the heat vibrates before you in waves, and I was in line for a frozen coke. I had done a pretty good job of avoiding Shane since the previous year. This time, though, there was no avoiding him. I didn't want to lose my place in line.

"Didja get it?" he said, glancing downward, kicking the stray blades of grass that grow through cement squares. There was no need to question what "it" was. I could tell this was difficult for him.

"Yup."

"You gonna go? It's gonna be great. It's at the Ventura Club. There's gonna be a band."

"Yeah, maybe."

"Great."

That was it. We got on with our lives, and I literally spoke not one word to him until the big event three weeks later.

I went because Mom told me I had to go. I was bummed out, because it was picture day at my Little League. When I got the yearbook at the end of the season, it was as if I didn't exist. There was my team, but I was missing. Story of my life, I thought at the time.

She bought me a suit at Sears for the occasion, in a color I had never heard of, called "taupe." She packed me up with a ten-dollar savings bond inside one of those cards that have a money slit.

The religious stuff was held at a temple in Tarzana; afterward, we caravaned to the Ventura Club. After we were seated, Shane made a grand entrance, complete with a Las Vegas introduction by the toupeed bandleader with the ruffled tux. The geezers with the thick rings around their wrinkled fingers broke into applause that continued until he made his way to the center of the table at which I sat. It was the only rectangular table in a spirograph of round tables that were covered in bright-white tablecloths that looked like oversized doilies. From our table, we could look out at all those rosy, sagging faces with false teeth smiles who glanced our way.

Shane wore a shit brown suit with an orange shirt and a brown tie. The Pioneer Chicken colors. I was surprised (and a little disappointed) that the greasy bird wasn't on the menu or that company mascot Pioneer Pete didn't burst out to sing a guest vocal with the band, perhaps a rendition of "I Got You Under My Skin" before dancing the *hora* with Great Auntie Zelda, who flew out from Fort Lauderdale for the occasion, while looking mere minutes away from death.

Of course, I was nice to Shane, though he wasn't around much. He spent much of the celebration working the room, shuffling from table to table, accepting the cheek pinches of relatives. I was a good sport, though. I shook his hand, made funny comments, and basically pretended that the last year never happened. That it was still summer. That we were still friends. I even helped hoist him into the chair for the obligatory Chair Dance, a silly Jewish ritual I never understood. That chair weighed a fucking ton, the legs of the chair were pressing against the palms of my hands, which were starting to sweat. I imagined his tits bouncing underneath those polyester layers like Jell-O jiggling in the fridge.

Two days later, back in school, I walked past Shane in the hallway before second period. I didn't say a word. Saw right through him. Yet, a week later, tit for tat, I sent him an invitation to my Bar Mitzvah. Only one parent was listed on the invite.

It was hardly the Ventura Club. Through the relatives looked the same (don't all Jewish relatives look alike?), the room, the vibe was completely different. Because our party was small, Nob Hill put us in the wedding chapel room. My name was misspelled on the marquee on Van Nuys Boulevard. The rabbi flirted with my mom, who I remember as beaming and radiant, but who, when I view photos, looks unhealthily thin and stressed. My uncle did all the stuff usually reserved for the dad. I felt self-conscious about this — no dad showed up at all that day — but no one else seemed to mind. Not even Shane. This time, it was his turn to act, and he did a fine job. He was in his element, after all. At a Bar Mitzvah, Shane was at home.

In retrospect, because of its seat-of-the-pants organization (a friend of mom's was the photographer; my uncle's golf buddy led the band), the event had a bit more soul than the usual Bar Mitzvah by the numbers. But I wanted it to be like everybody else's. I didn't want to stand out and be different. I wanted to blend in. If I wasn't so myopic, I could have learned something from Shane. He was different. He knew he was different. But at least he was honest about who he was. He took his beatings, but he didn't change for anyone. I certainly couldn't say that about myself. It took a lot of years to come to terms with that.

Now, sometimes, when I'm out, I take a look around for Shane. I wonder what he's doing, what he looks like, although I'd bet he looks just the same. If I ever do run into him, at some bar, say, I like to think I'll buy him a round. "Manischevitz on the rocks, Shane?" I'll joke, punching him in the arm. And we'll sit down, and make some small talk, and after we've tossed back a few, he'll look at me, and ask in that Jackie Mason voice, "So, why were you such an asshole? I thought we were friends." And I will shrug my shoulders uncomfortably, words frozen in my mouth, and wonder the same thing.

MAGIC HOUR

Erika Schickel

A MONTH after moving to Los Angeles, I was still carrying my crumpled TWA flight folder, a souvenir from my leap of faith. The five baggage claim tickets remained fanned out there, neatly stapled to the cover by the airline clerk.

"Are you traveling alone?" she had asked, as her manicured hand came down on the stapler with an efficient crunch.

"Yes," I'd told her, feeling my stomach rush up to meet my larynx. I was in psychic freefall. I had decided, out of the blue, to leave New York. I was going to Hollywood to became a movie star.

Yet "traveling alone" had left me lonely, broke, and homesick. I could not remember who I was, who I had been, who I hoped to be. I was seeing the world through puce-colored glasses, and it had to stop. I needed to change my point of view.

There was only one solution. I dug in my purse for the flight folder. Scrawled across it, on the fuselage of the skyward-jetting 747, was the number of Mark the Pot Dealer.

Mark the Pot Dealer answered his phone on the first ring.

"Oh . . . hi!" I said. "Is this Mark?"

"Sure is."

"I'm Erika. I'm a friend of Greg's?"

"Um . . . oh, *yeah*, sure. Hey."

"Hey. How ya doing?"

"Pretty good. What's up?"

"Greg said you might be able to . . ." the fear of a DEA wiretap made me speak in a murky shorthand ". . . to . . . hook me up." There was a click on the line and I felt a squeeze of paranoia through my scapula. Was I busted? Was "hook me up" too obvious? As Mark's silence continued, I began to feel that maybe he wasn't grasping my meaning after all.

"You know, maybe you could do me an eighth?" More silence. "It's just that I'm new in town, and Greg said it would be cool to call you, and I . . ."

There was another click on the line, and then Mark said, "Sorry about that . . . I'm back, but I've gotta take this other call. That's no problem, come on by. Do you know where I live?"

Hanging up, I got out my Thomas Guide, which was already showing signs of wear. First I looked up his street in the index and found we both lived on page 593. This cheered me. Locating his address on the spidery grid, I counted five blocks between us. I looked at the names of the streets. First were a few short east/west blocks: Ogden, Spaulding, Genesee, Stanley. Golden Retriever names. I saw the blocks bounding past me, Frisbees held between velvety lips, tails spiraling. Then just three long north/south blocks — Melrose, Fountain, Sunset. I pictured lush, fragrant, garden boulevards.

This would be a refreshing stroll through my new neighborhood. Best of all, I would be crossing my dealer's threshold in fifteen minutes and sucking down a bong hit inside of twenty. The very idea of getting stoned made me feel giddy and energized. I grabbed my purse and headed for the door.

"I'm going out!" I yelled to whatever roommate might be listening. I unhooked the screen door and pushed it open — an act in which I took great pleasure. You see, I had been a lifelong apartment dweller. I had never lived anywhere even faintly suburban. My youth was spent gazing out of high-rise windows, dreaming of ordinary things — front porches, lawn sprinklers, screen doors — the set pieces of a normal life. Here I was at last, twenty-six years old and pushing open my very own screen door. I felt like Kitten going on a candy run. Perhaps this is what was meant by "reinventing yourself" in Los Angeles.

I stepped out into the blazing sunshine. I was living on Stanley Avenue, a vintage Hollywood street. Squat, shingled bungalows lined up like tidy

Monopoly houses, each one sporting a bib of nubby lawn. It felt more like a backlot than a city street. In fact, living in L.A. was like being permanently on location. Buildings looked two-dimensional in the flat sunlight. The palm trees had obviously been brought in. Everyone was from somewhere else, madly connecting before moving on to the next project. If only I knew what part I was supposed to be playing, I fretted as I started off down the street.

Being an actress in Hollywood made me an instant cliché. It made me self-conscious, ashamed, banal even to myself. How could I, such an original individual, persist in this hackneyed dream? I found it difficult to admit I was an actress. I hated the very word. Instead I said, "I'm an actor"—the masculine implying seriousness of craft. "Actress," on the other hand, meant vanity, oversensitivity, easy virtue.

Back in New York, we called them "Snacktresses." We scoffed and mocked them when we saw them flit down the street like flimsy butterflies. As beautiful and substantial as spun sugar, Snacktresses were far more comfortable with air-kisses than handshakes. Their wispy hands would fit inside my broad, knuckled grasp like tiny, bejeweled sparrows. (I would have an overwhelming desire to crush them.) Snacktresses had agents. While we "actors" worked our way through summer stock and labored earnestly in student films and mystery dinner theater, these girls were raking in the big bucks on the soaps and appearing at conventions.

But was I bitter? "Yes!" I cried softly, stepping over a dried newspaper at the foot of someone's driveway. It was this morning's paper and already it was yellowed and brittle. *I should have worn a hat.* How can one possibly stay moist in this climate? *I should go back to the house for a hat.* But I was almost to the corner, and the thought of developing a melanoma was only slightly less abhorrent than the thought of turning back. A good Snacktress would be wearing sun block and maybe a long-billed Hemingway cap, her blonde ponytail pulled through the back and swinging pertly with each step. A Snacktress would use this walk as an opportunity to get her heart rate up — maybe do some toning lunges. She would be on her way to meet her trainer, not her dealer.

Up until yesterday, I had been playing the part of a waitress at Swingers, a faux coffee shop for hipsters in Hollywood. I had even been given a costume: a tiny pleated miniskirt and a garage mechanics shirt. Sort of a Madeleine-meets-Rosie-the-Riveter kind of thing. At Swingers, waitresses were required to wear lug-soled workboots. Tattoos, piercings, and fishnets were all considered a plus. Next to my hipster-Snacktress coworkers I felt like a dancing Hippo, my teensie tu-tu barely covering my ten extra pounds as I leaned over to wipe down tables. After three weeks, the manager took me aside to fire me. He said it was because I was a shitty waitress, but we both knew it was because I had been miscast in this role. He wanted someone who would look cooler in the costume.

It was midday, midweek, mid-October. The sun blazed fiercely in the flat sky, causing me to rethink black as a wardrobe staple. My clothes had absorbed so much heat they were beginning to burn my skin. The Santa Anas were blowing — a condition that had always sounded tempestuous, but seemed, in reality, to be nothing more than a bad wind blowing in the wrong direction.

Crossing Ogden, I realized I had been completely wrong about the Golden Retriever thing. There was no frisk in this walk. It was a schlepp. Block two was much like block one. A long warp of sidewalk with a woof of driveways. A row of skinny palm trees provided as much shade as a row of Q-tips.

So if I wasn't cut out to play a waitress, what should I audition for next? Among my few marketable skills was typing. I had done my share of temp work. But how do you get to temp jobs without a car? And, for that matter, how was one supposed to get to a car without a job? This chicken/egg question looped through my hot brain for a full block.

I arrived at the corner of Genesee and Santa Monica with the dawning certainty that I had no purpose in the world. At that very moment I looked up and saw a sign taped to a phone box that said, "Extras Needed!" with a fringe of phone numbers cut into the bottom. It hit me: That's exactly what I was. An extra. Not a key player in anybody's story, but an adjunct adrift in a plotless vehicle. I tore off a phone number and pocketed it as I lunged off the high curb, into the street.

The blacktop felt molten, gluing my feet down. Before I had gotten halfway across the street the signal was already blinking back to red. "Thank goodness I only have four more blocks to go," I thought, barely making it to the other side as a speeding Miata almost mowed me down.

In the flat sunlight, Hollywood had all the close-up glamour of an aging starlet. It desperately needed the cinematic framing and fast-forward blur of a windshield. My walk was a slow pan, and it brought into focus things I didn't want to see: dog turds, cigarette butts, the crusted, yellow horn of nail on a bum's big toe. It made me feel sad and queasy.

Midway through block three, I encountered another pedestrian. An old woman shuffled past with an aluminum walker, tennis balls jammed on its legs, a filthy scrotum of plastic shopping bags hanging from the frame. I looked up to say hello, but she was deep in conversation with herself, eyes unfocused.

Is this what I would become? A Hollywood have-not? I was off to a good start. Have-not-a-car. Have-not-a-job. Have-not-a-boyfriend. Have-not-a-clue why I had come to live in this bland and arid place.

And there it was again, walking beside me — my dirty little secret. I knew exactly why I was here; to become a movie star. It was not enough to be an actor making a honest living in repertory. I secretly felt — no, I *knew* — I had a face the camera would love. In my heart I felt sure I would be the one to beat the odds and achieve celebrity. This sparkly dream hung before my eyes and held me hostage to chronic unemployment and constant disappointment.

The biggest film credit I had so far was a featured role in a Troma movie. I had played an evil, spandex-clad, sex-crazed Freudian psychiatrist in *The Toxic Avenger Part II*. A part, the director assured me, that would require all my talent and classical training. It was thus that I came to Hollywood with nothing on my reel but a scene of me in a miniskirt, straddling a mutant giant, screaming, "Daddy! Daddy! Daddy!"

My throat constricted with tears. What was I doing here? Had I made a terrible error in leaving friends, family, and the love of a perfectly good enough man to come to a place that called six wheezing buses public transportation? As I groped my way down Spaulding, I began to weep openly. The salty tears stung my dry eyeballs. I must have cried for three blocks, because by the time my eyes had dried and refocused in the glare, I was north of Sunset and looking for Mark's building.

Back home I had bought pot from a gaunt, nervous black man named Jesus. So I was shocked when I rang Mark's bell, and the door was answered by a clean-cut, slightly hunky Jewish guy.

"Hey, Erika, come on in." I stepped into the apartment, which was deliciously dark. Mark was wearing what seemed the official L.A. Dude outfit: T-shirt, baggy shorts, tech sandals, a cordless phone in his hand. I was aware of him giving me the once-over. "Wow, you look hot!"

"Oh, man, it's about a million degrees out there," I said, ungluing my purse strap from my sweaty shoulder.

"I wasn't talking about the weather," he responded with a cocked eyebrow. I stiffened, not yet ready to flirt. Then he smiled. "Just kidding." My fake laugh came out as a perfunctory snort, then a sigh, to show I really meant it.

"Can I offer you a liquid?"

"Some water would be great," I croaked. Mark retreated to the kitchen, leaving me to look around. The pad was Standard Bachelor: leather sofa, big screen TV, tinted glass coffee table, and a few dusty spider plants huddled by the window. A faded, curling *Cirque Du Soleil* poster. The miniblinds were drawn, but the fierce sunlight sliced through their gaps, streaking the walls in noirish stripes.

When Mark returned, he was carrying a small, frosty bottle of spring water. He handed it to me, and I gratefully broke the seal and drank it down. The sun and tears had wrung the moisture from my vital organs, making them dried sponges. I could feel the water flowing through my body, my innards swelling back into shape. Mark watched silently as I drained the bottle dry.

"Want another?"

"No thanks. I'm good."

The corners of Mark's mouth curled into a Grinchy smile. "Want a bong hit?"

"Oh, God, yes!"

He directed me to the sofa, and the leather squealed as I sat down. From behind an Infinity speaker, Mark withdrew an enormous, green fiberglass bong and a small Gerber's baby food jar of weed. He selected a bud and crumbled it up, packing it tightly into the one-hit bowl. He handed me the bong and said, "Mazel tov."

The bong stood as tall as a toddler. I took it between my knees and put my mouth on it while Mark flicked his Bic. The grass ignited as I sucked. The smoke gathered like a small thunderhead inside, hovering over the gurgling water like bad weather. When all of the weed had burned, I released the carb and the smoke shot back into my lungs.

At first the hit seemed just right, but then it expanded exponentially. It burst out of me and threw me back on the sofa in a fit of coughing. I sputtered and gasped and reached for my empty water bottle.

"Are you okay?" Mark asked, clearly amused.

I couldn't speak, but I gave him the thumbs-up as I held my head between my knees, hacking uncontrollably. The more I tried to suppress my coughing, the more explosively it erupted, raking my charred throat.

"More water?" he offered.

I nodded, giving him another thumbs-up. He repaired to the kitchen while I tried to gather myself. The coughing slowed, and I wiped the tears from under my eyes. Then I just concentrated on breathing through my nose. When Mark came back, he put another bottle of water and a tiny snack bag of weed on the coffee table and sat down beside me on the leather sofa. "That's sixty," he said, putting the bong away.

"Great," I rasped, as I cracked open the fresh Sparklett's bottle and took a long, soothing swig. Then I dug in my purse for three of the five twenty-dollar bills that I had left to my name.

"Good weed, huh?"

"Yeah, well . . . I'm stoned." It was no lie. The room had suddenly grown deep and full. A soothing hum filled me. I was intensely aware of my eyebrows.

"Man, I *hope* so," he said, lighting a cigarette and blowing out the smoke. "I thought I was going to have to give you mouth-to-mouth."

"Well, it's been a while since I've done that." The sentence came out sounding coy, like I was talking about fucking. Fortunately, I was already so red-faced from coughing that he couldn't see me blush. I never had this problem with Jesus.

"Make sure you really crumble it up first." He offered me a Marlboro, which I took, leaning into the flame of his lighter.

Just then, the phone in Mark's hand rang and he put it to his ear. "Yello. Hey, Sid! No, I'm not busy, what's up? Hold on, let me get my book." He got up and disappeared into a back bedroom. I tucked the bag of weed into my purse and stood up, feeling the room reel a little as I struggled to regain my equilibrium. If I was going to make the long trek home, I had better get going. Mark came back into the room, smiling. "That was my agent. I've got an audition for a game show at five-thirty. I gotta get in the shower."

"You're an actor?" I asked.

"Yep. You?" he said, with no discernible trace of embarrassment.

"Actually . . . yes."

"Be careful. This business is brutal." The cliché made me reach for the door. "I mean it," Mark continued. "Girls especially have to be strong."

"Yeah, well . . ." I twisted the doorknob fruitlessly.

Mark leaned in, his spit pulled to a fine gauze in the corners of his mouth. "You know," he said, "I heard about this one girl . . . an actress . . . she beat her brains out with a blow dryer."

"What?"

"She killed herself with her blow dryer."

"No way."

"I swear!"

"It's physically impossible!"

"I tell you, it's true."

I tried to picture this Snacktress having a really, really bad hair day and bringing her Conair crashing down on her own lovely head. I saw this woman using every ounce of strength in her aerobicized body to end it swiftly, saw her falling to the floor, diffuser clattering on the Spanish tile, power cord wound around her long, graceful neck.

The image hooked into me, and I exploded in an inelegant guffaw, startling both Mark and myself, and causing him to withdraw. Once triggered, though, my laughter fed upon itself. It felt safe and familiar, and I stretched out in it. I fell into my laughter as if it were a soft bed. *"Here I am,"* I thought, "here I am!" Two fat tears rolled down my face.

Mark looked at his watch. "I really gotta jam out to Burbank."

"Right," I sputtered. "I'll be on my way. Thanks so much for the bud, Mark."

"No problem, Erika. Anytime." Mark reached around me and firmly threw open the deadbolt. I stepped off his stoop, and into Oz.

The wind had changed direction. It was coming off the ocean, and it scrubbed the air clean. The light had changed, too. It was as if a big UV filter had been placed over the low-slung sun. Shadow had returned, adding depth of field. The golden light turned the landscape Technicolor. Magic Hour had arrived.

I struck out, back toward Stanley Avenue, feeling as though I'd been filled with helium. I floated down the street, over the chunks of sidewalk cracked by earthquakes and pushed up by ficus roots. In the buttery light, Hollywood had become a natural beauty. I stopped seeing the trash and instead saw the plants. They seemed to burst out of every crack and crevice of the city.

In the east leaves were dropping, but in Los Angeles nature was in full riot. A purple bougainvillea scrambled up the exterior of a dry cleaner's shop. A passionflower vine lushly upholstered a chain-link fence. Telephone poles were maypoled in morning glory. Purple salvia grew in an undulating wave along a curb. A concrete planter held an agave the size of a bus wheel. The plants were immense and prehistoric seeming. How had I missed them? Gathered in the corner of a Mobil station was a flock of birds of paradise, their orange heads tilted back, wings arching toward the sky.

For all their exotic beauty, these plants were tough and sinewy — full of their own juices. None of them were native. They had all been transplanted from somewhere else. I stopped to stare down the crimson throat of a yellow hibiscus the size of a phonograph bell. I had tried growing this plant on my windowsill back in New York. I fed it and kept it warm in its little pot; it lived for a long time, but it never once flowered. Here, it was a profusely blooming hedge in front of a dental office. Like everything else, all it needed was the right location in order to root and bloom.

DEAR AMERICA

Jeffrey McDaniel

I am but a river boat, hopelessly in touch with my inner
canoe. On my first day of nursery school, I cried

in my mother's arms. It wasn't separation anxiety.
I was scared she would come back. In high school

I was voted most likely to secede. In college, the teachers
looked at samples of my urine to know what books

I'd been reading. I'm a narcissist trapped in the third
person. The sound of my own head being shaved

is my all-time favorite song. I approach people
on the street, show them pictures of myself as a child,

ask them *have you seen this boy? He's been missing*
for a long time. His eyes are the last swig of whisky

before stumbling from a bar on a sunny afternoon.
His cheeks are twirling ballerinas. His cheeks, revolving

doors. I'm all out of cheeks to turn. I'm all out
of cheeks. My ego is a spiral staircase inside a tornado.

My eyebrows are that furry feeling in your gut
when you're about to tell a lie. My tongue is a dolphin

passed out in an elevator. My tongue is a red carpet
I only roll out for you. My penis is a wise ass

in the back of the classroom, who doesn't know
the answer, but sticks his hand up anyway. My heart

hangs in my chest like a Salem witch. My heart
is a turtle that's been ripped from its shell. My heart

is an alley so dark nymphomaniacs are afraid
to kiss. My heart, America, my heart.

THE MUTILATED MAN

Sesshu Foster

SEE it for yourself. I don't know if you'll ever get a chance, but if you do, check it out. I mean open heart surgery.

After batteries of tests, some in the middle of the night, drawing fluids, electrocardiograms, administering nitroglycerin, etc. After thousands of dollars of blood pressure and anti-clotting medications, all the costly and interesting procedures the patient will never see itemized unless he's so unlucky as to be uninsured.

I'm going to have to look into this. I want to find out more about it.

The patient is on his back, blinking at the bright lights and trying not to be apprehensive, trying not to think ahead. The — you want to say victim but, okay, patient — has been sedated via intramuscular demerol or something stiffer. Ruefully, he has already submitted to all sorts of indignities. A man like himself — with his prejudices — being handled by all these women, telling him what to do at his age, surrounded by the disdainfully cold glances of these young people, black and Filipino nurses as he is prodded, injected, sampled, questioned, shaved, salved, and prepped. They must have an IV drip going before the anesthesiologist puts him under. I imagine that's when they gather as a team around the man on the tray.

It's not really a tray. But to me the gurney or operating table or whatever it is looks like the little carts in the morgue they use when they wheel the bodies up to the USC med students on the fourth floor to dissect for class. I always just thought of it as a tray. I'm sure my cousin's husband, the one who moved to the Northwest and who is doing really well in sales, would know what I'm talking about. He has catalogs in his office with the names and order numbers of all that stuff. Whatever, metal cart, wheels, dolly, folding bed, slop bucket, bedpans, the IV stand like a coat rack the old folks are moving step-by-step as they move down the hall. All of that stuff, I'm sure, has its own official name; the plastic lidded trashcans lined by plastic bags with yellow biohazard warning stickers on top and on the side, the ones the orderly pushes down the hall from room to room during the cleaning shift, even the baggies and the little vials and sacks he collects that not even he knows the names or contents of. I'm sure they all have *names;* it's all accounted for in some administrator's computer; she has to order so many of them from the supplier every so often.

Like, BD-1204s and BD-1208s (the half-size larger).

All of that's great business.

I don't know that much about it, but lots of the family are in medicine. They talk about it all the time. They say it's great.

I'm thinking about one uncle in particular.

He had open heart surgery three times!

So there he was in the operating room, prepped and all, and I assume that he had nodded off before they started drawing on him. Maybe he's still awake, grunting at the slightly chilly gloved touch of the nurses baring his chest and abdomen under the lamps. And what do they use? Magic Markers?

How about that? Magic Markers!

They wouldn't let me hang around there. (One time I was in the ER interpreting for this Japanese karate guy who was in a lot of pain, but he was a lot younger and tougher than the rest of us so he was taking it very well except it interfered with his use of English idioms and medical terminology, so I was in there helping him out, making sure he understood the questions from the physicians and nurses, getting him X-rayed and taking care of his insurance, and he was writhing a little, but controlling it well, and I had the doctors get him something for the pain, and when the technician brought the X-ray I looked at it and told my friend that it didn't look bad at all; the tech and I showed him the break in his wrist, and he was relieved for a moment until the doctors came back and explained that his wrist was broken in three places, one of the little bones just shattered, and told him he was going to have to be operated on right away, and that a pin was going to be inserted to stabilize the worst of the fracture but they could not be absolutely certain that the break would heal right the first time, etc., and that he was looking at months in a cast before therapy, out of commission at least for the remainder of the year, and they whisked him away to get prepped.) Though I often look like I am exactly where I belong.

If I could do it all over, I'd be right there by my uncle's side.

The old guy would be flat on his back as the surgical team gathered around. Support team milling about in the background, like shadows. Heart-lung machine wheeled into place. I assume the head surgeon supervises even as the nurses lay him out. My uncle's large chest has shrunken somewhat as heart disease limited his movement in later years. Both his parents died of strokes, and he has their history of diseases and more: high blood pressure, arrhythmia, diabetes, arteriosclerosis, high cholesterol, angina, arthritis, a history of systemic problems, all that and more. He had TB as a child and his brother and sister both died of TB, and others in his family had it, too. His family were dirt poor farmworkers, and he sucked in the bitterness of that life just like he sucked his thumb. They went straight from the fields to a concentration camp in the Arizona desert. Well, the next generation, the generation after him, produced a long line of doctors, nurses, social workers, hospital administrators, medical technicians, and I once worked as a pharmaceutical orderly myself. So I fit in. And every time I fill out a medical history form for insurance or employment, all the diseases I list on it are his. I'm sure I forget to list some. No epilepsy or fainting spells or dizziness (except that one time he had a heart attack when he was driving down the freeway) (well, he pulled over and blacked out in the emergency stopping lane and then he woke up — he thought — a few minutes later, and holding on his chest with one hand drove slowly home with the other, trying not to black out, and really pissed off at his doctors, who, of course, admitted him immediately and decided, finally, yes, he probably did have a heart attack, and yes, he probably needed a triple bypass operation where they take a vein out of your leg, unplug the aorta, pop that sucker from your leg right there on your heart, suction whatever they can out of the exposed veins and valves, I suppose, suction out the yellowish cholesterase, whatever compound that hardened fat turns into when it coagulates in and around your heart, giving you that *angina* all the time — but I don't remember if that was his first triple bypass or his second) so, whatever, when I fill out forms I just check off anything and everything.

It's all pertinent.

On the other side of my family (the side people never talk about) we have some of the rest: alcoholism, cancer, blood clotting, rheumatic fever, rickets, depression, dizzy stupefaction over things like Christianity, and chickenshit behavior. That side of the family doesn't bother me, so I don't think about them. Maybe they drink so much, they tend to leave other people alone unless they catch you the wrong way on a bad night on the highway.

I wish I would have known. I wish I could have been there for my uncle.

Anyway, I knew they wouldn't let me do the Magic Marker thing myself. His arms (IV tubes taped on at wrist and elbow) akimbo like chicken wings, withered biceps wrinkled and the skin yellowing with age, liver spots on the dry, sunblackened arms. When he nods off, slack mouth slightly agape, his dry lips brusque — as ever — firmly stung by disappointment. His pectorals gone, maybe the few hairs around his dark nipples shaved off. Maybe the nipples shaved off. Maybe the nipples cold, shriveled, purple, flat as an old bruise. His skin translucent as chicken skin across his breastbone and the ribcage jutting, the way he lies on his back as if uncomfortable, in spite of his large gut. His paunch, its girth, its retention of muscle definition, looks like that of a younger man, though not necessarily a healthier man.

All that would be revealed immediately — you suppose the surgical team may have familiarized themselves with it once or twice already, talking to him as they size him up. At his bedside, comforting him with small talk, off-hand jokes, because of that genial manner that he puts on when at the disposal of those whom he considers his superiors. Perhaps the surgeon has met him, sat with him, and outlined the plan. The surgeon will look into his big dark face and not really know how much he understands. The head surgeon pleasant and businesslike, leaving the real questions and real follow-up to his physicians. Who the old man does not trust as much as the specialists, since both his doctors — he thinks — allowed his condition to progress without proper diagnosis or treatment until surgery was absolutely necessary or he would die. He's probably right about that.

(Physicians in our family have, on occasion, tried to second-guess for the old man, and hook him up with other specialists in the city; but he keeps going back to this same hospital because it is close to where he lives and accepts his preferred payment plan. As is his way, he prefers to berate the doctors over the phone, barking at them as he stands in the hall of his one-room life with the TV going in the background, and make no mistake, he returns ever faithful to his next appointment, grinning sheepishly as they prod him with their supercilious manner.)

He is still a big man who walks with a heavy tread. Flat-footed. His large torso reclining slablike on the gurney is still imposing, if a little withered and wasted by age. His forearms more dry and blackened and less burnt red-brown by the sun, ending in the broad, blunted, mute paws like worn instruments. (The first time they will draw their design on the waxy, seamless, shining skin. The second or third times they will have to draw it upon the broad scars of previous operations, with their stippled outer edges in raised relief like a thick melted zipper stretching from throat to navel.)

I suppose that they draw on him with a black grease pen like a woman's eyeliner. It would be cool if there's something going on between the doctor and one of the nurses, if the nurse offers the doctor her eyeliner and he uses that, but I suppose if the procedure goes by the book they go in for some expensive art pencil that costs the hospital a good deal and that the cost is passed on in the billing department (where my friend, the poet, works).

They would not let me, but if they did I would select a fat red marker and draw something like this:

Or something like this:

Or, perhaps I'd just copy the surgeon's diagram with slight modifications of my own design.

I never did visit him in the hospital, because I figured it would be boring. (I'm always wrong about things like that.) I mean I've worked in hospitals, and I knew I'd end up wandering away from the family, snatching an ID badge from a desk or jacket hanging in an office, and prowling the premises looking for a little action. Nothing that would make me real money, not like when I worked in pharmaceutics, just fidgeting, fooling around, remembering the old days. Chatting with the clerks and orderlies, looking to meet someone with pretty eyes.

The usual.

Sure, after the second or third time, I had to go.

Hey. It's worth a look. Here was this guy, flat-footed nasty Buddha of a man, sturdy as a stump, who'd worked the fields as a boy and spent his life as a Japanese gardener, groundskeeping for white people around their San Marino and Beverly Hills homes, who mowed the green strips in front of their corporate offices in City of Commerce and City of Industry and Montebello, who watered and planted and soaked the sun into his deep mahogany skin and never took a day off, so any day of the week including Saturday he could be seen, Chaplinesque under the beating sun, plastered with a curtain of smoggy haze, walking back and forth in front of some corporate office (fast-forward this video and it reveals his work as truly senseless), making their landscape tidy, green, replanting flower beds, snipping off old brown leaves, edging and blowing the detritus into the gutter with the two-HP blower on his back, the cap with green plastic sun visor stained with perspiration.

He bragged to us that he never had to advertise, that all his "accounts" came by word of mouth. He'd stand on the broad expanse of immaculate lawn with his supervisor, the "plant manager" or "operations supervisor" or "environmental maintenance engineer" and make small talk, clear up a few details related to scheduling his route, and wax sardonic in reply to his supervisor's remarks about wife, vacation, or company business.

Then he'd come back to the van where I'd be waiting, sitting in the passenger seat and watching him through the windshield, having loaded the equipment and coiled the hoses in the back. He'd haul himself into his seat with an asthmatic wheeze, and for a moment stare forward into the glare of the dazzled windshield and clench his jaw. It was then that he'd explode.

Without a word—though, of course, he must have known that I was sitting there expecting it, even he was not so stupid (though at the time I believed him not just stupid but incapable of such thought) that he would not know what I was feeling, stiff with apprehension (or my brother, if he was unlucky enough to have to substitute for me — before my brother would characteristically refuse to go and was kicked out at thirteen years old to work and live on his own). For years, I envied my brother with his drugs and teenage alcoholism, and I felt sorry for myself—my brother had abandoned me, I thought—as I sat in the passenger seat listening to the old man try to breathe when he sat behind the wheel, and he'd reach across the space and cuff the side of my head, and curse me for "making a god damned shitty mess of the cuttings by the driveway" or punch his knuckles in the side of my head, involuntarily driving tears into my eyes and tossing an old stained canvas glove that I had accidentally dropped while mowing into the side of my face ("you stupid little fucking idiot") (the other glove, which I had thought was the pair, clutched in my lap), and my uncle would curse me long and hard for being a no-good useless piece of shit scum of the earth just like my father.

Or, sometimes, he'd just unclench his jaws and sigh. He'd strip cellophane off a pack of Pall Malls from the box he kept between the seats and light a cigarette and puff and turn the key in the ignition to drive to the next site.

For years, I never knew what he'd do next. They had decided that, with my mother working full-time and my old man long gone, my uncle would raise me while I helped him on the job. Before I knew better, I thought he had something personal against me.

Maybe he knew that. He was more cunning than he let on. I used to wonder if the sun on his head, on the thick bulletlike skull behind the visor, made him smarter like a lizard.

He was more stupid than cunning, though, I believed that then; and I thought he was crazier than fried lizards, too. You could tell by how the veins in his forehead and neck stood out under the skin; how he looked at you through those red eyes, trying to think of some excuse to spit curses and beat on you. If he couldn't think of an excuse, if you did nothing wrong, if you coiled the hoses and packed the tools just how he liked, if you made sure to forget nothing and hurried to help him clear the sacks of hedge cuttings and grass from the lawn, he could only look at you regretfully and sigh and smoke his Pall Malls. He might exhale smoke and sigh, "Shit . . ." Looking out through the glare on the windshield at the long expanses of lawns in the Southern California sun. If he did think of something and cussed you or slapped the back of your head and you said nothing, said nothing during the shitty years they forced you to be with him, it was because you had learned how long he kept a grudge (he remembered the tiniest incidents for weeks and months and they inflamed him again and again when he thought of them) and that it was best never to speak to him and never to say anything except "Yes."

If I was lucky, he might just spit out the window, cuss a little bit, exhale raggedly, and ask if I wanted to eat at my favorite place for lunch. Bits of grass stuck to his massive hands, the skin callused and chapped and fingernails thick and yellow. Then, driving, sooner or later he'd launch into one of his rants (he got psychotic when he was inspired — he'd stutter on unblinking); (if he passed a car with black men in it) he'd lecture about the goddamned stupid niggers, the coloreds, burning their own neighborhoods to the ground and killing anybody like they did, they had no more sense than apes in the jungle, they should all be shipped off back to Africa. He'd point to an empty lot and say, see what that is? That's the unions. They're destroying this country. The coloreds and the unions.

I'd look at the empty lot next to a liquor store or whatever as we drove down the avenue.

He'd go on, "That's your urban renewal for you. That's why there's nothing there. That's why this whole town looks like *shit*. Because the unions have this big building in Washington D.C., it's probably the biggest building in Washington, and they don't want people to work if they ain't union. Because they want everybody to be union. So stuff doesn't get built. They don't let companies just build wherever. Environmentalists. So that's one of the reasons why this country is so fucked up, because of them and the coloreds burning down the buildings that we do got. Then we got kids like you. The next generation. Supposed to be the fucking future of this country. Christ almighty, I'm glad I'll be dead when that day comes, I'm telling you. Shit, I will be glad to be dead."

It seemed like I went down the avenues in that van for years, and I guess I did, waiting for the day to get finished for years, waiting for the traffic to move for years, waiting to get out of that van for years, waiting for the light to change, waiting for the summer to be over, waiting for him to come out of a delicatessen and thrust the sandwiches into my hands, waiting and thinking about if everything was in its place and did I forget any of the tools. He'd buy me one Coca-Cola, two if he was feeling good. In the last couple years that they made me work for him, he got to liking me, so — though he still cussed me regularly and tried to hit me whenever he got a chance, he never flew off the handle anymore and tried to hurt me like he had when I was small. He'd say things like, "You're a pretty damned quiet kid, you know that?" He might reach across the van, and though I'd lean away, he'd affectionately hold his arm out till he located the side of my head and he'd rap my skull with his knuckles hard, and joke, "Hello? Hello? Anyone home? Ha ha ha. Lights are on. Anyone home?" (Rap with knuckles.) "Ha ha ha. Well, I know some thinking's going on in there. That's good. That's real good. Maybe I'm learning you something after all. Ha ha ha."

He'd smoke and say things like, "I see you don't smoke. That's good. Shows more goddamned sense than I gave you credit for. I bet your friends smoke anything they get their grubby fingers on. Maybe you won't grow up to be a shithead like your old man after all. Tell you what, I'll mow this next place if you wash the sidewalks down good with the hose."

He played muzak from the easy listening stations on the radio and some-
times he hummed along and I did my level best to ignore him happy or
otherwise. Seems like at the last he was happy with me, as happy as he ever
got. He thought I was his fucking dog.

He bought me a pair of seventy-five-dollar Redwing steel-toed boots,
double E at the Redwing Store, just my size, best pair of boots I ever had.
He started giving me a dollar or two on top of the dollar an hour he had
told them he'd pay me (and had not the first year).

He was a professional Japanese gardener and he made the properties on
his route immaculate and we worked sunup to sundown whenever I wasn't
in school. He drove down the freeways and boulevards talking to me about
how the politicians were just plain crooks but Nixon was *a victim of the
media,* the media were like, well, he didn't know what the media was *like,*
but if it weren't for *the media* most likely we wouldn't have had no trouble
in Vietnam, and he couldn't see how Mexican women could work as hard
as they did and support the damned *Mexicans* who were almost as bad as
niggers, and why those women *let* their men live off them the way they
did, and why they had to have so many snotty-faced kids when they
couldn't take care of the ones they did have, it was *no wonder* people
thought they were stupid. But he wouldn't say Mexicans were lazy, at least
not the women. 'Cause he'd seen them working, now that there weren't
hardly any more Japanese gardeners — most of 'em were Mexican now.
He'd talk about the coloreds and all that shit and I didn't hear it any more.
I just thought about whatever I wanted and answered when I had to and
he talked on and on.

Soon as I got a chance I quit and I never worked for him again or talked
to him ever. I hit the streets at fifteen and never had to work for him again.
I was moving.

I missed his open heart surgery.

I would have liked to see him that first time. Or any of the times, really.
It must be something to look at. They just ripped him down the center;
they must've ripped a quick and easy neat slice with a razor-sharp scalpel

that just opened him up. His insides must have just about popped right out. The blood must be flying; the team must be all elbows, frantic fingers, bent heads, mopping, suctioning. . . . Maybe they sliced him in sections, but my guess is they did it all at once. Slice straight through the pectoral muscles down to the breastbone; and then they use that hot little saw. At the speed that little saw spins, it must fill the room with the stink of burnt bone and blood. The surgeon has to wear safety goggles. So he doesn't get a bone chip in his eye. Some nurse is probably standing at his shoulder holding the serrated bone saw just in case. And when the circular saw cuts through the breastbone, they aren't going to stand around waiting. The team is cooking, suctioning the blood, peeling back the skin, applying the two clamps that tattoo bruised and dented impressions in the flesh *for months*. And, oh, *the impressive part:* They've got people standing at his head, keeping his face-mask in place, keeping him breathing, monitoring his vital signs, ready to hook him up to the heart-lung machine; and they fasten on the clamps and pull his ribcage apart like they are pinning a butterfly to a board. You can imagine a human being with their chest spread open like that, exposing the heart and lungs and internal organs. What did his heart look like?

I would have liked to see it.

I saw him afterward, in a contingent, with my sisters or somebody else in the family. My brother made fun of me for going, when I told him. "I wouldn't go see that old bastard; he's the only person I can think of—and I've met some shitty motherfuckers—that I wish was dead."

"But you should've seen him," I told my brother. "They really did a number on him."

"I don't care," my brother said, "I don't care about him at all. I don't ever want to think about him."

But I told my brother about how we visited the old man in intensive care, how he looked even older now, and smaller, like they had cut something out of the inside of him. (My brother said, "His heart is probably all black and greasy with tar from Pall Malls.") I hadn't talked to him, just stood in back of everybody and the old man saw me in back and was too tired to say anything except hello. I saw he was surprised to see me. He looked like he was ready to go under, like a jack had slipped out from under a car and the car had landed on his chest. He had this sick look on his brown and yellow face, trying to smile for all his visitors with their flowers and cards and cheery sympathy. I think I made him nervous, standing in the back not saying anything, not smiling and just watching, because he wouldn't look at me. It had been years since he'd seen me last, and they said he'd asked about me. The nurse told us we'd better let him rest, he had to have some tests done in a little while. And we all hurried out of there.

They kept bugging me about it, so I went back with them again. It was a few weeks later, maybe a month or more, but he was sitting up, and the bed had a button he could push to get the end of the bed to rise up so he could watch TV or read (the *Reader's Digest*), and he had more color in his face. But I was happy to see he still looked older. And weaker, and that it showed in his face where everyone could see it, and he didn't seem to like that; I sensed a new fear in him. The doctors told us he was doing great, that everything was going fine. They made some jokes and he grinned, happy to be alive. We all stood around his bed and wished him well and laughed. I laughed; you could see his days were numbered.

Before we all left, he showed us his chest. My cousin — the one who'd brought a teddy bear wearing a "get well soon" T-shirt — walked out in the hall because she didn't want to see it. The rest of us stared at it. His torso was amazing. It looked like a side of beef swinging on a hook in the slaughterhouse. It looked like his history; all the bitterness he'd held inside stewing his internal organs. The skin was discolored from getting sliced open and spliced together again, with big black stitches holding together two lips in the long welt that ran from his throat to his solar plexus. The swollen skin looked like meat that couldn't decide whether to live or die. It was a raw color, mottled, white where it was pulled taut by the stitching and darker where it was creased or folded into the cut. "Inside," he said, "they put me together with staples. I got big metal staples to hold my breast and ribs together." He held his green gown up so everyone could see and he grinned, proudly.

I had vowed never to speak to him again, but I couldn't stop myself, and I asked, "Does it hurt to laugh?"

"Yes," he said, "Yes, it does." And he winced, and laughed.

I hurried out of the room shortly after, sick that I had actually spoken to him.

He could no longer work his groundskeeping route after that. He gave it up, and invested in a line of indoor plants that he maintained for branches of the Bank of America. All he had to do all day was go from bank to bank, walk around the lobby and behind the counter watering the potted plants, removing the sick ones and grinning like a death's-head, responding with clumsy small-talk to the pert young tellers and clerks whose plants he tended like his own. They'd go on counting their money and ignore him. He boasted to the family that he made more money with this line of indoor plants than he ever made working outdoors. He could even take vacations now, and trained a Mexican kid to watch his plants for a few days at a time. He'd disappear off by himself. He'd charter a fishing boat to go down off the Mexican coast or drive up the eastern side of the Sierras to Lake Crowley when trout season opened.

He survived fifteen years after his first operation. I didn't pay attention, but he had another bypass once or twice after that. Finally he had to sell the indoor plant business and limit his trips to driving out to the beach and sitting in the van in the parking lot. He did stop smoking but he never followed the diet the doctors ordered. At the end, the doctors told him that if they didn't unplug another vein out of his (now spindly) scarred thighs and graft it onto his heart, this time he was going to die. He said, okay, he'd die — no more operations.

The morphine didn't work at the end. He lingered for days after the last heart attack. Some of the family came to see him (not me). He told them all to get out of the room when the pain hit him. He lost consciousness. His kidneys failed. He writhed in pain for days without ever regaining consciousness. His lungs filled with fluid. The doctors kept draining them. His body kept trying to breathe. He died approaching midnight on a Monday.

I hope I was making love at that moment. I hope I spent the hours of his final agony making squishy noises and moaning and making our room smell like the sea. I hope I was busy making a woman happy, that she went to sleep happy, happy.

They cremated him, as per his request. I never got a chance to look at that heart. I wanted to see the color of this rage we shared, squirming in us like a headless snake.

Years earlier, they had asked me if I wanted his indoor plant business. I considered taking it over and setting it up so a couple kids I know could run it. But it would mean that I would have to retrace his steps and negotiate with him and go through his paperwork. I told them to give it to somebody else. It was bought by someone outside the family.

Me and my brother were joking about the old man. My brother said, "You know, he never had a woman in his life."

"That's right! You know, you're right!"

"I wonder why."

"Probably because he was scared of white women and Nisei women couldn't stand him."

"Could you see him with a Mexican woman or a black woman?"

We both laughed.

But my brother refused to go to the funeral. He refused to have anything to do with the old bastard. "He's dead!" I said. "He's dead and gone!"

"No way." He shook his head. "No way. He went his way and I went mine a long time ago. I'm sorry I ever met that son of a bitch."

"It was a long time ago. I'm telling you he's dead."

"You can go if you want. He always did like you better."

"The food's gonna be good, I'm telling you."

"You go. I couldn't stand to see all those people in the same place. I know them too well. They'll all be standing around talking and laughing and I'll remember how they treated us and what they did to each other."

So my brother didn't go to the funeral nor on the fishing boat off

Guadeloupe Beach where we tossed the old man's ashes overboard nor to the banquet afterward. I had told him the food was going to be great and I was right. At times like these the family really cooks.

ENTER THE YEAR OF THE DRAGON, 2000

Russell Charles Leong

for Frank Chin

I enter the dragon
careful not to waken any napping animals
or dreaming ancestors, for
if a hero falls alone in the forest
who will hear him fall?

Now turn the sound down
because Romeo must die.
Jet Li & Chow Yun Fat, Jackie Chan
battle it out on video
on my nine-inch TV screen, Korean-brand name,
assembled in Mexico.
The tape snags.
The screen goes gray, then white.

White is the color of loss.
Because Bruce Lee
left us a long time ago
kicking the air into architecture
art & essence.

To enter the dragon, head East.
East into the San Gabriel Valley
way past Pasadena, Altadena
the Santa Anita Racetrack
Arcadia, Monrovia

inching behind a thousand taillights
seven o'clock the eve of the New Year.

Enter the dragon. Make a left
off Irwindale Boulevard, home
to small industries like
metal Olympic torches,
veneer & laminate furniture
paper, cardboard, & electronic parts
assembled minimum wage
by Salvadoran & Vietnamese refugees.

You don't quite expect it
coming up on you
as you turn your car onto Foothill Boulevard
cinderblock & concrete
spaces yearning to be filled.
A dark, moonless sky
lonesome, somehow.

To enter the dragon
step gently on your brakes
when you see neon glowing red.
A parking lot
for one thousand cars
Pacific Pearl Seafood Buffet
all you can eat
$7.99 dinner special:
It's the Year of the Dragon!

To enter the dragon
Walk directly through the glass doors
past plastic pink roses & plastic purple grape

clusters stuffed in porcelain vases;
one side of the enormous room
Latinos, Filipinos, & whites
neighborhood folks
pile eggrolls, pizza slices, steak
& broccoli onto white plastic plates
squeeze themselves into vinyl booths
go back for seconds and thirds.

Other side of the room
rented for the night
Chinese women all primped-up
bound tightly in jackets that
shimmer red & green
dangly jade pendants & diamond earrings
middle-aged men don pin-striped suits
eyeing stacks of gold & red foiled boxes
hoping their raffle ticket will win them a DVD machine
or Sony color television, the grand prize.

Enter the Dragon.
Silver & gold tinsel pineapples
hang from aluminum air-conditioning ducts
red squares with the character
"Chwun," for Spring,
turned upside down.

Brown busboys pour
buckets of buddhist bamboo shoots
sliced pizza
fried shrimp
smoked tea duck
California sushi roll

kung bao chicken
ham fried rice
onto steel platters.

"Tonight, we enter
the Year of the Dragon!
To each of you sitting here
from China, Taipei, Tibet, Hong Kong,
Hawaii, Wisconsin, New York, Florida,
Los Alamos, New Mexico
& from Norman, Oklahoma,
Wan Swei! Wan Swei!
Ten thousand years more!"

Between each karaoke song
Miss Peony Wang Lin & Mister Bronson Kao
(well-known local newscasters)
call out five-digit ticket numbers
hand out red & gold boxes:

"Ganbei! Ganbei!
Bottoms up! A toast to each of you
bobbing your handsome
round heads up & down!
Pretty ladies, too!
Drink up! No one's gonna go home
empty-handed tonight!
Everyone's a winner here!"

(Lucky ones tear the foil off their
packages of ginseng tea, dried mushrooms,
silk scarves, gloves, & more of the same.)

After three hours we are tossed
& fried & digesting each others'
fluids & sweat & eating aromas:
drowning in the perfumed river
of the Pacific Pearl Seafood Buffet.

I step outside to the parking lot,
pass out of this world & into my own.
From below my belly
I find my breath
touch the roof of my mouth
with the tip of my tongue, exhale.

I pay homage to a moonless sky.
My life is a recycled koan
one hand clapping; one hero falling
over & over again.
I enter the restaurant
through another entrance.

Through the Western & Eastern door
Through the Northern & Southern door
I enter the dragon from four directions.

I enter flesh, bone & blood.
I return to my chi.
Following my fingers
crystal & concrete-block walls shatter.
Following my heels
tables buckle & chairs collapse
Following my breath
Plastic grapes & artificial roses melt.
Following my form

Swiss watches leave their wrists.
Gold coins escape their pockets.
Jade rings slip off their fingers.
Return back all plunder to the people
through the Little Dragon's breath.

Through buffet aisles
I turn platters of sizzling meat & noodles
into boomerangs. Until the cops come.
Arrest & book me.
By this time I'm naked.
A fifty-year-old bowlegged Chinaman.
Black-dyed hair purple under the neon.
No suit, no shirt, no tie, no pants
No nylon socks, underwear, shoes
No fake Rolex. No dyed jade. No shiny manicured nails.

Naked. Nothing. Nada.
Essence. Original Body.

I've entered the dragon.
Sweet & sour blood flowing red
from the corners of my mouth
arms & legs bruised and cut
a number & a white band
Clipped securely around my wrist
Like other brown & black guys
we're here in L.A. County Hospital
Here in the Year of the Dragon.

The County will hold me for observation.
The restaurant will sue me for damages.

The customers will file suit, too.
They will impound my car for unpaid speeding tickets.

Because today is February 4th, 2000.
Irwindale, San Gabriel Valley, Los Angeles,
United States of America.

Today is the world without the Dragon.
Today is the world without Bruce Lee.
If a hero falls alone in the forest
who will hear him fall?

NAKED CHINESE PEOPLE

Diane Lefer

W E were always finding naked Chinese people in the shower. We called them Chinese, though one was Korean and one was half Korean with a father who was an American G.I. She was the first. She'd wandered away from a rave in the desert and came upon our cabin where she walked right in and stood under the shower until the water ran out. We found her slumped in the stall, incoherent and already almost dry. The other Korean had been invited to a friend's, took a wrong turn, ended up at our place and, unwittingly, made himself at home. The third, who may or may not have been Korean or Chinese, was jabbering incomprehensibly in what may or may not have been his mother tongue. He spoke no English and could not give any account of himself. The police arrived accompanied by two white men who claimed to be doctors, but something about them seemed undoctorlike, including the fact that one of them spoke to the man fluently in his own language. Also, they had arrived within minutes of our phone call, though we are not on a paved road and are aware of no hospital in the vicinity.

Things come in threes, and so we could have gone on as we were, expecting no further intrusions, but after the third Chinese man was carried off by the so-called doctors, Richard and I decided it was time to put a lock on the door.

It's in and around our weekend cabin in the desert, now equipped with a lock, in which the events I'm about to narrate took place. The lock on the door is irrelevant, as are the naked Chinese.

We call it a cabin though it's actually a trailer which the high winds might at any time overturn. The winds scare me. There have been times driving out there when tractor-trailers going through the Cajon Pass have been blown right over on the freeway and so when a truck passes me, or I pass a truck, I'm always braced for disaster. Even so, we used to go most weekends.

Up until the dirt turnoff, there's only one road, and yet we often feel we've taken a wrong turn. In one direction, the way is flat and without interest. In the other, it's a marvel of rock formations and distant peaks, high cacti and even lush stands of leafy trees. Even after years of making the trip, I often panic partway there to ask, Where are we?

The land about seems so flat, I can't explain how hidden our place turns out to be from view, how you don't see it until you come right on it.

There are other trailers scattered about the land, none within sight of ours, but all so similar and surrounded by Joshua trees that vary only in the slightest degree, you can understand how people might confuse them. It's as if the desert's already laid out in a grid to be filled in with one cookie-cutter dwelling nudged up against the next. Our weekend homes retain their mass-proliferating quality though empty miles still intervene between them and one person hangs wind chimes and another *chile ristras* on the door because for all our fear of difference, uniformity has its own fearful shame.

So it wasn't all that strange that Chinese strangers came to our door by mistake, or that my ex-husband, who would be alive if he had only found us, lost his way.

When I was a child, riding the subway, whenever I saw a Chinese person, I used my index fingers at the corners of my eyes to pull the skin aslant. Happily, I chanted *Chinky Chinky Chinaman.* I loved the Chinese and did this to greet them, to say *Hello! I see you! Welcome to America!* It never occurred to me these Chinese people might be in fact Americans. Ah, to see through the eyes of a child! It never occurred to me they would interpret my greeting as anything other than a friendly gesture.

But all that's past. In twenty-first-century America, history no longer counts and race, I'm told, is history, so I'm not sure a story can be "about" race anymore. Of course it can be, but maybe it shouldn't be. Race is background, perhaps, environment. The way we see things, informing the way we see others, speak to others, think of others, but as an undercurrent, rarely admitted, just there, a constant subtext. The Other used to be invisible. Now unavoidably visible, we (in this case White) see and in our clearsightedness dismiss without seeing. Irrelevant.

I was telling you about the cabin.

All of a sudden it seemed people kept giving me things I couldn't hang on the walls. For example, a poster for a French film, *Comment faire l'amour avec un nègre sans se fatiguer.* I'm more comfortable saying the title in French, although the poster displays it prominently in English: HOW TO MAKE LOVE TO A NEGRO WITHOUT GETTING TIRED. There's a white woman and a black man reclining, but not together. She lies in the foreground reading a book, dressed in socks and underwear. He is stretched out on the bed, draped in a sheet. What appears to be the Washington Monument rises from his midsection. His face is covered.

We tacked the poster up in the cabin. It was a private joke, just to emphasize how private the cabin was supposed to be. A place to get away, a place where no one would ever be invited, especially not Richard's grown children. A place so far from others, I imagined Richard and I would have very noisy sex.

One of the police officers was black and I wondered what he thought of the poster.

Did he wonder why Richard let me hang it? Did he think we chose it together? Or was it Richard's choice? Was it some pointed reference to me?

Which part embarrassed me the most? The word *Negro*?

Sometimes I wonder how did I become a white woman married to a white man. When you have an unhappy childhood, surely the Other always looks better. White woman/white man. I imagine that's what the black cop saw. I felt defined, confined, less than who or what I am. I wanted to say: *But that's not me.*

When Skee and I were still married, I never stopped to wonder who I was, though eventually I had to wonder who he was. A brain tumor will do that to a person, though the tumor is not what killed me. I mean *him;* I meant to write "him." It killed, rather it did *not* kill *him,* at least not directly, but I didn't write "him," I wrote "me." You see how closely the two of us were tied together.

I had never wanted to be "taken care of" by a man, a phrase I always heard as threat. But when I lay my head on Skee's chest and he held me, I felt safe and cared for in a way I'd never before known. It was not that I felt he would protect me, but that I didn't have to protect myself against him. I suppose what I'm describing is trust.

Early on, Skee warned me: "A black man isn't used to being loved. There's times I'm going to push you away. I don't want to — it's the panic. Please wait it out when it happens. Please let me go and let me come back. Remember that I wouldn't panic if I didn't love you."

So when things started to go wrong, I attributed it to blackness. I was patient.

I may be a white girl, but my life hasn't been without pain. When I was twelve, I was raped by a man dressed up as a priest. We were Jewish, but I had been raised to respect priests and nuns, partly out of pity. They hadn't chosen such a life, I was told. Their parents had given them to the Church. It sounded so much like human sacrifice, like throwing young girls into volcanos, I was not surprised that what the man did to me was so painful. I arrived home dazed and bleeding and told my mother. "Did you come?" she asked. I had no idea what this meant. The priest had said "Come with me," and afterward, I'd come straight home. Yes, I said, and she hit me.

Neither my mother nor the police seemed to think it strange that a priest would rape a child. They only knew he was a fake because he'd drawn a knife across my thigh and left a wound. "A priest wouldn't do that," said the cop, and I said, "He said he wouldn't hurt me."

In *The Turner Diaries*, women like me get hanged from lampposts.

"Let me in!" he kept saying, while I kept saying, "Where are you?"

What if I'd said, "You're not acting like yourself." What if I'd said, slyly, "Hey, shouldn't we have an annual physical?" What if I'd seen a man changing every day before my eyes, instead of seeing a black man?

What if they'd diagnosed and caught it earlier? They saved his life, but could they have saved his mind, his brilliant reflective consciousness, the man who had been my life-partner until he was suddenly, irrevocably, gone?

After we divorced, there were nights I slept with his science journals piled around me, or clutching one of his notebooks written in his almost microscopic hand. During the good days, there had been times when we just looked at each other and burst out laughing at the sheer unlikely joyful luck of having met. Once he was gone, I spent hours at his computer, trying to guess passwords, half-believing that the answer to this misery was there to read in one of his locked files.

I didn't know where he had gone. I didn't know he'd lost his job. I didn't know he'd been arrested. And at the university where he'd taught (and then grabbed his crotch in front of students and grabbed at women's breasts) and in the courtroom where he was arraigned (after a wild scene in a 99¢ Store), no one saw a man who'd lived for years an honorable, exemplary life. No one saw that what was happening wasn't normal.

"Let me in!" Skee was just trying to find me in the cabin where I'd gone for the weekend with Richard.

The night Skee and Richard first met: Skee showed up at my apartment. Richard and I were half-undressed on my bed. It was the third night we'd had sex. We were new enough I was still keeping count. I would have ignored anyone else at the door, but it was Skee and I leapt immediately from the bed, covered up and let him in. It was clear something terrible had happened. He wouldn't tell me. He kept saying *If I couldn't have come here, if I couldn't have come here, but of course I could, I knew I could.* Do you know there were mornings I walked out the door to go to work and found him sitting on the sidewalk, banging his head against concrete, and then all I'd have to do was say his name or touch his shoulder and he'd stop? Do you know what it is to feel so much power over someone, the power that you alone can make him stop hurting? I made up the couch for him and went back to bed with Richard, and though we had to do so quietly, we made love. His fingers were electric on my body and it wasn't that I felt I was making love to them both or that I was jubilant to be with a man who was so vigorous and healthy when Skee, much as I loved him, was so ruined and it was not the *frisson* of having sex with my new lover while my ex-husband lay only several yards away. It was that Richard had not known who Skee was or why I was so quick to care for him, he merely saw that Skee mattered to me, and he had treated him in a gracious and welcoming way and then left the room to leave us alone and I knew then I wanted Richard because I knew he would never try to come between us. In bed, though we muffled our sounds, I looked up at him and said, "I'm falling in love with you. You know that, don't you?" and in retrospect, I think that was the closest I ever came to loving Richard.

I loved our cat. Though she was an indoor cat, safe from city traffic, Richard and I never had her declawed, thinking that someday we might move to the country and she'd enjoy the outdoors. The first time we took her to the cabin, she was afraid to go outside — inconvenient as we hadn't brought the litter box. The second time, she ventured out and something ate her.

Don't say I loved seeing Skee reduced to *this*, a black man like a pet or a helpless child.

What's true is marriage is indeed a contract in which each of two adults has responsibilities. It was only after Skee's brain was mutilated that my anger against him disappeared. I could no longer hold him responsible and so could regard him again with that original and so emotionally satisfying unconditional love. There was nothing to resent, no reciprocity to expect. It was the passionate attachment one might feel for a Down's syndrome child or for God. A commitment so unabashedly and exaltingly one-sided, it could only end with death.

When he died, I stopped feeling. I could no longer bear to have Richard touch me. Let me be specific about the kind of touch: Richard lost all interest in sex years ago but we had continued to hold hands or throw an arm around a shoulder in a friendly and fraternal kind of way. This was something I could no longer do.

There was a kind of overload which seems strange because I felt so little. What I felt was not sensation itself, but the feeling of always being pestered. Richard talked too much. It may not have been very much at all, but whenever he spoke I wished he would be still. His words meant nothing to me. They were pebbles thrown against my head. And when he touched me it was like having a rough seamstress fitting clothing I hadn't ordered to my form. His hands were like dead things up against me, perhaps they disgusted me because they proved to me my own unresponsive flesh was dead.

I wanted to roll myself up in a ball and cover my head with my arms. All I wanted was to be left alone.

The cat would have understood. She was dependent on us, she formed attachments, but we knew not to touch her when she didn't want to be touched. After she was eaten, there was no one, no one left to understand me. Sometimes I thought about being eaten by a tiger. I wanted to be eaten alive though I know the way it works is first a swipe of the paw to break the neck.

And I thought of what it had been like to lie in Skee's arms so many years ago and no matter how our senses merged, it was always possible, except in the most profound darkness, to see where he began and I left off.

"Let me in!" he said.

When people lose their way, you try to help.

We drove the naked Chinese woman to the nearest emergency room, a good half hour away. The Korean man laughed, dressed, apologized, and drove off in his car, a Volvo. With the third man, the police and the men who called themselves doctors appeared at our door as if they'd been tracking him.

I remember the beautiful delicacy of Skee's ears. How pleased I was he never pierced them. They were perfect.

And I remember lying with Richard, him inside me, and how I jumped up at the sound of Skee's voice on the answering machine. "Here I am, Skee. It's all right. I'm here." And if I'd been there for him when he first got sick maybe none of it would have happened. And I felt a moment's guilt towards Richard, but he showed no sign and never said a word and so I told myself I hadn't hurt him.

It's a misconception that people die because something inside goes wrong. I think we die from the outside in. A bullet, for example, penetrating a body, or in my case, it started with my skin. If I turned on the fan, and stood in front of a mirror, I could see the breeze move my hair, but there was no tingle in my scalp. My arms stopped feeling the air. The circulation of my blood, it seemed, had retreated deep into the interior, leaving no sensation where my body met the world.

Early in our marriage, when Richard first let me down, I remember how hurt and anger tied my stomach up in knots. Then, in time, it seemed I no longer had a stomach. My mind could register the disappointment, but to my surprise, there was no more physical response. My husband didn't make me happy, but at least he no longer made me sick.

I was driving to the cabin alone one night when I heard a siren and saw a motorcycle cop in the rearview. I had no idea what I had done. I pulled over. He stopped yards behind me, and as I watched him walk toward me, I felt something I had forgotten beating hard inside me.

How do I remember my best-loved best? When he held me close, or when he hit his head against concrete till I said no?

He wandered the streets and sometimes slept there. I gave him a cell phone and paid the bills. "So you can reach me whenever you need me."

Maybe the doctors who came for the third Chinese were real and there was a mental hospital in the area after all. I wished I knew where because I understood it might not be a bad idea for me to go there.

He took a bus, he hitchhiked, he walked, who the hell knows how he got to the desert.

The phone rang. He said, "Let me in. Please let me in."

He had been here before. We had brought him.

I opened the door. Skee wasn't there.

"Please," he said. "Please."

"Are you in L.A.?" I asked him. Our phone rings both places. I said, "We're at the cabin."

"I'm at the cabin," he said. "I'm in the desert. At the cabin. At the trailer. Please," he said. "Please."

"I don't see you," I said. "The door is open."

"Why have you locked me out?" he said.

I said, "The door is open." I said, "I'm right here. Where are you, Skee?"

"Let me in!"

He was at someone else's trailer. A black man trying to get in.

"Where are you?" I said. "You're lost. Don't do anything. Where are you?"

I heard shouting, and then I heard gunfire.

They said the suspect turned with something in his hand. The mobile phone I gave him.

People deal with grief in different ways. I went to a rave just like our first naked person. Paid ten dollars for a map and drove out into the barren flats.

In the sixties, we were so uptight, for a white person to dance with abandon and throw her body around was shocking liberation. In the sixties, we tried to overcome history but we did not pretend it didn't exist.

In the seventies, we had the Latin hustle — hustle almost a dirty word, how surprising then how orderly the movement, how precise the steps.

At the rave they dance as in a trance. In the firelight, everyone's skin glows. You can't tell color. And these days everyone wears dreadlocks. Not everyone, of course, what I mean is anyone who wants to. The locks bob and tremble and flail, like a headdress, in the firelight, and I think of the Spanish padres watching the Indians dance, how they saw not men but devils.

Everyone was uninhibited. I felt very old. I was sure they were using drugs I'd never even heard of. At my age, everything *me fatigue*. No one cared what I did. No one watched me. I squatted in the dirt and cried for my sweet darling cat who got eaten.

I wasn't stoned. But these days, I don't like driving because I find myself forgetting to look or staring without seeing or seeing without registering or looking in the wrong direction and so I drive very slowly because I can no longer remember to be careful.

The Highway Patrol pulled me over for going too slow.

It was the black cop, and so I thought, *He's not the one,* and I wondered if he remembered the poster.

They say sometimes it starts with a peculiar smell. Sometimes with an auditory hallucination. Do you think it can start with thoughts of race? Thoughts of race as a symptom of psychopathology, the first manifestation of psychotic break.

We went back to Los Angeles and a terrible man stormed in firing at the Jewish Community Center and then he killed Mr. Joseph Ileto who was delivering mail.

Richard said, "Where do you think you're going?"

I was going out into the street. I imagined wearing a sign that said *Race*

Traitor. I imagined shouting, *I'm a Jew! I loved a black man!*, shouting *Kill me! Here's my heart! Shoot me now!*

I hardly leave the apartment. Richard goes with me when I need Advil, as if a pill made in a factory can ease the pain.

The girl behind the counter looked Filipina.

"My condolences," I said. "For your Mr. Ileto."

Just because she's Filipina, or looks it, does that make his murder important to her, does that entitle her to condolences from strangers?

"Do you think," I asked, "that when one becomes acutely aware of race, it's advisable to put oneself under a doctor's care?"

I said, "I'm not going to hurt you," which is what the rapist says to the woman or the child, so it's no wonder the Filipina girl seemed frightened.

I said, "They shot him."

By the register, they were selling guardian angels in the form of pins you pin to your lapel. I took one from its cardboard backing and, before Richard could stop me, stabbed it into my hand, just to see.

I remember slanting my eyes on the subway and calling the naked people Chinese even after we knew that they weren't and I remember the watercolor set I got for my birthday as a child. It had a color called French Green. Later, when I lived in Maine, there were houses painted in just that color and the people who lived in those houses were invariably of French-Canadian descent. French Green, the Yankees said, and French was not descriptive but pejorative. And remember when they called black people "colored." If they'd been called brown, it would have been fine, but they were "colored" which meant someone had done something to them, they had been painted. If I got close, the color would rub off. If it came off on my skin, I wouldn't mind, but if I came home with brown stains on my clothes, my mom would hit me.

After I brought Skee to meet my parents, no one mentioned race.

And I think about the scar on my thigh that Skee kissed and Richard pretended not to see. And I think that Skee is dead and that They killed him.

We stay in L.A. I don't want to go back to the cabin. We've left the door unlocked in case anyone needs to get in and sometimes I wonder if I had made Skee go to the doctor if they could have saved all of him. Or if he had been diagnosed before our marriage crumbled, would we have stayed together? Would I have devoted my life to caring for him? I think he and I both know I would have been willing. It's not so easy to say whether he would have let himself be cared for.

In the poster, the man lies draped in a sheet, his face covered. His prick stiff with — it could be rigor mortis. He could be dead.

Driving down Highland, I went through a red light on purpose, hoping a cop would stop me. I wanted to see if my heart would pound.

He asked for my license.

I asked, "Were you there? I want to know what happened in the desert. I want to know what happened to my husband."

"Stay in the car," said the white cop, but I opened the door and stepped out, daring him to hit me.

"Are you the one?" I asked. "Are you the one who killed him?"

I could see he wanted to shoot me, but he didn't.

"Racist pig!" I said. "If I were a black man, you would kill me. If I were a Latino male, you'd cuff me and shoot me in the head." I had the sudden thought that I could pull up my dress and show my thigh and say, *Look! Look at this! Do you see what that white man did to me?* I could say, *Hang me from the lamppost!* Instead I said, "Reverse discrimination! What are you going to do? Ticket me? Send me to Traffic School?" I said, "Just because I'm a white woman. Kill me. Why don't you kill me? It's skin privilege, dammit. Why won't you kill me?"

When Skee acted crazy, that was normal for a black man. When I acted crazy, it was decided that what I needed was Richard's care and the latest meds.

Richard takes care of me, at least for now, and at least for now I let him.

This is normal life. He goes to work. Like a woman, I stay home. Most nights, we stay in and watch TV.

On Fridays, we go out to eat.

We go to the Korean barbecue. I'm learning not to stare at the Korean people, but discreetly, very discreetly, I watch to see what they do. Use the lettuce leaves like a tortilla, wrap up meat and *kim chee* and eat it like a taco.

My heart is hard. I'm going to get better.

All around us, Asian people are eating. They are fully clothed, and so are we.

before

Amy Uyematsu

Such unwelcome commotion how long the walk home crying after the other kids

Peek under my skirt an echo of giggling then louder the lure of sycamore and pine that purples flowering on lacy jacaranda and eucalyptus-filled skies whose perfume

Is always dizzying and sweet the surprise of sliding down poles at recess legs tightly entwined pelvis against steel what to call this unexpected friction still nameless between soft and hard this secret to repeat if no one's looking the grip of Mr. Goto's hand when I'm eleven his fingers holding my hip bone for speechless seconds and

I want to run away not sure why he studies me so strangely long before I lie awake

In the dark not knowing the words as I call on my hands to answer

CACTUS

Tara Ison

I HAVEN'T left the apartment in nine months. My current boyfriend Paul has tried. He's tried to lure me outside with tickets to the Hollywood Bowl or the Greek, lobster dinners on the Santa Monica Pier, a drive to the outlet mall in Camarillo for shoes. He combs *LA Weekly* in search of compelling exterior events. He seeks to entice me with unmuggy, azure-sky'd days, with dove gray rain days, with his twilight-walk-on-the-beach idea of romance. He brought me a kite, a neon lime rhombus with an optimistic mile of spooled nylon string, and proposed Laguna. He bought me a pair of rollerblades, then he bought me a JetSki. Actually, his parents bought it, for both of us. But his parents have always liked me. Paul thinks going outside will be good for me, scrub off dull cells of skin, freshen my blood, inspire bloom. You need some sun, he says hopefully, light and fresh air. A change of atmosphere. You're pale. You need to go outside. He talks about the necessary vitamin D absorption from ultraviolet rays. He cajoles, pleads, pouts, but in the end I give him shopping lists, and he comes back with everything I've asked.

I don't need to go outside. My computer is right there on my desk, and my work, mail, faxes, contact, come to me. Light and sky, a vertical swatch of the Hollywood Hills, all come to me through the faux bay window in the living room. I can plant myself safely in the window seat I rigged up and look out, see pavement, Laurel Avenue, cars, the streetcleaner on Tuesday mornings, a sleeping ceramic child and the ugly, treacherous, stolen cactus in our small plot of front yard. Paul has refused to water the cactus, thinking that will get me to rise, but I remind him: It's a *cactus*. Go on, with-hold water. It'll just mock us. It'll outlive us both. Just try to master it, and, more likely, you'll be the one to get hurt. This cactus stabbed me once, so I know what I'm talking about.

Josh, my former boyfriend, dug the cactus out of the ground in front of me on our only trip to the Mojave Desert. He had a job leading overnight hiking excursions for junior high and high school kids. He had a stock of whistles and white cotton French Foreign Legion–style caps. He'd drive a herd of bored, sweating students out to places like Death Valley, Anza-Borrego, Indian Canyon, in a renovated bus donated by the L.A. City School District, and explain how crashing tectonic plates thrust up the mountains and granite shafts, how melting glaciers once filled the basins with lakes, about global warming patterns and elevation and evolving ecosystems, how the water burrowed itself deeper underground as if look-ing to hide while harsh, parching winds swept soil into dunes. He showed them bedrock worn down and exposed like picked-clean bones. He taught them about the pleistocene Pinto People, and the Serrano Indians who lived on pinyon nuts, cactus fruit, and mesquite beans, wove sandals and baskets from the shredded, curly fibers of Mojave yucca, and left behind their pottery and rock paintings. He explained how explorers a hundred years ago dammed up the last trickles of water, plundered the desert for gold, and left a honeycomb of mines. He pointed out arroyos, playas, and alluvial fans baked down to dust, the stump of a basalt volcano, aplite and gneiss glinting in the sun. At dusk he showed them emerging kangaroo rats and desert iguanas and burrowing owls, explained how roadrunners get all the moisture they need from the bodily fluids of reptiles, insects, and rodents they eat, taught them how every desert animal has adapted in body shape or metabolism or special skill to hang on to its place as predator or prey. At night he and his students would all lie in their mummy bags under the black celestial dome, undimmed by any fake municipal glow, and watch the elliptic path of the planets, the zodiacal chase of stars. It's the *vastness* of it all, he would always tell them, me, sounding drug-fried or stupid, neither of which he is. His favorite word, *vast*—vast desert, landscape, atmosphere, universe, space. Earth: a core of rock, a crumbled mantle, a thin, forsaken crust, and a mere us between it and the vast and boundless sky. He said it was the vastness that got to them every time, what they succumbed to, the letting go of small things, but I know what got to them was him. I pictured the cynical, trooping teenagers rolling their eyes, elbowing each other, then finally cracking smiles. I pictured them losing their cool urban sheaths and succumbing to his desert varnish, his energized mirage, his pulse. Succumbing to this oasis of a person. He said it was the vastness that got to them, but I know that's what got to *him*, rooted him, somehow made him feel peace. I didn't get it. All that quiet just sounded lonely to me. The idea of succumbing to all that space made me feel aimless and lost. I could never understand why he'd want to feel so insignificant.

I used to watch him pack for his trips. He'd squeeze one spare everything into a small duffel bag and reel off the desert's vast beauties he couldn't wait to get back to, while in my head I listed ways he might get hurt. A blistering third-degree burn, despite the sunblock. Heatstroke, despite the cap. The skull-splitting fall from a rock. A flash flood while he slept. In my mind he'd go to retrieve a student who'd wandered into a forbidden, abandoned mine, only to have it collapse on top of him in a thundering billow of rock. He always packed a topographic map and compass, but I suspected he'd get lost one day in the pirouetting cactus-boulder cow skull, cactus-boulder-cow skull backdrop of the cartoon Southwest. I'd watch him load the bus with plastic five-gallon barrels of water—*I want you guys guzzling two gallons per person per day,* I'd hear him warn students on the phone in his teacher's voice, *you gotta replace that sweat!* — and think: evaporation, dehydration. I pictured him desperately sucking a chunk of cactus. I pictured him writhing with heat cramp. He always packed a shovel, in case the bus got mired in sand, and I'd picture a fresh-dug desert grave, his body wrapped in the shiny green Hefty bags he took along for trash and already melting into his skin in the sun. He had a cooler the size of a steamer trunk packed with food and bricks of ice, and I'd think: starvation, botulism. The first aid kit didn't reassure me; it confirmed my fears. There were desert tarantulas and desert snakes, and I'd watch him sharpen his jackknife and scissors and imagine him coming back in a limp, drained stagger, his body marked with a cross where some student had X'd over a fanged puncture to suck out and spit the poison from his blood. Every time he came home, a mere him, hair burnt a lighter blond, his fruit-leather skin covered in a gritty sweat and his nape bright as tomato from having loaned his neck-flap cap to a student too arrogant to bring his own, I'd busy myself with a special dinner, something cool with mint and cucumber, draw him a tepid bath, bustle and fuss all to avoid an hysteric relief at having him back and okay. Each time he came back unhurt I stockpiled the fear, carried it over to the next time, weighed the increase of odds that meant nothing bad had happened yet and so next time, of course, it would.

When we were first together, he'd always asked me to go along. When we were first together, I wasn't scared at all, and I always shrugged and said No, I don't feel like it, I'm not much of an outdoors person, You go, we're not joined at the hip, You go, we're going to grow old together, right? plenty of time, You go, we don't have to do everything together, we don't have to share all the same interests, right? Plus the lack of privacy, the adolescent throng, the harsh and lunar-sounding landscape, the herding and the rules — *bag up and ziplock your toilet paper, you guys, leave no trace!* — always made it sound more like work than play. And I didn't want to be part of his work, just one more thing he had to pack and take along. I wanted to carry more weight than that. But then after a while I thought maybe if it were just us two. I wasn't seeing him that much. He was being successful and busy at his job, scheduling extra excursions. That's what so great about you, Holly, he'd say to me, leaving, You're so independent. He was away a lot of weekends, then a lot of weekdays, too, and getting an edgy, cramped look sometimes when he was home. So I finally suggested it, my going with him and just us two, and he wanted to know why I'd changed my mind. He wanted to know what I possibly thought I'd get out of it. You're not very adaptable, Holly, he mumbled into my neck one night over the whir of the window fan. And I said, See? That's the point, I don't understand the appeal. This will expand my horizon. But when I said that, I realized it was his horizon that worried me; his was getting too big and far away for me to be more than a speck in it. A mere me. I was a dot on his landscape, and I wanted to be a vast and boundless thing for him. I wanted him to succumb to me. I went to the outlet mall and bought hiking boots, a special sunscreen with alpha-hydroxy. But by that time, I wasn't just worried, I was also getting scared, for him, and he had stopped asking me to go.

Then one bland, humid Friday morning last April, the phone rang with someone telling me that weekend's excursion to Joshua Tree was called off due to an outbreak of flu at some East L.A. junior high. Josh was outside loading the bus, and, when I told him, got his edgy, penned-up animal look, the one that says *let me out.*

Shit, he said. He sighed, regarded the bus a moment. Then he turned back to me. Okay, let's go. We'll go, just us two.

Now? I said.

I'm packed up. I have the permit. It's April. I can't stay here all weekend, he said, gesturing at the street and pavement. He had refused to plant grass on our little front plot, saying lawn in Los Angeles was an environmental insult. I'd thought maybe just a rose bush would be nice, but instead we had a found-rock garden. We'd spot lost-looking rocks in alleys or streets, bring them home. At first I'd thought it was fun, kitschy, but today the rocks just looked forced. Horns honked down on Sunset Boulevard; there was a siren's rise and ebb, a jet, a helicopter's anxious drone, the hot gasp of wetted city cement, the smell of exhaust.

What's the problem, Holly? he said. You said you wanted to go.

I saw us going back inside the apartment where it was safe and where he didn't want to be, saw us spending a weekend together, just us two, with four walls and a roof and a window unit that cooled and filtered air. Then I saw him saying, I'll go, I'll just go myself, and then going by himself. Leaving me in favor of all those dangers. Wandering off and never coming back. I saw the snake venom coursing through and no one ready with a knife; I saw him dead from exposure and no one there to dig his grave. I saw turkey vultures swooping in to pick his bones clean. This wasn't him wanting to *leave* me, I realized with relief; this was him *needing* me. This was him not wanting to get hurt, not wanting to be alone, not wanting to let go. Wanting to let me in to fill up all his precious space.

I went inside, and put on my boots and sunblock. We transferred mummy bags and shovel and cooler and first aid kit and wheelbarrow and gallons of water from the school bus to his truck, left Hollywood, and drove a few hours' east from Los Angeles along the 10, where the world went dull and beige, full of highway and dirt without nap, tired motels and shopping malls and hamburger drive-thrus collapsed at the foot of mountains as if dumped off cliffs. Then, somewhere beyond the turnoff for Palm Springs, higher and higher up and further on Route 62, the dunnish air cleared and the Mojave Desert slowly unrolled into vast, lucid bloom. Magentas, lemons, purples, oranges, whites, from the horizon to us, a sudden extravagance, and the wind-snap of sage, nectar, honest rock, succulent air.

See? he said. April.

I pictured it all dead, I said.

It's never dead. It looks dead in fall and winter, sometimes, when a lot of it's dormant. But then it all explodes.

I took off my boots and hung my feet out the window, so my toes could breathe. I leaned back against him, and he put his arm around me, poked his nose in my ear. He kissed my throat and said, See?

Yes, I said.

No, look, a Joshua tree, he said, pointing.

We were passing a lanky, trunked thing, its branches outstretched in stiff torsion, each one ending in a tuft of spines. We passed another one, then three.

Joshua trees, he said. This is the only place in the world they live. And they live hundreds of years. The Mormons called them that. They drove out in their wagons to California and suddenly saw all of these and said they looked like Joshua, his arms up, welcoming them to the Promised Land.

He slowed the truck. The tree didn't look like a welcoming prophet to me. Its trunk was covered in spikes scaled like a chain mail of daggers. The raised branch-arms looked deformed. It looked like an armored soldier with boiling oil poured down his back, caught in the first moment of pan-icked, agonized cringe.

We passed more, and then many, and then they were everywhere. It was a whole field of trapped and seared Joshuas trying desperately to grip the sky, shaking twisted, crippled fists at God.

We stopped at the Oasis Visitor Center in Twentynine Palms. Josh reg-istered the truck at the backcountry board while I examined glass jars of jewel-colored cactus marmalades, cactus pickles, cactus candy. The labels showed a thorny cactus fruit split in half, revealing tender, pulpy insides. I bought granola bars and another half-liter bottle of water and leafed through a book called *Common Cacti of the Southwest*.

Look, I said to him, showing. I'm learning all about cactus. We should get this.

Holly, he said. He took the book from me and put it back. You're here. You don't need a book to *show* you here.

All right, you teach me.

Just be patient. He smiled at me as I tore the wrapper off a chocolate chip granola bar and ate it. You have to be patient in the desert, Holly. Give it up.

Before leaving we walked up close to a smallish Joshua tree. A wood-pecker tapped at a branch. Josh showed me wrens nesting in the tree's top-most spines, and thumbnail moths collecting pollen from the blossom clusters, laying eggs. He nudged a toppled, decaying limb with his foot; a kangaroo rat scuttled away, and termites surged.

It's the perfect ecosystem, he said in his teacher's voice. All in itself. The living tree is food and home for birds and insects and rodents. And then even when it's dead, it's food and home. The energy just keeps cycling, being transformed. There's life everywhere, if you just look for it.

Oh, God, I said, ducking. In front of me was a fat lizard impaled on a spike through its belly. Hanging on a low Joshua tree branch I almost walked into. Its sleepy lizard-eyes were just starting to crust; flies buzzed.

Who would do that? I asked.

A shrike, probably, he said. Or a hawk. Saving it for dinner.

I thought the desert was so peaceful, I said.

No, the desert is so honest, he said.

He saw a bit of trash nearby, a dirty paper flap. He picked it up and tossed it along with my granola bar wrapper into the forest green Hefty bag in the bed of the truck. He'd brought along a whole collection of plastic bags, from tiny ziplock to body-bag-size. *Leave no trace.*

I screamed at the stab to my leg. Josh always camped with his students at official sites with tables and fire grates, but he'd wanted the two of us out in the middle of nowhere. And there we were, only us and the desert and a sere, planeless sky. We'd parked the truck and put on our French Foreign Legion caps and hiked hot silent miles into the wild brush from the road, as requested by park rules for "wilderness camps." The Joshua trees had thinned out as we went farther east. We'd passed rock formations that looked like animals and gourds and human skulls, hiked across bajadas and around granite outcrops. Josh pointed out iguana, skulking coyote, rabbits, squirrels. Desert dandelions and mallow, flame-tipped ocotillo, beavertail, prickly pear. He was walking ahead of me, pushing water and supplies in the small wheelbarrow; he'd told me to walk behind, to obliterate the wheel's track.

Tire marks can live out here for years, he'd said. And they don't belong here. Scars in the desert heal slowly.

Thank you, teacher, I said. But my footsteps don't belong here, either. Don't footsteps count as scars?

We wove our way through creosote bushes and gray-green cactus scrub, breathing hostile air that heated, dusted, and dried my lungs, when I felt my leg seized by sudden hot pierces in the flesh of my right calf, just above my boot. I shrieked. A cylindrical piece of gray-green cactus half a foot long clung to my leg as if velcro'd, its spines lodged in my skin.

Josh dropped the wagon and ran to me, grabbed my hand before I could reach down.

Uh uh, he said. Don't touch.

Out of nowhere, I said. This thing attacked me out of nowhere. I bit my lip, determined not to cry, split open, fall apart.

Jumping cholla. They're everywhere. He pointed to a shrubby, fuzzy cactus nearby, three or four feet high, pale green and flowerless. It looked like a bristled balloon animal, twisted from those long, skinny balloons into joints, and covered with spiky hair. It looked mocking.

You must've brushed against it, he said. You step too close to one of those joints, they sense the moisture or heat or energy or something, and attack. They jump, and cling on.

This is like getting all your childhood vaccinations at once, I said. I wasn't crying, yet.

I told you to be careful.

You told me to be *patient.*

Same thing, he said. He rummaged in his duffel bag. They also call it teddy bear cholla.

Adorable, I said. I pulled the bottle from my backpack and gulped water.

Or silver cholla. They have these silver sheaths on their spines. Look at it, see the sunlight through the spines? See how it shimmers? They're sort of luminous, huh? Pretty?

Josh.

That's good, keep drinking your water. You're breaking out in a sweat. And breathe, Holly.

He came to me with a comb and a pair of pliers. He helped me sit down, and propped my leg up on his thighs. A lot of people think chollas are sort of ugly, he said. Stiff. Stunted-looking. I think they're sort of cool. They get little violet flowers around this time of year. And they're edible, you know? They taste great, sweet, you just have to peel them and —

Josh, do something.

Yeah, hold on.

He slid the comb between my leg and the cactus, threading its teeth among the spines. I swallowed a long drink of water so I wouldn't scream again, maybe my two gallons worth.

These're called glochids. These little spines, see? They're barbed. They lock in under the top layer of skin. That's how this thing reproduces. The joints cling to whatever passes by. Whatever'll carry it around. Then it lands somewhere, and takes root. Chollas are tough. Ranchers hate them, they're like weeds. But medicine men used cholla on people during prayer ceremonies. They believed the spines drew out the sickness.

Josh.

Okay, hold on.

He gripped the comb then flipped the cactus joint off and away from me, leaving a dozen golden needles still imbedded in my leg, and despite myself, I shrieked again.

Why didn't you warn me? I asked.

I'm sorry.

No, about the cactus. If they're so dangerous.

Okay. I'm warning you now. This is going to hurt. Take a few deep breaths. Try to relax.

One by one he pulled the spines out with pliers. My leg bristled and I shivered at the fierce, tiny burns. I chewed my tongue and swallowed blood while he tried to distract me by teaching me all about cactus. Their survival strategies. How their spines evolved from leaves as a defense against predators, how the reduced leaf surface helped them endure the desert. How their thick, waxy skins retard evaporation, how they're misers, hoarding water in their fleshy stems, in their ribs or barrels or pads of tissue, how during and after a rain they gorge on water, expand and swell to hold as much as they can, how their root systems are shallow but extensive, spreading out wide under a thin surface of dirt to pick up and store moisture from the lightest desert shower. He talked in a smoothing, soothing voice, while pulling out the spines. Each spine barb tugged with it a small divot of flesh, a brief welling of blood, and with each tug I thought Why didn't he warn me? Why did he bring me here, drag me out in the middle of vast nowhere, if this was just going to hurt? He's trying to get me to relax and succumb to all the landscape and space, to feeling, to feeling small and not clinging to anything, to letting go. As if that weren't dangerous, as if there's any peace in that.

Cacti are actually related to the rose family, did you know that? he was asking. You can see it when they bloom. They blow roses away. Sometimes you can actually watch a cactus flower unfold, the petals open up and uncurl. Actually, they're more beautiful than roses. You expect a rose to be beautiful. It's more interesting to find all that beauty in a cactus. The split personality, you know?

I didn't say anything. I was too angry, I didn't trust myself to speak. Or breathe. I didn't trust the only air there.

Okay, he said. Your spines are gone.

He squeezed my calf hard to bring out the last of the blood, blotted it away with a piece of gauze, then applied antiseptic ointment from the first aid kit. I wiped the sweat off my upper lip. My T shirt, one of Josh's, was sticking all over; I was sweating too much and too fast for the air to burn it off my skin.

Are you okay? he asked me. He leaned over and pressed his mouth against my damp forehead.

I'm okay, I said.

Drink more water, he mumbled against my hair. I want you guzzling, like, two gallons a day. You need to replace all those fluids.

I nodded, just a small dip of a nod so he wouldn't move his mouth. But he did. He wrapped more gauze in a bandage around my leg, then carefully disposed of the bloodstained gauze in the Hefty garbage bag.

I wasn't going to make love that night. My leg still throbbed, I felt filmed with sweat and sunblock, I wanted to punish Josh for not taking better care of me. We'd zipped our two mummy bags together and I crawled inside with him, determined to stay separate and stiff as wood. But he named the stars for me, and I pressed against him for a sense of scale. He wove his legs between mine so my bandaged calf would rest on top, and I bent my other leg to help. He raised his hand up to trace the constellations, but the parallax distorted their forms; I reached up with him to clasp his hand, trace the sky with him and share his view, horizon, galaxy. He kissed me and then I could breathe again, fully, breathe in the air that was him, breathe in the having him to hold on to, what always made me feel found and unbound, blessed. His touch always split me open into something tender and sweet. He saw in me something luminous, ready to bloom. But it was all him, and he never realized that. I didn't deserve such significance. I didn't deserve him. An elemental, pure, and infinite him, a man who saw the life in a dead lizard, who saw more beauty in a cactus than a rose, who could find the pulse in a petrified limb. A man who didn't realize that I was just a mere me, and that I lived on, drank from, him. And that without him forever as wellspring, as font, I would shrivel up to a small, withered, petty thing and die.

A cactus, I said the next morning. I want my very own.

Come on, you *have* your very own. He stopped rolling up our mummy bags to strike an iconic cactus pose.

That's a saguaro, I told him, remembering from *Common Cacti of the Southwest*. They only live in Arizona.

Hey, good.

At the saguaro festival in July they make cactus wine, I told him. It symbolizes rain replenishing the earth.

I'm very proud of you.

And you're a lovely cactus, I said, but this way if you ever leave me, I will always have the real thing. See? I pointed to a small Joshua tree in the distance, an isolated straggler. I waited for him to ask *Why do you think I would ever leave you?* but he did not.

Ah, he said, smiling his teacher's smile. It said *You are about to learn something,* and I was sick of it. But a Joshua tree is not a cactus. It's a yucca. It's actually part of the lily family.

All right.

Not every desert plant is a cactus, he said. There's yucca and agave and bear-grass and ocotillo and creosote and—

All *right!*

He pointed to the ugly killer cholla that had attacked me. *That's* a cactus. Chollas are cactus.

Fine. I'll make do with a cholla. A lowly, ugly, common desert weed.

No.

You thought they were beautiful, I said.

We're not taking a cactus home, he said.

Why not?

He pointed out that the cactus had already wounded me, that I was still complaining about my throbbing leg, and that getting it home would be impossible.

You're scared of a few glochids? I asked. Embrace what you fear.

He sighed. I waited. I waited for him to tell me we can't disrupt the ecosystem of the desert. That tough as cacti are, they're also vulnerable, that we might get it all the way home just to have it refuse to take root and then die. I waited for him to talk about indigenous nutrients in the desert soil, about fungal spores and etiolation. That we didn't have room for the cactus at home, or space for its root system, that the concrete would snuff it out, choke it dead.

This is a national park, he said finally. Everything is protected here.

I wasn't, I said.

We just looked at each other. Then he came and knelt next to me. He put his hand on the back of my skull, wove his fingers through my hair and tugged my head back, put his arms around me. He wanted me to clasp him back, I knew, but I wouldn't give him that. We just sat there for a moment in silence, a heated, taut desert silence. I waited. He gave up first. He got up, took a bottle of water, and hiked all the way back to the truck for the shovel, twine, gloves, a tarpaulin, returned, and dug. I kept watch. We roped the cholla, steadied it in the wheelbarrow, strapped it to the bed of the truck with twine, camouflaged it with Hefty garbage bags, and drove home without talk. We planted the cactus in our found-rock-garden front yard. A week later, I found a chipped ceramic Mexican child sleeping beneath its huge ceramic sombrero near a dumpster in the Fairfax district and brought it home. I tried to get Josh to debate whether the ceramic child was racist kitsch or just kitsch, but he only rolled his eyes at me. In the end we put it next to the cactus, facing the street. I called him our little ceramic son. And, as a little ceramic child, it had no moisture or heat or energy, so I knew it would always be safe from the cactus spines, and could sleep in peace.

My leg healed, of course. The wound became a spray of small roseate scars. And the cactus did take root in our found-rock plot, did just fine. For two more months, it lived and breathed and grew, did very well. I hoped it would blossom, soon, give us showy violet flowers. It didn't, but I smiled at it every time I came and went, every time I looked out the window. I admired how the sun on its silvery spines made it shimmer, made it luminous. And every time, I thought with pleasure that stealing the cactus was the type of unwholesome, dishonest thing Josh would never have done in front of the junior high and high school kids, or by himself. But I got him to do it for me. I got him to break into the desert for me, plunder it to bring me jewels. I got him to tear a piece off the vastness, chain it down to a bound and finite space. Looking at the cactus always made me feel victorious. I would look at my healed leg scars and think *I am inoculated, now, I'm safe.* I felt very peaceful and secure, until two months later, when Josh left me.

Josh was killed in a plane crash. Not the kind where you're on the plane. The kind where you start a fight with your girlfriend who loves you to death but whom you say won't let you breathe, is too clingy, so you decide to go off hiking by yourself because you need the space, you don't want to do every single thing together, all the time, take and share every single breath with the woman who loves you to death, so you drive out to the Mojave by yourself in your truck, park it and trek across the desert like Moses, through a field of Joshua trees with their grotesque, outstretched-to-God arms, to sleep under the stars and feel profoundly, vastly insignificant, and far overhead a Cessna Skyhawk SP with engine trouble sails downward, into the welcoming arms, and doesn't see you because you're a mere dot in the landscape, and you don't see it, you just barely awake at the sputter, the swooping whine of what perhaps sounded like a very large desert bird, a hawk, or a screeching owl, or maybe the death cry of a lizard pierced by spikes, and so just as the plane crashes down — *then* you see it, yes, but it's too late — and lands on top of you in a blaze of oil and shredding metal and burning yucca, creosote, ocotillo, maybe, your last thought is I should have kissed the woman I love good-bye when I left, or I should have never left her to go outside where it's harsh, unforgiving, dangerous, or at least I should have brought her with me so we could die together. That kind of plane crash. When they dug him out of the cratered brush and found his driver's license, unsinged but the laminate melted into his thigh, they called and told me, and my first thought was, It's not fair to die in a plane crash if you're not actually on the plane. Then I realized I was shaking and couldn't walk properly, so I crawled into the bathtub. The porcelain was cold, wonderfully solid, anesthetic, and I could pull the shower curtain around to make myself a terrarium. I figured I could sleep there, bathe there, have a water source, have someone bring me packages of ramen to make, I could even shit and pee right there forever, a perfect ecosystem, for the rest of my life, and not ever have to go anywhere or outside again. That worked just fine for three or four days, except for the ramen because I didn't have any, so I just drank a lot of water from the faucet instead, and then Josh's younger brother Paul drove down from Santa Barbara, banged on the front door for a while, then decided to break through the bathroom window to come get me.

He made me get out of the terrarium-tub, and then he decided to stay the night, just to make sure I was okay. He was a sophomore at UC Santa Barbara, studying biology or pre-med or something. Josh had shown me photos of his brother. Paul was seven or eight years younger and unripe-looking, a laundered sweatshirt and ironed jeans, a Josh's kind of hair but combed and darker, a Josh's face but paler, unvarnished. He looked just like the photos, but now he also looked scared, stunned. He got me towels and one of Josh's clean T-shirts, and made me take a shower, which seemed ridiculous, given that I'd been living in a bathtub for four days, but fine. When I came out he told me not to worry about anything, that everything had been taken care of, their parents had had Josh's body brought home to Ventura. They'd wanted to find me, have me come for the service, but I'd never answered the phone. They'd always liked me. They thought I was a stabilizing influence on their wandering son. That I could root him. Now they were worried that I was all right. So after the service, because there wasn't time before, Paul had driven down to check. He could stay a few days, he said, then drive back up. I said okay. He'd found sheets and a pillow for the couch. He asked me if I wanted to go out for pizza or something. I looked outside the living room window, at the ugly, treacherous, stolen cholla cactus in the front yard. It had beaten me, gotten me back. I'd stolen Josh, too, and the cactus had punished me for both of them. No, I told Paul, I really didn't feel like going out.

I climbed into bed. Since Josh had left I'd slept far to one side, almost on the edge, so as not to disturb his blanket and mattress space. So his imprint was still there, and a strand of hair, the smell of rock. I thought of his body burned into the California desert, wondered if the heat had turned the desert sand to glass. I wondered how long the scar of his footsteps' trek would last. I wondered if they searched for and found every last shred of him, packed up every scrap in tiny ziplock bags. *Leave no trace.* Or if a limb was left behind. A dead, rotting Josh limb, now food and home for the termites and kangaroo rats, his energy recycled, transformed. He would have liked that.

I got up and went back to sleep in the bathtub.

After a few weeks, Paul had the idea to transfer to UCLA. He decided to just forget about fall quarter at UCSB, so he could stay in L.A. and hang out with me, then start winter quarter down here. What he *really* wanted to do, he confided one night, was drop out altogether and do something really cool and free-spirited like Josh. He didn't *really want* to be a doctor, he had the feeling, but his parents were pretty invested in it. In one of their sons being achieving, successful. And *now*, you know . . . his voice trailed off. He asked me if I had talked to my parents. If maybe I wanted him to call them for me. And I said No, they never even met Josh, I haven't even seem them for a few years. We've never been very close. They're not your kind of parents, all nurturing and invested, I told him. My parents were always off being very busy, always leaving me to go off by themselves.

Paul was sleeping in the bed by then. I'd given him Josh's space. I was sleeping in the bathtub, but I'd leave the door open and the shower curtain tugged open to talk at night until we fell asleep. And after a few months, he decided he didn't *really* need to get his own apartment, that he should probably stay with me so I wouldn't be all alone and he could take care of me. I gave him Josh's clothing to wear, all of which is too big for him and full of threadbare spots, but he likes it. He wears Josh's French Foreign Legion caps. Josh would have liked that, too. Their parents call every few weeks to see how we're doing. I hear Paul tell them he's worried about me. They tell Paul they read an article that says the first year is the hardest, but then it gets better. They tell Paul they're going to fax the article, so that I can read it. They say they want to come visit us. None of them seem to realize it's my fault we all lost him. That it's because of me we all have to cling to each other and shrivel up and pay.

Paul tries so hard. He goes to the grocery store and makes us pizza from scratch. He goes to the laundromat. He goes to video stores and brings home armloads of the newest releases, because I won't even debate the idea of going out. He seems to think I'm very fragile, about to wilt and expire, or explode. He says he doesn't like to leave me alone, but I think he just doesn't like to go out by himself. I urge him to go. I tell him We don't have to spend all of our time together, do we? I tell him to make some friends from school. I tell him he needs to give me more space, and his scared look has started coming back.

I'm asleep the night he comes home sometime in April, after hanging out with his new friends from school. I wake up because he's loud and stumbling, a little drunk, and comes into the bathroom to tug on my arm. *Please, Holly,* he says, *wake up. Please come sleep in the bed with me tonight.* He strokes my hair and my shoulder. We've never touched. We've been together almost a year, and we've never even slightly brushed against each other. I barely even sense him in the apartment, rarely sense his energy or heat. He starts crying now, *I miss Josh,* he says, trying to grip me, *I'm lonely, please, isn't it time, aren't you lonely?* and I think, What difference does it make? I let him pull me out of the tub's cool hug, and pull me into the bedroom. We get in the bed together, both of us in Josh's T-shirts, and he's fondling, clutching at me. My skin just feels numb. It's dead skin, and he's rubbing me as if trying to make it alive. He enters me, I'm dry as dust and I don't even feel it. He's trying to get further inside me, and I realize, then, what he's really trying to do. Get me to unfold, to pulse. It's April, and he's trying to get me to flower again. He's trying to peel back a layer of me to get where it's pulpy and soft. He's feeling so much, and he's trying to make me feel, too, expose me to where it's dangerous and full of unseen, searing threat. He's touching me as if he's capable of that. But he isn't. He's weak, insignificant, a pale imitation. And he's just clutching at me because I'm here, not because I mean anything, am anything to him, really, he's just clinging to whatever happened by. Anyway, I won't let it happen. I suddenly see myself making love to Josh, then, opening up to all of it, I feel myself start to get wet and I chew my tongue to bleed and keep me from it, so I won't cry, fall apart, split open into the tenderness and the sweet. I hold myself stiff as wood, I gulp and gulp to hoard up all the wet, keep it inside of me, and when he finally finishes, I gasp and prickle with relief.

I like to keep the front door triple-locked and it takes me a moment to remember, deadbolt first, that's right, then knob. I leave the chain on, and peek out through the gap at the empty street, sleeping ceramic child, the cactus. It's grown bigger. It's taller than I am now, cuddly and blameless-looking, its spines silver and luminous in the moonlight. I unchain the front door and step outside. The outside air feels exactly the same as the inside air, and I think, Of course, there is no difference. It isn't safe anywhere you go.

The cactus is waiting for me, and very welcoming. It isn't punishing or mocking; it's kind. It knows I want my spines back. It knows my moisture, heat, energy, and yearns toward me. It yearns toward my legs, first, my thighs, then the insides of my open arms, my throat, embraces me even before I've pressed against it with my breasts, attaches to every inch of my skin with its greedy tines. The cactus needs me. It finds me significant, and I embrace it back, hard, to feel its spines enter and become mine. Each pierce creates a vivid bloom. Each spine taps my blood, then my bones, and this makes me feel boundless, and vast. And this is something I can succumb to, this is something I can feel.

ATWATER

Jacqueline De Angelis

I

If I am on the river, if I am staring in the water, if I see all the
      plastic cups,
a whiffle ball, sharp objects swiftly moving, miscellaneous
      wrappers, no buttons,

then, *where do I enter?*

II

You can walk
under bridges, through one city

and then another without noticing. *Look, a drowning shopping
      cart.* In it a list:
toothpaste,
candles,
juice,
pink dishwashing soap.

III

The water isn't potable. It doesn't irrigate. It will not serve us.
The river is passing. Ends at Playa del Rey.

IV

This river is no river of future.

V

There is a boy with black hair. His father passes the kite string.
The boy looks up. The kite is yellow and probably black.
     Certainly dark in spots. A bee
maybe? The string slips. The boy doesn't want.

The kite is going one way, the river another.

VI

Pure snow melt, pure rain runoff rushes down San Gabriel
     mountain canyons. It mixes
with our gray water. If we are unlucky the sewers run into it.
     Ends in Playa del Rey.

King of beaches. Sun on the beach. Sunny beach. Playa del
     Rey, beach
where airplanes run low. Where sound diminishes.

VII

We are wry about it.
We do not sit and reminisce about the night we rode this river,
self-sufficient, the moon fragments in waves.

We do not yearn for the slap of river on shore.

It is us this river. We slough off. We ride back and forth and
     over and over and do

not call its name. We do not turn
in the dark to spell it on the broad back of someone we love.

We have an ocean. But that is another story.

VIII

The Mississippi is commerce. The Mahoning is canoeing clubs.
The Ganges, religious. In the Amazon swim fish that can bite
        OFF your feet. Now look at how
movies have made rivers so frightening they appear in my
        dreams.

IX

Why are you surprised; it is a river therefore people drown.
They watch too much TV and consequently have no
        experience.
The swift deep is something they learn too late.

We don't stand, stare,
throw coins,
think of it as travel, commerce,
salvation, *escape.*

X

People have jumped. From the spanning bridges. Off the
        viaducts.
They heard the laugh concrete has.

I don't actually remember the story of the woman who leapt
        from the bridge with her baby.

I heard it. I saw the daughter in Thursday's paper. The details
    are hazy.
I remember the part where it said she was lonely. That struck
    me.
Who isn't really?

XI

I live on the river bank. Not the current but the real shore.
Some hot nights the river smells. Damp clothes left in a plastic
    bag. Some sort
of excremental mold. Something the cat dragged in.

I do not stand and stare. I do not whisper its name to the broad
    back of my lover.
If this is a river . . .

XII

The daughter, all grown sitting at her kitchen table, said, in the
    Life & Times section, that she
forgave
her mother. "My mother was just lonely." We can all
    understand that.
This forgiving daughter with unkempt hair fascinates me. See
    her in the shabby
four-color of newspapers. The printer's rosette off-register;
she is cyan, yellow, black, redder than dreams.

XIII

We are wry about her mother at dinner. Wire monkey mother.
    Mother that dresses you up
to jump off a bridge.

XIV

If this is a river it has no dreams.

XV

No, it has one dream.

XVI

Where do I enter?

XVII

When you live this near you have frogs and June bugs. If you
      lived one street away
you would have the June bugs but not the frogs. You would
      not hear
the cars on the freeway, either.

Some years the June bugs stay until July. The frogs less regular.
You have more in your yard if you have a dog and not a cat.
If you go down to the river at night you can hear frogs in the
      stream of vehicles.

You would not want to go down to the river at night.
      Remember, this isn't a river
of dreams, you do not toss coins for wishes, there is no
      salvation at this shore, no one
whispers its name into your ear.

XVIII

Here is the historia of el Río.
Listen. This is before the Spanish altered the world.

"Some of the old men were smoking pipes well made of baked clay and they puffed at us three mouthfuls of smoke. We gave them a little tobacco and glass beads, and they went away well pleased . . . After crossing the river we entered a large vineyard of wild grapes and an infinity of rosebushes in full bloom . . . After traveling about half a league we came to the village of this region, the people of which on seeing us, came out into the road. As they drew near they began to howl like wolves; they greeted us and wished to give us seeds, but we did not accept them. Seeing this, they threw some handfuls of them on the ground and the rest in the air." (Bolton 1927:147)

XIX

The neighborhood ice cream truck plays "Fascination."
In the winds, in the blasting heat, right through the fall, it *is* the
    background. Fascination.
I stop. Look around the room. Notice what I can.

It never fails, I sing a line, I do not know the real words to this
    song.

The train follows the river like a fascination.

The freeway follows the river like a snake. No, that's not it. The
    freeway
hems the river. That's not it . . .

The wild grasses break through the concrete channel and grow
promiscuous. They regreen her in clumps.

The foreign reeds grow straight down her spine.

XX

The river goes one way, people another.

My neighbor Moselle never liked the smell
of this river. When Moselle first laid her eyes on it — it was
        when people took pride —
it was when you could trust what was in the water and who
        came to your front door.
She couldn't speak for anyone else.

It smelled like *an infinity of roses.*

XXI

Floribunda I am promised at the Home Depot nursery.

"Blaze
Masses of bright-red 3" blooms cover this
popular climber spring through fall.
Strong canes reaching . . . display a profusion of eye-
catching, brilliant color . . .

Water thoroughly, weekly."

Plant it at the corner of the house and it will climb like the
        climbing
roses of Spain.

My mother says, you'll be sorry. My mother sees it attack the
        roof tiles. My father
the plumbing. I am going to see *an infinity of roses.*

XXII

This river is paying for its past anarchy. It is under observation,
    police copters, news choppers.
I often wonder can they scan for floating bodies?
How can anyone decipher the homeless life under the Los
    Feliz bridge?

We who live here do so at our own peril. We who live on the
    shore ignore or just plain don't
believe it.
We live with mortgages, landlords, out of old Winnebagos
    parked riverside.
They never tell you a thing about this channel when you live
    here.

It's a channel, isn't it? It isn't a river, is it?

XXIII

*"We forded the Rio . . . which descends with great rapidity from the
canyon through which it leaves the mountains and enters the plains. All
the country that we saw on this day's march appeared to us most suitable
for the production of all kinds of grain and fruit." (Teggart 1911:181)*
Batata,
maize,
tomatl,
ahuacatl (ah'-wah-cah-tl),
chicle,
cacauatl (kah-kah'-wah-tl)
papas.

"When early British golfers were playing with a ball made of
feathers packed into a leather cover, Indians were playing a game

with a ball made of rubber." . . . *they began to howl like wolves; they*
greeted us and wished to give us seeds . . .

XXIV

Coming home. Stuck in traffic. All of us resigned but cunning.
On the viaduct, over the river, we do not move, *it* moves.
Here transportation is a toy; speed's a memory. All our
        achievements fallow
misrepresentations. We've missed the mark somehow.
We've missed appointments, births, love. Pain is will, away.
        Dinner cool; down
on our luck, death in the air, we are struck with the smell of
        rotting dog.

What if the river is liquid god?

I can't get that mother out of my mind.
I bring her up at lunch. Boss asks, *Who do you think you are?*
Singular, lonely, had enough fiction for one life.
I laugh, the arugula leaves, alligators at the tip of my fork, flap.

XXV

I am the jumping woman. I think of diving all the time. *Let me*
        out of this car . . .
The water is fine . . . End in Playa del Rey . . . *An infinity of*
        roses, . . . seeds flung in the air.
We know this. We ALL know the KNOCK in our ear.

If god is a liquid, if this is a river . . .

XXVI

There is nothing you can be told that you don't already know.
Don't ask a river.
Don't run your firm hand along its slippery thigh.
Don't spill your drunk guts out, pat your belly and think
you gave yourself to it, fed your real self to this deep slim
    channel.
Hollow, hollow your friends yawn on the shore. There is
    nothing
I can tell you that you don't already know.

XXVII

chan.nel (chan'el) n. Abbr. chan. 1. The bed of a stream or river.
2. The deeper part of a river or harbor, especially a deep
navigable passage. 3. A trench, furrow, or groove. 4. *Electronics.* A
specified frequency band for the transmission and reception of
electromagnetic signals, as for television signals. 5. The medium
through which a spirit guide purportedly communicates with
the physical world.

XXVIII

Sit and look at it, *go ahead,* come on, *hurry up,* scoot, pick it up,
go on go.

Sit on slanted concrete. Watch water. *Look,* eddies. See the
    pied-billed grebe
dive rather than fly. Ignore the traffic. *Over there,* the great
    cosmopolitan egret —
nuptial plumage — stands, reflects in the current. Sit,
sit by the river and want.

XXIX

Clean the air and your own heart.
Drink all the bottled water you can.
Drink it all day long if need be.
Look, we are water. Our veins: What are they but a personal river?

Do you stare at water and think of your affinities? Have you ever?
When you see it (hostage) follow a cement course, what do
        you see?

XXX

You can walk under bridges, through one city without noticing

you are in another.
Where is our empathy?

Life shouldn't be so hard. All we want is to be liked, admired if
        possible, just

not hated.

But, we do not leave well enough alone. We do not let things
        set. We do not give things
peace.

XXXI

The mother who leapt got up and got dressed then dressed the
        baby.

The mother broke. The baby daughter bounced.
Was it notoriety she wanted them to land in?

Was it more of the same? The ordinary list?
Toothpaste,
dishwashing soap,
pink juice.

At the sink scrubbing pans the cinematic me
jumps off buildings, drives cars into walls, off the edge of cliffs.
I am lonely, the dishwater is tepid.
I don't have the energy to cleanser the sink so
I jump, crash, drown. Very dramatic.
So's the funeral.
Fewer people come than in the past. I've grown more realistic.
But they still regret my cold body laid out.
They should have called me more.
They might have had me over *for a little something* once in awhile.

Have I told you about this pain I have? I've been talking about
it for years but no one listens. I've gone from one thing to the
next and it never leaves me. The number of things I've tried, the
amount of money I've thrown at it. The time it has eaten away.
Legion, all of it.

And what good does it do to tell you about it!

XXXII

Had enough fiction for one life?

XXXIII

Let me gather my heart and lock it. A raven settles
in the apricot tree. All green, all hard, all raven waver.

There are so many ways to be famous but to be happy you
   must trust the small.

XXXIV

What do you know of loneliness?

Don't turn away.
Without quizzes
without note pads
with all of the years brushed away;
think.

Don't turn to me,

XXXV

Here is where I enter, proctor
in these cold times brought by various product lines.
Elicits desired response.
I fail myself in check-out lines.
Always out of something.

XXXVI

Here is where I am a part of the whole,
a part of the problem, and I *can't* make myself *stop*
the purchase. Home late from work
I can't deal with recycling plastic and one slips to the trash.

If this river is liquid god, *What have I done?*

This morning I stood on the porch staring.
Should I paint it again or tile it once and for all?

Is it a bad entrance?

Anything happens when answers are not the point.

XXXVII

There is no prayer wheel turning over the rush of water; *this*
    isn't Tibet.
The ancestors are not burned at the shore, *this isn't India.*
No gold in pan, *there's no Rush.* No fish spawn.
No bend in this river that isn't planned.
No *roses,* no, not anymore.

Because we can.
Because we can
Man's nasty eye and hand.

We are in a lot of trouble but *carpe diem, don't worry* we do not
    live that long.

XXXVIII

Deal the cards, as we say in my family when somebody talks too
    long.

Here I stand at the sandy brink of this river with my particular
    set of genes in hand.

Deal the cards.

NATIVE TO THE PLACE

Lynell George

Some evenings, when I drive west on Beverly Boulevard — downtown Los Angeles melting away in my rearview — I see a man planted in the very place along the road where the incline suddenly slopes downward then tips for a moment north before it yanks itself west again.

He is bare-chested. His belly sun-poached, salmon in the sun. Though I haven't double-checked this detail, I assume he wears shorts, or long pants rolled, since his shins — spindly, the hair like moss covering them — are exposed as well.

He stands, feet wide apart, sizable paunch thrust forward, with two objects, possibly bowling pins, clutched in either hand. He raises them sky-high as each car passes. A blessing? A curse? I'm not certain, because his face — distorted by a cartoonish, too-broad smile — is partly obscured by a yellowed Santa Claus beard and, of course, glasses to black out the sun.

This spectacle doesn't stop traffic, nor does it even cause it to snarl. When the green arrow appears, drivers' feet glide from brake to accelerator and take that curve.

This, you see, is normal.

It's normal in the same way that tuxedos in the afternoon are. Or sunglasses at night. Or that the earth roils unexpectedly sometimes; rises like a scared cat's back beneath one's feet.

It's normal.

I grew up in a place where you wore sundresses to school well into October. Where a field trip was not a museum visit, but a studio tour.

Where a summer job as a tuxedoed theater usherette could lead to work as an extra, or at the very least find you enmeshed on some strange adventure with a fast-talking dreamer (or schemer) who claimed to be employed as one.

I don't remember how or when I first began to separate exaggeration and extrapolation from the truth—the L.A. that is the "official story" from the one I navigated daily on steel-wheeled Street Kings, then on a banana seat, and finally in my very first American four-door. At face it seemed a growing-up terrain like any other, except our hometown bread-and-butter industries—movies and aerospace—were there to test the borders, always questioning, "How high the sky?"

Living in Los Angeles calls into question, every day, just what is "normal": The routine becomes a healthy rhetorical puzzle. What *is* "normal" is that the boundaries are always stretched, allowing for wiggle room; and that wiggle room sometimes plays host to chaos and uncertainty. Everything operates just a shade differently here—age, race, class, gender. Yet if there's something to be said about a constant mad push forward, the heady sensation of always peering around the corner to see what's coming, it also means you risk all for playing so close to the machinery and its heat.

Coming of age in Los Angeles, then, means you get to kiss your idols. Or discover that they are balding, date minors, and—despite being married and father to three—have an insatiable appetite for transvestites. In other words: They are human, too. And though all this, as well, is normal—blemished and unfiltered—for a time, I could no longer bear it.

But somehow you wander back.

Now I live in a place where helicopters and sirens sound nightly. At the end of a particularly intense, sun-streaked day, maybe the *pop-pop-pop* of a .22. Helicopter searchlights sometimes slash through my darkened rooms, shatter the mood, lighting everything hot like a set. But even that becomes normal. Becomes part of the landscape—as expected as sunrise or sunset. It blends in like the bleat of horns from the mariachis strolling the as yet "un-beautified" eastern fringes of Sunset Boulevard many stories below, or the sharp spray of night jasmine releasing.

All of this is normal, too — determined and self-defining.

All of this is home.

"It's vair-ree *ray-air*," my friend Sonia, who is from Rio de Janeiro, crisply enunciates. Her eyes go wide while she displays me to friends, as if I, not she, were the long-stemmed exotic, cut and out of water. "Vair-ree *ray-air!*"

It is a summer evening; but it is winter. It is a Tuesday; but the crowd gathered within this open-air venue under vaulted white tents suggests Saturday. Sonia is between sets, this tiny woman with an amphitheater-sized voice, wrapped head-to-toe in canary yellow. She's been on stage for hours and hours it seems, singing, tossing out dressed-up sambas and other forget-me-not postcards from Brazil. She is alive and grateful, a conductor of energy.

Still, her friends collect in wonder around me, their numbers growing, as if I've sprouted an eleventh digit.

No. Not from Bahia.

Not from Rio. Not from New York.

From here.

"There is no such thing as a native. Not from this place," I've been told.

I don't know how we — we natives — became so well hidden, or rather so misrepresented. How we born-to-it Angelenos developed such a stubborn tarnish.

Part of it, perhaps, has to do with the region's fast-forward evolution. No longer quaint horizontal pueblo, Los Angeles is now modern and vertical — augmented by angles of glass and steel. For many years afraid to build too high, we have stanched our earthquake paranoia with scientific assurance and architectural advances, not to mention our own stubborn persistence — clear evidence of our invincibility — in the face of perpetual change.

It's this perpetual change I've gotten used to, history often razed, painted over, obscured, or simply rewritten to be made "more grand." Life here requires constant reassessment.

Because I find myself always considering the past, curious about antecedents, I tend to create confusion. I stick out painfully from the rest. Countless times, I've been told, "You don't seem like you're from L.A." The statement, always announced in burnished, approving tones, is offered like a blessing. The underlying message: "You were saved."

I've also been told: "It must have been strange to grow up here." Strange, they say, because "there are no seasons." Or because "there is no center." Or "it's not a real city." But now I read between the lines and think "strange" because to live here and successfully acclimate, people often throw off many layers of convention. Once they relieve themselves of the weight of abstract commitments and expectations, they are suddenly liberated to wander away from a more recognizable and "responsible" adult self. That gauntlet thrown down to "normal" is what kicks up resentment, challenges a life that doesn't ask questions or stretch out to explore.

I often tell people that Los Angeles makes no sense if you talk about it out loud: The land of slow-float car chases and girls with Mercurochrome hair. So my L.A. exists in the mind, in fragments — a conflation of time, space, and reality. It involves things that can't be put on postcards or projected on wide screens. I'm uncertain when I first realized that my existence here was so far different from how the outside world characterized it. But I began collecting, honing my own defining details, way back, as if I knew I'd need to. Back when a thirty-minute drive could throw you out into the sticks, under a spill of stars, smelling eucalyptus and mustard. It was *rustic:* a term I equated with the sudden presence of coyotes and skunks; or the slap-dash souvenirs-of-the-journey décor found within the homes of canyon dwellers; or simply the barefoot meander. Rustic, I later came to understand, was a polite euphemism used by decorum-bound easterners and southern-ers to describe the haphazard existence we had jerry-rigged for ourselves. Rustic was this desert marked by summer days with blade-sharp heat that would suddenly soften — the ocean breeze running in for a rescue. The reward on days like this was a vast glittering canyon view at the very moment when the hills unexpectedly stepped aside in the turn of the road.

But — I know — those bits and pieces have sunk quick and deep into my consciousness.

I live in this city with a healthy mixture of infatuation and infuriation.

It's a place where the pattern of life can be disturbed just as easily by a location shoot shutting off several crucial city blocks at rush hour as by a riot long put on simmer, now coming to a boil. I sometimes marvel at how easily we learn to fall into place, to adjust to what at first looks or feels absurd by assigning some idea or out-of-air explanation for what many would find utterly inexplicable.

Not long after 1992's much euphemized . . . insurrection, riot, revolt, response, or (my favorite) "unpleasantries," I was moderating a Sunday afternoon program at the downtown library — a respected jazz musician's oral history of the dapper days of Central Avenue and the evolution of West Coast style. Everything was in place: the auditorium to capacity; the sound system piping in jazz sides of the era. Suddenly, moments before our microphones went live, the woman who had organized the program darted out from the wings, jamming a sheet of paper into my hands. On it were instructions to give the assembled guests: that the "gunshots, tire screeches, and explosions" they might hear outside were not another riot, just high-tech FX for a new film starring Harvey Keitel and Robert De Niro. Nobody should be alarmed. And nobody was. Well versed, bombs and sirens and whatever else erupting around us, we simply pressed forward. As so many of us already had — long ago.

That's just it.

I grew up in the place of new beginnings. The place where people start from scratch. I grew up hearing about the road here. The whys here, ultimately the frustrations and ruin of here: too tall an order even for paradise.

What happens when the possibilities run out? And what if, like me, you are already here?

It's an existence that constantly sets up the interior conflict, laid out black and white on the page — Los Angeles is both all that is real, and all that is not. It builds it up then tears it down. It raises expectations and strikes them as efficiently as a set. And though you want to protect what stands before you, fragile as it is, you also know it wasn't meant to last. It's fleeting and temporary. The glue: anticipation and memory.

You have to learn, or else the joke's on you.

My junior high school was the set for *James at 15* starring Lance Kerwin. The series was as short-lived as the actor's teen idol fame. Though we had Midwest-style trees that turned an array of vibrant seasonal tones, and though the homes surrounding the campus were primarily brick and wood bungalows that could easily represent a small, tidy neighborhood someplace east of us, we couldn't help but wonder at the choice. What about all this suggested *Anywhere?*

A short walk across campus offered no answers, only the realization that we were in the midst of some yet-to-be-understood sociological process. There was no firm center, only loose orbits. Within this quickly merging world, identity, for so many of us, was a set of daily costume changes. Only the brave ones had the confidence to pick and choose—and ultimately add on at will.

Here, then, Cuban car club members took their lead from the mini-Mack Daddies in Qiana and sansabelt slacks. Japanese-American kids flashed signs, claiming to be "Baby Crips" and sauntering around in blue nylon bomber jackets edged in orange. Even the surfers, once largely blue-eyed with shaggy hair bleached blond, now included a varied sea of faces—white, black, and brown. Along with their velvet rubber thongs or Vans, they wore Pendletons with white triangles of T-shirt flashing. When they wandered into class long after last bell, their shirts, still damp, pressed against the skin, the stains spreading shapes like countries, continents.

As with so much else, the city was changing at the base. It wasn't just the languages—those strange pauses and stresses—spoken across the grocery store aisles. Nor the new Christmas Eve traditions of tamales and samosas. Nor even the wars about music piped over the PA at Friday night dances—Led Zeppelin or Heatwave; P. Funk or Aerosmith. It was instead how everything was pressing fast-forward. Much faster than we had time to think about, let alone put together. Opportunity and disappointment, past and present all colliding. Reality was confusion. Like us, the city was figuring out what—and how—to be.

In its earlier incarnations, Culver City had been home to Spanish bungalows, palm tree–flanked duplexes for starlets-in-training—a city of a different kind of new beginnings: clean-cut "juveniles," first bachelor pads, B-movie girls rooming with ingénues in the 1930s. Not long before that, before this patch of land, dotted by avocado orchards, was even deemed a city proper, its founder, Harry Culver, had rented spotlights and with them nightly raked the sky. Calling attention to what he hoped would be a big bonanza coming attraction. It was Thomas H. Ince, who, in 1915, made Culver City an "industry town." Scouting locations, Ince was looking for a perfect stream to float three "Indian rafts" and found La Ballona Creek, which, with its lush surrounding foliage, could substitute easily enough for the wilds. Subsequently, Ince would make Culver City his studio's home.

By the mid-1970s, Ince's "perfect stream" had become little more than a fenced-in greenish trickle, running along the north side of Jefferson Boulevard just below what was left of the MGM backlot—a pitch-colored jungle gym of wood and metal that had been set afire in 1939 to serve as Rhett and Scarlett's Civil War–era Atlanta — director Victor Fleming's attempt at history restaged. Meanwhile, on the south side of that utility road, condominiums and town house developments were beginning to spring up in what had once been Metro's vast holdings. The developers named them, like nostalgic scrapbook captions—Raintree and Tara Hill—after two films that had made these nondescript patches of land cameo-famous.

The impossible-to-ignore irony was that Tara Hill, home to Culver City's most sizable black community, was named after Miss Scarlett's plantation. But in 1975, no one wanted to pause over this detail too long. Sights were set on the broad view, the notion that we were, collectively, a model for the future, a new set of hopefuls. No matter that Boston was erupting nightly on the news, or that so much of the South, under a different sort of reconstruction, remained an italicized racial epithet. Despite "race relations" West Coast–style—a language of symbols and wide-berth avoidance —it could, we knew, be different here.

Movie magic — wasn't. Not for us. My best friend's father worked the property department at MGM. Their home often reflected how well—or badly — a particular show was faring: "It's done in early *Little House*," Joanne's mother would announce, arms a-flutter, with Carol Merrill flair. How simple it looked to build a world: It was modular and take-away.

It wasn't so much that we were jaded, but early on, you figure out "day-for-night"—the quality of light, the angle of it; or how a storm brews and rages. It's like watching smoke in a beaker after you know the steps, the chemistry. Compelling, but mapable. We wanted to see something jagged. Incomplete. Complicated and elusive as the lives we were living. Proximity played gracious host to possibility—for those who waited around to see.

The year James turned fifteen, so did we. We took it all in, as our quaint brick-and-cement quad became a weekly tangle of cable, Andy Gumps, honey wagons, Teamsters in faded-blue Wranglers watching the pep rallies on Friday mornings with an uncomfortable degree of unblinking interest. But what we saw in front of us confirmed something different, sent a competing message. We studied — like it was language, or math — ringed around the action, as our blooming, wild-weed world was rendered moot. Lance Kerwin could be 1950s Wally Cleaver. Could be 1960s Robbie Douglas. And we already had Greg Brady — notebook in hand, powder brush making matte of the shine. He gets girl; he loses girl. He gets paid. Take after take. Stop. Go.

A chance to do it again. Do it better.

Looking at him and the extras they carted in from elsewhere left most everyone without words. There was no Meenah or Soraya. Sumalong or Darnell. Puppet or Armando. We were standing in the wings, far out of frame, watching the cameras rolling. All of us sworn to silence; secrets afraid to breathe.

That is until Puppet began to chuckle, over the teachers' and crew's "shhhs" and "hushes": "*Mentira!*"

Then, Mando, air released with a hiss and curl of Marlboro smoke. "Bullshit." The lit butt hit a cable, "Lies." Then asphalt. Quickly extinguished with the heel of his black canvas shoe walking away.

Cinema verite . . .

"*Mentira.*"

The two sides to every story:
The truth.
And the lie.

Still, I'm trying to understand what the camera does.

There are simple rules. Too close up, it distorts, erases shadow and shadings that create character and depth. Too far away and you will not get a sense of what's happened or what's beginning to transpire. There is a middle place to find.

In my head, I fan a montage of pictures. Separately they all mean something; collectively I'm left with a curious jumble of what all these Los Angeleses signify.

Even Los Angeles's organizing thesis is really just a backdrop open to interpretation — the edge of the world, the beginning or ending of things — depending on your life philosophy. The ocean then becomes the establishing shot for it all. Each day ends, curls at the edges right before our eyes. See it drop into the sea?

The southern end of the West Coast — both gentle curves and jutting angles, warm and relatively peaceful waters — is altar to those who don't want to be hemmed in. Whether it was Frankie and Annette's perpetual beach blanket weenie roasts or Malibu's messy boys in Hang Ten and O.P., the ocean provided a daily baptismal — if not the soul, the head washed clean.

Growing up, Dockwieler. Marina del Rey. Venice Beach. Playa del Rey. Those were ours. The picture-postcard beaches—Leo Carillo, Zuma, Point Mugu — were much farther north — heaven — or may as well have been. To get to our beaches only took one bus, maybe a hitched ride along Venice Boulevard. Most, however, were in the noisy, gritty flight path of LAX, and at least one offered a contemplative landscape of smokestacks and industrial tubing that you'd never see on TV.

By the time a classmate of mine fell off a longboard, which then slammed into the small of his back so that, at fifteen, he was enthroned in a wheelchair to navigate the halls, the stares, paralyzed — forever — I'd already stopped idealizing the ocean.

Gray and smelling like steel, gasoline, its scent hung in my hair for hours.

You didn't swim or wade in it after a certain age, unless you had a wet-suit or just liked to tip the balance. Maybe you were part of the surf tribes gathered along it, worshiping it, bobbing in its vastness — weightless.

Giving yourself over to it. Protecting what's left of it.

Those who know the city well understand that Los Angeles puts on its face before it steps out into the world. And those of us who have been here and have watched from up close know that in a place as frenzied and unruly as this, truth, as Oscar Wilde once quipped, is simply "one's last mood."

Natives know. L.A. is messy outside of its curated center. For anyone who has grown up and wise in it, it provides a modular set of truths, ways of understanding. Does knowing that there is no "fourth wall" or that Gilligan's island lies within a faux-pond on a Fairfax-district soundstage make you more cynical? Perhaps. But "Do we ever get *that* deep?" is, of course, the main punch line, the jab we lob back and forth among our-selves. If nothing else, this place equips you with a handy mantra that should be engraved on every Angeleno's side view: "Objects in the mirror are a lot more fucked up than they appear."

Things do get handed down here. Good and bad. Stories that are really cautionary survival tales.

My great-aunt Hilda came from Louisiana during the deep winter of Jim Crow. She arrived with her dapper Pullman Porter husband, Algernon, who traveled sometimes east to west, but mostly his weekly runs were south to north.

I barely knew her. Scrapbook pictures animate her features: wide smile; large arms open into an embracing hug. It was Hilda who collected my mother at the end of the line from New Orleans to L.A., who planted the first Los Angeles seed with the family. But she had been tipped off-balance early. Her railroad-man husband went out on a shift one day and rode away into middle space.

The accompanying absence, though no one talked about it, was like walking around a hole plunged deep in the living room. Hilda continued cleaning Hollywood houses. She kept her own in display-floor order—cut gladiolas and birds of paradise in heavy crystal vases; hardwood floors polished to a mirror shine; linen so white it smarted the eye in sunlight. Outside there were oranges in the trees along with apricots and lemons. It would be lovely—even if you had to make it so.

Proximity wills you double knowledge. You know all of it, or much of it, isn't smoke and mirrors, but plywood and drywall. Los Angeles is a city that can be shorthand or stand-in for anywhere, from Manhattan's Upper West Side to Lorne Green and James Arness's turn-of-the-last century wild west. And yet because Los Angeles is able or willing to be everything, I wonder, as a woman wonders about another who alters herself unceasingly to answer someone else's whim—is that why it tends to be dismissed as a trifle or, worse, as nothing?

The heightened state to strive toward: to be flexible but not toss away too much.

A waiter friend of mine, who arrived here twenty-five years ago with acting aspirations, is now graying at the temples. He realized mid-effort that it wasn't what he wanted—stage or screen, big or small. The realization was like opening a bay window. Back home his family simply didn't understand any part of this: not the initial aspiration, nor this current resting place. Even he wonders how he ended up embodying the cliché—waiting—but in a sense, he says, this place has allowed him much more grace, more latitude, "It doesn't hurt to be broad-based."

Some people don't give as easily. Some people don't know how to make themselves go slack and see where it all takes them—which is essential to the ride.

My father came here from the East. He came to have some space. He'd tried on a handful of careers—armed forces, policeman, teacher, ultimately administrator.

When I was in college, in the 1980s, he was an assistant principal at Hollywood High School. It was an unruly time. His principal had a fake tree with fake birds that would chirp and tweet. One afternoon when I visited, he smiled stiffly, like a Disney Imagineering-invention, and took my hand, offering one bit of caution, with a wink: "Be careful. There's evil out in those streets." The scent of his cologne lingered in my nose, on my skin, for hours afterward.

One day, my father said, the principal simply stopped showing up. Left his books in the cases, his pens in the holder, the birds in the tree. Maybe it all was too much for him. This was about when punk exploded. It carved itself on the city's consciousness. It careered out of clubs and face-lifted Hollywood palaces left for ruin—The Mask, the Anti-Club, the Starwood, the No Name, the Lingerie. All of it slashing through its territory with twisting fury.

It was around this same time that Southside and Eastside gangs began to pump up the murder stats as if they were a spinning tote board with no reconciliation in sight. It was one of L.A.'s angriest moments; it was one of L.A.'s most alive moments—as if we'd all been suddenly shaken awake to get a good glimpse behind the screen, at the levers working. It sent the works in the air for a while. It was as if everyone had figured it out and called the bluff. It was generations of waiting for the main act that fails to take the stage.

In those years, at nutrition and again at lunchtime, my father could be found filling in for the missing principal, standing on the corner of Sunset and Highland, making sure the pimps wouldn't approach the girls and boys leaving campus—and vice versa. Also there were the dealers to tend to. More than once, I got a call from some concerned friend or another, who didn't know how to tell me that he or she had seen my father—six foot three, poker-faced, mustachioed, unmistakable in one of his serious gray or navy three-piece suits—standing on the corner of Sunset and Highland in the middle of the day, talking to a little girl in platforms and a bare midriff, who rocked back and forth on the rise of her shoes, astonished at not simply being caught, her plan interrupted, but being recognized—seen through.

If you were honest and just let the needle drop, the soundtrack for Los Angeles would not be the Beach Boys, but cruising music: the slow glide of cars, asphalt like a pencil smear curve, widening outward. It's the ragged, piecemeal rhythms of a street band like War and its marriage of soul music congas and fraying rock guitars. L.A. is broken edges and patched-together lives. It's the struggles and the conflicts and the injustices obscured. It's a life full of competing melodies and the few, but ever growing, clearings of common ground.

L.A. has long been too narrowly defined — surf guitar, beach bunnies, Cool School, and Hockney's blue pools. L.A. is a loud cacophony. It is unwieldy and inexplicable: think Ornette Coleman's screaming sax, not just Chet Baker's restrained atonal whisper. It's a region too often critiqued and summarized by those on the outside who can't quite discern its nuances, who become transfixed by the projection, who can't seem to push their way beyond, though it is now long cliché, the city's illusion industry.

How is it, I've often wondered, that those who come from elsewhere become the definition of Angeleno, that *what* and *whom* the place attracts has overwhelmed what it actually *is?* All of this — the endless carnival ride — has obscured so much else, that particular beauty of living within the splatter of a mix, this pieced-together endeavor as grand yet precarious as Simon Rodia's Watts Towers. a 3-D mosaic, a monument to the tossaway that questions what is exactly temporary or throwaway? That truly is Los Angeles, what makes it hum or hmm It is a Latin city, a catholic city — broad-based, augmented, and enhanced by all that adorns it.

So how does one revise, update what's been handed you — an inaccurate legacy? Why has *what attracts* obscured *what is?*

What *is,* is the space. The room to see and live a life not bordered by a solid line, but one broken — merging.

I like the possibilities:

A wind-scrubbed night. An aging penthouse apartment. A kitchen with parquet floors. On the old stove both back burners are busy. On the left is a pot of black beans from a Cuban recipe. On the right, red beans, a recipe from the host's old New Orleans lover. There is a band playing meringues on the roof. In another room, someone is spinning records, old-fashioned LPs with cracks and pops, blues and jazz — minor keys and complex changes. There are conversations in Spanish, Armenian, Korean, English swirling around us. Someone has lit candles and arranged them on the ground like lanterns. And if you stand at the lip of this crumbling high-rise you can look out upon the mirror of MacArthur Park Lake, beyond it the city, a map of light, as you only see it from the sky.

It's ineffable — even to me at times. How can you love something so multipronged or so duplicitous? I've gotten quite adept at reading between the lines, knowing where to sink my roots. Knowing how to pick out what is pure or what is bauble, as effortlessly as picking fruit. It's easy enough to let all that occupies the center of the frame overwrite all else. But for all that is random and cruel, there is forgiveness about Los Angeles. It allows a generous and broad berth. It allows for a life with many acts, many costumes, and a handful of tries, like a roll of new coins.

For me, there is beauty in the confusion and chaos, within the elusiveness and the nonsense. I've come to realize that the real stories will always be told outside of the frame. That Los Angeles will always churn out something different — polished and stylized, for those paying to see it. For the others who are willing to take a self-guided journey, there is something as seductive and untamed as the old drives along the canyon passes awaiting them. There is joy in having the space to create or journey towards something new everyday, to be an expatriate on my own soil.

And so this night, like so many, when people broach the subject, the details of their journey, I listen to them intently.

Curious, we natives are always susceptible to good stories — the there-to-here stories.

I like to hear what yanked them west — employment, passion, boredom, fury. I'm eager to hear the beginnings, the middles, the denouements yet, and most likely never, to be resolved.

We sit in a circle, old friends and new, breathing life into our stories, playing shadow pictures on the wall.

WHEN MOTHER NATURE VISITS
SOUTHERN CALIFORNIA

David Hernandez

Before we knew it the palm trees
were shaking like pompoms, seagulls
were pinned flat against buildings
like pressed flowers, and the billboards
down Sunset Boulevard took to the air
with the swiftness of a magician's card trick.

The wind's howling kept us up all night.
Imagine a blowdryer as big as a 747 engine
outside your front door. Imagine that sound
at three in the morning, windows rattling.
car alarms caterwauling in the distance.

Although the windstorm eventually dwindled
to a breeze, some of us knew She would return,
lugging stadium-size buckets of water, or wielding
a jackhammer with a blueprint of our fault lines
rolled under one of Her massive arms.

We surrounded our homes with sandbags.
We slept under doorframes and dinner tables.
We waited for Her to remind us
whose turf we were on.

JOB'S JOBS

Aimee Bender

GOD put a gun to the writer's head.

I'm making a rule, said God. You can't write another word or I'll shoot you. Agreed? God had an east coast accent, tough like a mobster, but his lined face was frail and ethereal.

The writer agreed. He had a wife and family. He was sad because he loved words as much as he loved people, because words were the way he said what he wanted about people, but this was God and God was the real deal, and he didn't want to spend too much time dwelling on it. So he packed up his typewriter and paper and tucked them in the hall closet, and within two days, to comfort his loss, went to the art supply store and bought oil paints and a canvas and a palette and set up in the garage amongst the old clothes and broken appliances. He'd always liked painting. He thought he had a good sense of color. He painted every morning for hours, until he started to paint something real.

He was working on his eighteenth canvas, blues and reds in sharp rows blurring in the middle, making a confrontation with purple, when God entered his studio, this time holding a dagger.

Cut the painting too, said God. No words, no images. Or — he made a slicing motion near his stringy throat.

Why? cried the painter, already missing the sharp smell of the oils, how the colors mixed to become brand new again, an exotic blush of yellow, a blueish greenish grayish, a new way to show trees, with white!; he missed the slow time he took washing his hands with turpentine, the way his wife liked the new rugged scent of him.

God lifted the dagger to the lightbulb of the garage and it glinted, unpolished silver, speckled with brown. Do not question God, said God.

So the painter packed away his paints, inside that hall closet, next to the typewriter and reams of white paper. He felt sad again but within a week, signed up for a drama class, held in a church where the ceilings were high, the air cool, and every scene took on particular gravity with those stained-glass windows acting as set. He played a few roles, and he wasn't very good at first but was enjoying it anyway, shy man that he was, liking the way he would feel his feeling and then use it and look around at the other people in the class, faces split into red and yellow triangles from the windows, and see they were feeling the same feeling with him, how contagious it all was. He needed a lot of reassurance as an actor, but he was starting to under-stand its ultimate camaraderie and loneliness, the connection which is tight as laces then broken quick as the curtain's fall.

So of course one afternoon, walking out of the church, spanking a new script against his knee, he found God in the backseat of his car, gripping a bayonet.

No more, God said. In my house no less, said God.

The actor started to cry. I love acting, he said. I'm just getting it right, he said. My wife thinks I'm coming out of my shell.

God shook his head.

Mime? pleaded the actor.

God poked the actor's side with the sweet triangular tip of the bayonet.

The actor sat in the car, gripping the steering wheel, already missing the applause, the sight of the woman in the front row with tears in her eyes that were from the same pool of tears he'd visited to do the scene, the entire town fetching water from the same well.

God exited the car. He waited at the crosswalk. He didn't cross on the flashing hand but waited for the green walking man.

The actor was depressed for a while which his wife didn't like much, but finally slogged himself out of it and took up cooking. He studied the basics in the cookbook and told himself that patience was a virtue and would be put to good use here. Sure enough, in three months, he'd made his first soup from scratch—potato leek nutmeg—and it was very good. His wife loved it. You're amazing, she told him in bed, his hands smelling of chicken guts; I married the most amazingly artistic man, she said.

He kissed her. He'd made a dessert too and brought it into bed — a chocolate torte with peanut butter frosting. He kissed her again. After two bites they forgot all about it.

God was apparently busy, he took longer this time, but showed up after a big dinner party where the chef served leg of lamb with rosemary on a bed of wild rice with lemongrass chutney. It was a huge hit, and everyone left, drunk, gorgeous with flush, blessed. The chef's wife went to the bathroom and guess who sauntered through the screen door, swinging a noose.

No! moaned the chef, washing a dish.

This is it, said God. Stop making beautiful food. Stop *talking* while you're at it. What is with you?

The chef hung his head. Then hung up his spoons in the cupboard with the typewriter, paints, playbooks and wigs. With the pens, turpentine, and volumes of Shakespeare. The shelf was getting crowded so he had to shove some towels aside to make room. He spent the week eating food raw from the refrigerator, and somehow found the will to dial up a piano teacher. But right when he glimpsed the way a chord works, how it fits inside itself, the most intricate and simple puzzle, when he heard how a fourth made him weep and a fifth made him soar, the rejoice of c major, the ache of d minor, God returned with a baseball bat tucked into his belt.

Don't even think about it, barked God.

The man attempted dance.

Backstage, God waved his rifle high in the air.

The man took a year off of life. He learned accounting. He was certain this would be no problem, but after a few weeks the way the numbers made truths about people's lives was interesting to him; he tried law but kept beginning a duet with the jury; he found the stock market reminded him of a wriggling animal. God showed up at the workplace and stuck pins near his eyes.

So the man sat in a chair. He went to a park and looked at people. A young woman was writing in her journal under a tree; she was writing and writing, and he caught her eye and sent her waves of company and she kept his gaze and wrote more, looked up again, wrote more, circled his bench and sat down and when she asked him questions he said nothing but just looked at her, deep and real, and she stood and went away, got a drink at the drinking fountain, circled back. After an hour of this, she said Thank You, tears in her eyes, and left. The pathway of her feet looped to the bench and back and away and back, swirls and curls and lines.

God was irritated. Close your eyes! said God, shaking a bottle of pills like a maraca.

The man's wife was unhappy. She was doing the cooking now and her husband didn't move or speak anymore. She missed their discussions, his paintings, his stories, his pliés. She missed talking to him about her job with the troubled people and how at certain moments there was an understanding held between her and the person, sitting there, crying or not crying, mad or not mad, happy or unhappy, bland or lively, and it was like, at that moment, she said, they were stepping all over a canvas together. It's like, she said, the room is full of invisible beetles. Or water. Or pillows. Or concrete. She told him all about it and his eyes were closed but she could feel, from his skin, that he was listening. She went to him and undressed him slowly and they made love there on the sofa, and he hardly moved but just pressed his warmth to her, his body into hers, and she held him close and the man gave her all he could without speaking, without barely shifting, lips and hips, and she started to cry.

Afterward she pressed her head to his chest and told him all the things she had thought about, the particular flower he made her feel, the blade, the chocolate torte.

They slept on the sofa together.

God put the man in a box with no windows. He tied his hands behind his back and knotted a blindfold over his eyes. He stuck duct tape over his lips. God said: Not a peep out of you. Don't you interact with anybody. The man sat with his head full of dreams. He thought of flying fish and the smell

of his wife's skin: white powder and clear sweat. He thought of basil break-
ing open and the drawing of a tomato with red and black paint and the
word tomato, consonant vowel, consonant vowel, consonant vowel, and the
perfect taste of tomato with basil together, and the rounded curve of a man's
back, buttons of spine visible. He wondered where the girl with the journal
was right then. He thought of his wife making bridges of air over air. He
listened to the sound of wind outside the box, loud and soft as his breath.

FASCIST ISLAND

Gerald Locklin

it's the sort of shopping center
that makes you realize
that even if a rich aunt died
and remembered you in her will
she just wouldn't really be
rich *enough.*

LOS ANGELES

Richard Rayner

I LIVE in a Spanish-style villa in Los Angeles, at the corner of Franklin and Grace, two blocks from Hollywood Boulevard and only one block from Yucca and Wilcox, known as "crack alley." One morning, my girlfriend walked down into the garage beneath the building and found human excrement on the windscreen of our car. The excrement had not been thrown or carelessly daubed, but somehow painted in a perfect rectangle, thick, four feet by two. Someone had gone to a lot of trouble. From a distance the excrement looked like a nasty modern painting; it also smelled powerfully and took over an hour to wash and scrape off. "Why didn't they just steal the fucking car?" she said. I did my best to be urbane about another unpleasant reminder of the nature of our neighborhood. The homeless, I told her, couldn't afford the gas, and the homeboys wouldn't be seen dead in a Volvo; they preferred old Cadillacs and new BMWs, white, loaded with extras.

Several times during the past year, I'd watched from my study window as officers of the Los Angeles Police Department staged elaborate busts on the streets. The officers, always white, wore sunglasses and had Zapata mustaches and carried shotguns or had handguns strapped to their thighs. A car was surrounded and stopped. The suspects, always black, usually young, often well-dressed, were dragged out and made to lie on the ground. They were cuffed with plastic thongs that, from a distance, looked like the tags with which I closed up bags of rubbish. Then they were searched and made to kneel, one on this side of the street, one on the other, while the officers talked among themselves or, swaggering to and fro, conducted an ad hoc interrogation: "Shut the fuck up and don't move," I heard on one occasion. "Feel clever now, black boy?" "Be careful now, I'm in the mood to hit me a homer." Every now and then a helicopter would appear, a roaring accompaniment to the scene's edgy surrealism. Sometimes my neighbors came out: an old lady who used to sit in her car, although she never drove it (that was what she did most mornings: She sat there, in her car, not driving it); a long-haired heavy metal musician; a blonde from Texas, pretty, but probably not pretty enough to make it in the movies; a black onetime boxer whose presence was always a comfort. They watched without any sign of animation — it was all fairly routine — and after fifteen minutes or so, the suspects were driven away in the back of a black-and-white police, car, known to the officers as "a black and normal" ever since police chief Daryl Gates said that the reason why so many blacks died from the carotid chokehold — the controversial technique once used to detain suspects — was that "their veins and arteries do not open up as fast as they do on normal people."

I was surprised, not by the fact that this was happening in my neighborhood, but by the fact that the people of my neighborhood accepted it all with such indifference. There was, it was apparent, nothing remarkable about the behavior of the LAPD, which was seen less as a police force than an army at war, a perception encouraged by the department's chief. Gates referred to black drug dealers as "Viet Cong." He told a senate committee that even casual drug users "ought to be taken out and shot." And part of his strategy, Gates said on another occasion, "is to put a lot of police officers on the street and harass people and make arrests for inconsequential kinds of things." Gates was known to model his police department on the U.S. Marines; its stated aims were to be fast, mobile, and extremely aggressive.

"You're *supposed* to be frightened of the LAPD," a friend told me. "The question is why you live in the neighborhood you do."

My apartment, I explained, was a particularly beautiful piece of history, designed and built in the 1920s by the movie director Cecil B. DeMille.

"Are you insane?" my friend said. "Move somewhere else, move away from that shit, move to the Westside," by which he meant a small rectangle within the new 310 area telephone code: west of La Cienega Boulevard and north of the Santa Monica freeway. My friend stressed the borders: These weren't just streets; they were magical divides. By entering this area, I would be safe, secure, and white. Hispanics would be the people who didn't speak English; they would clean the house and clip the lawn, then get on the RTD and disappear back to the netherworlds of East and South Los Angeles. And blacks wouldn't exist at all, unless they wore Armani and worked at CAA.

Seeing a black in Los Angeles, I had come to realize, wasn't the same experience as seeing a black in New York. I found myself making categories. There were the smart professional blacks — lawyers, entertainers, film industry schmoozers. These I greeted with a smiling "Ciao!" There were middle-class blacks, who ran businesses and owned property in more or less exclusively black and Hispanic areas — Inglewood, Compton, Crenshaw. These I knew about but never met: our worlds didn't intersect. There were the bums on Hollywood Boulevard, asking for a quarter or shouting their rage among the tourists, the runaways, the hustlers and hookers, the followers of L. Ron Hubbard and his Scientology Church. These it was safe to ignore. And then there were the homeboys, the gang-bangers, who pulled up alongside at a stoplight, or ran whooping through the aisles of smart movie theaters in Westwood or Century City, or strutted along that same stretch of Hollywood Boulevard in Nike Air Jordans, baggy shorts, Gucci T-shirts, and baseball caps with an X on the front. Perhaps they really were in a gang, perhaps not, but they behaved with an anger, an arrogance, an aura of fearlessness that suggested they might be. With them, I was the one who became nonexistent. Staring straight ahead, I would quicken my step, but not enough to attract attention, and was most comfortable if I happened to be wearing sunglasses, so that no eye contact was possible. I would hold my breath. I would be invisible.

I knew that my fear was out of all proportion to the true nature of the threat, but, like the earthquake that must happen eventually, the black street gangs of South Los Angeles were a part of the city's apocalyptic demonology. They were armed with Uzis and AK-47s and even rocket launchers, killing each other, and sometimes innocent bystanders, not just for money or "turf," but for wearing the wrong color of shoelace or baseball cap. There were said to be as many as 100,000 hard-core gang members. Their tags were sprayed on the wall of our building and on the sidewalk outside, an indecipherable crossword, a labyrinth of black paint on white concrete that our Mexican gardener washed away with Clorox and whitewash. A few days later the crossword was always back.

So it was: Don't go here, don't go there, lock the car doors, never spend more time than you have to in parking lots, avoid eye contact on the freeway. This wasn't *just* paranoia. One Friday night, I happened to glance at an old Cadillac Coupe de Ville cruising alongside us on the Hollywood freeway. I saw a black kid hand a gun to a friend in the back, not even looking, passing the gun over his shoulder as casually as if it were a pack of cigarettes. So it was: Don't go south of Wilshire, here's a homeboy, here's a cop car, a black and white, a black and *normal*. Good. The police spoke about perimeters and containment and points of control. They spoke about South Central as if it were a township.

Los Angeles was a lot like South Africa. The apartheid wasn't enshrined by law, but by economics and geography, and it was just as powerful. In Los Angeles I was afraid of blacks in a way I never had been. I behaved in a way that would have disgusted me in New York or London. I was a racist.

The Taser stun gun was introduced by the LAPD in 1980, and it was used against Rodney King, the black motorist whom LAPD officers Lawrence Powell, Ted Briseno, Timothy Wind, and Sergeant Stacey Koon were accused of unlawfully beating shortly after midnight on 3 March 1991. Despite all that had been written about the incident, I had read very little about the operation of the Taser. It was, I discovered, a weird-looking device, a crude, chunky gray pistol which fired darts into people. The darts were attached to wires, which on pushing a button administered a shock of 50,000 volts. "Seems to cool off most people pretty good," said a representative of Ray's Guns of Hollywood. It had been used more and more to restrain suspects following the banning of the carotid chokehold in 1984.

Rodney King was stopped after a high-speed pursuit, first on the Foothill freeway, and then on the streets of Pacoima, during which he drove at speeds in excess of 100 miles per hour and ignored a number of red lights. The initial pursuit was made by Melanie and Timothy Singer, a husband-and-wife team of the California Highway Patrol, but when LAPD cars arrived on the scene it was Sergeant Stacey Koon who took charge. As Koon notes in an as yet unpublished autobiography, he looked at the petite Melanie Singer and then at the six foot, three inch, 225-pound Rodney King (who, according to Koon, had dropped his trousers and was waving his buttocks in the air), and decided that this was about to develop into "a Mandingo type sex encounter," a reference to a Hollywood movie which involved black slaves raping white women.

Koon used his Taser stun gun, firing two darts into Rodney King and giving him two shocks. One was enough to subdue most suspects and even the Mandingo Rodney King himself was on the ground by now, showing little sign of resistance. Koon and the three other officers then kicked him and hit him fifty-six times with their batons, breaking his ankle, his cheekbone, and causing eleven fractures at the base of his skull, as well as concussion and nerve damage to the face. The force of the blows knocked fillings from his teeth.

The last of the not guilty verdicts was announced in Simi Valley at three-forty-five P.M. on Wednesday, 29 April 1992. As Stacey Koon left the courthouse, it was declared that he had hired an entertainment attorney to sell the movie and book rights to his story, which would be titled *The Ides of March,* since he had been indicted on 15 March of the previous year.

After the verdict, I went to the Mayfair Market, to a bookstore, to a bar on Franklin. People were nervous, excited. Something was going to happen in South Central; the question was how bad it would be. When I got home, the phone was ringing. Crowds had gathered downtown at the Parker Center, LAPD headquarters. A police car had been turned over.

Looting was said to have started in other places, though the moment when the riots began in earnest was easy to spot: It was broadcast live on TV.

At six-thirty P.M., Reginald Denny stopped at a traffic light at the intersection of Florence and Normandie. He was on his way to deliver twenty-seven tons of sand to a cement-mixing plant in Inglewood. Denny, thirty-six, would have been driving through South Central to avoid the rush-hour traffic on the freeways. It was the territory of the Eight-Trey Gangster Crips, one of the city's most famous gangs. While waiting for the light to change, he was pulled from his rig by five or six black youths. Two news helicopters were overhead, watching the crowd which had been gathering since the verdict was announced, and the incident turned into an uncanny mirror-image of the Rodney King beating, though where the King video had been dim and murky, captured by an onlooker from his balcony with a newly acquired Sony camcorder (a few days earlier, on the same tape, he'd bagged Arnold Schwarzenegger, filming a scene from *Terminator 2* in a nearby bar), what I saw now was shot by professionals — the camera zooming in and out, the images well defined and horribly colorful.

Denny was kneeling in the middle of the street, now empty. Two blacks entered the frame and beat Denny's head with their fists and then kicked him. Another black raised his arms and hurled the truck's fire-extinguisher, hitting Denny on the side of his head, which lurched from the impact. Denny tried to move and rolled onto his side. The helicopter circled for a better angle. You could now see how Denny's white T-shirt, which had slipped up his belly, was saturated with blood. A black appeared briefly, smashing what appeared to be a lamp-base over Denny's head. He collapsed again. Another black appeared: This one was holding a shotgun at arm's length, very casual, and shot Denny in the leg. A black was wheeling a bicycle in the background. A black ran up, leaped athletically in the air and kicked him in the head. Denny tried to stand up. The right side of his face was a mess of red, as if it were melting. A black hit him with a tire iron; Denny went down. A black hit him with a beer bottle and then raised his arms in triumph. Another black appeared, went through Denny's left pocket, right pocket, back pocket, and then ran away with his wallet. A black in baggy shorts stepped up and kicked Denny in the head and danced away on one leg very slowly.

It happened in silence since the scene was filmed from a helicopter, but later I watched a video shot by an eyewitness — again the uncanny mirror image. In this one there was sound; you could hear the voices: "No mercy for the white man, no mercy for the white man." It seemed to be choreographed and went on for a very long time — thirty minutes. Watching the Rodney King video, I had thought it reasonable for American blacks to hate the police and be suspicious of all whites. This didn't make me suspicious of these particular blacks; it made me want to kill them. If any of them had been in my power in that moment, as Reginald Denny was in theirs, I would have done it gladly. I actually saw myself with a gun in my hand. Pow. Pow. Pow.

A few feet from Reginald Denny's truck was Tom's Liquor and Deli; it was the first store looted. The first fire-call was received thirty minutes later at seven-thirty P.M. Forty-five minutes later was the first fatality, Louis Watson, thirty-two blocks and three miles from where Denny's truck had been, yet still in the heart of South Central. Watson, an eighteen-year-old black who had wanted to be an artist, was shot to death at Vernon and Vermont, hit by a stray bullet while waiting for a bus.

The TV showed a fire, then another, and still more. Soon there were so many that fires normally requiring ten trucks were dealt with by one. A fire captain was threatened with an AK-47 to the head by a gangbanger called "Psycho." Another fireman was shot in the throat, and more people began to die, a lot more people. Dwight Taylor, forty-two, was shot to death at 446 Martin Luther King Boulevard. He had been on his way to buy milk. Arturo Miranda, twenty, was shot to death in his car on the way back from soccer practice. Edward Travens, a fifteen-year-old white youth, was shot to death in a drive-by attack in the San Fernando Valley. Patrick Bettan, a white security guard, was shot to death in a Korean supermarket at 2740 West Olympic. But the dead were mostly black. Two unnamed blacks were shot to death in a gun battle with the LAPD at Nickerson Gardens

Housing Project. A robber was shot to death at Century and Van Ness. *Shot to death:* The phrase itself had a velocity, a connectedness to the violence it described, that even constant repetition couldn't reduce to TV babble. At ten-forty: Anthony Netherly, twenty-one, was shot to death at 78th and San Pedro. At eleven-fifteen: Elbert Wilkins, thirty-three, was shot to death in a drive-by attack at 92nd and Western. Ernest Neal, twenty-seven, was shot to death in the same incident. Time unknown: An unknown black male shot to death at 10720 Buren Street. A man *of unknown race and age* was dead of "riot-related injuries" at Daniel Freeman Memorial Hospital: what possible state was he found in?

Thirteen dead by the end of the night, 1,600 fire-calls, and in the moments when TV stations had nothing new to show, they always went back to Reginald Denny, a white man, forever on his knees, being beaten. Outside, the choking, fried-plastic smell of the fires wafted across the city.

On Thursday morning, people were wanting the riots to be over, hoping they were, believing that they had been a one-day affair. At nine-thirty the radio weatherman was still trying to be wacky. "Our weather today calls for hazy sunshine. Let's change that," he chortled, "smoky sunshine." If the riots were going to start again, I wanted to see them for myself, and I wanted to see them with a black, not, I'm afraid, because I thought I'd get a special insight (although that was the way it turned out), but because I knew I'd be safer. I called Jake, a black screenwriter. He had grown up in Los Angeles, in South Central, in fact, where his father had been a preacher, and he had gone to college in New York. He had only recently moved back. "I've been talking to people, not just the gangbangers, and they're saying they just ain't gonna take it. They've been resting a couple of hours, but it's all going to start up again." Today, he predicted, the rioters and looters would march across the city. He said he's pick me up soon.

Jake arrived by eleven and we drove down Normandie, a helicopter overhead, following us south.

Hispanic families stood in doorways, waiting. A street was taped off where a building had burned the previous night, and twice we were passed by LAPD cars, not moving singly, or even in pairs, but in groups of four and five. "For safety," said Jake. "Those guys are nervous. The LAPD got burned last night." He exchanged a fisted salute with the black driver of a Chevrolet. "The way they left that guy there at the intersection? The *police*," he said, as if it were the rock group he were talking about. "The homies think they've got something on them *forever*."

A palm tree was on fire. Flames ran up from the base to the leaves above and seconds later the entire tree was ablaze. Five or six young black kids were running. For a moment I thought they were frightened, running away, and then I realized, of course, they'd set it alight. There was the sound of a gunshot, though it wasn't clear who had fired it; it seemed some way off.

But it was my first experience of the riot close at hand. I was afraid and began to babble. I explained to Jake that I hated gunfire. Americans were obsessed with guns. Before New Year's Day the city authorities had found it necessary to place billboards all over Los Angeles, in English and Spanish, warning people not to fire their guns into the air at midnight. So lots of people fired their guns *into the ground*. Sometimes, lying in bed, or finishing dinner in our Cecil B. DeMille dining room, with its wood beam ceiling and baronial stone fireplace, I hear shots outside the building. "Car backfiring again," I'd say, and my girlfriend would roll her eyes.

"I'm the sort of person," I told Jake, "who lies awake in bed thinking someone's about to break in and slit my throat." No doubt I'd be like that if I lived in the Cotswolds or on the Isle of Skye. Unfortunately I lived in a neighborhood where corpses were found stuffed into our garbage bins or decomposing in closets in nearby apartments. These stories never made it into the *Los Angeles Times*.

"Move to the Westside," said Jake, and I presumed he was joking, though I remembered the first time he'd visited our apartment when he walked around checking the locks; then he'd gone around the block and advised us not to walk on Yucca.

Jake wasn't joking. "You can afford to move away. Move the fuck away," he said. "What's your problem?" He'd been living down at the ocean in

Santa Monica since returning from New York. He said, "You live in a mar-
ginal neighborhood, so it's real for you, because you know it's there, but at
the same time it's not real, it's just the big bad boogie thing you glimpse
from time to time." The "it" he was talking about was violence. "But it's
never reached out and really hurt you."

I agreed; I was lucky.

"I was lucky too. I grew up in a bad neighborhood. Guys I went to
school with are in jail now, or long dead, or crippled in wheelchairs, or have
had twelve feet of intestine ripped out by a gunshot."

On Vermont we passed a furniture store, burnt out and still smoking,
and then a minimall from which people were running with armloads of
loot, or calmly wheeling laden checkout trolleys. It seemed extraordinary
that traffic was moving about quite normally at these places, and that these
events were visible as we cruised about, snug inside Jake's Honda with the
radio and air conditioning on. We drove past a Blockbuster video store —
its window already smashed — as two police officers struggled to cuff a
black who was kicking out at them from the ground. Three black kids were
getting out of a white Toyota that had just driven up. They walked past the
black on the ground and the two officers trying to hold him there, entered
the shop, and started filling up their arms with videos.

I wanted to say, this is it, we're really in the riot now, it's starting up again,
but Jake was so casual about it all. He said that these kids had no hope of
getting out as he had. Everything about society told them they were worth-
less, nonpeople. They had nothing, so they had nothing to lose, something
I'd hear a lot of blacks say over the next days.

We drove east on Pico, past blocks that were quiet, then past blocks
where crowds had gathered in anticipation of something happening, and
then, once again, past blocks where something *was* happening already.
There was a mob inside a Payless shoe store, and a black kid, very young,
emerged running with two boxes, stopped for a moment, then sat down in
the parking lot to try the shoes on. There was a Vons supermarket that Jake
had passed some hours before, while it was being looted, which was now
on fire, flames leaping through the roof, a fire truck yet to arrive.

Jake said, "Sometimes they do it at the same time, other times they clean it out and come back hours later and burn it then. Keeps the cops on their toes."

I nodded, as if to say, yes, I could see the logic of that. Two Hispanic youths appeared, casually wheeling a piano around a corner. I was beginning to get a sense of the sheer scale of what was going on. It was huge. The radio was announcing a curfew. After sundown tonight people on the streets anywhere in Los Angeles would be stopped and questioned. The National Guard was on its way, and 2,400 federal troops, veterans of the Gulf War, were set to follow.

"Hubba, hubba," said Jake.

By one o'clock we were looping back to the east. We came up to Third and Vermont. There was a big crowd and a fire in the distance, and now another one, closer, but just starting, and to my left, a column of thick black smoke which made my eyes water and got into my throat almost at once. I began to cough. Twenty or so young men of various races, not running and not walking either, but hurrying as if toward a very serious appointment, crossed the street and kicked down the door of a toy shop. The Korean owner stood by, offering no resistance, shaking his head. On the other side of the intersection three black looters were running, away from the Unocal station, lugging cans of oil in either hand. I didn't need a diagram to figure out what they were going to do with the cans. A hydrant was shooting a plume of water high into the air. At the Thrifty Drug Store, there was a line of people waiting to enter through a door, its glass smashed out, while others made their way out with plastic bags or carts filled with stolen goods. A man kicked some glass aside and emerged leaning backwards like in a Monty Python silly walk, his cradled arms piled so high with white and brown boxes that I couldn't see his face.

The traffic lights were out at the intersection. Making a left turn, not a simple exercise at the best of times in Los Angeles, was now a game of chicken, with fire trucks speeding up the hill and drivers nosing forward anxiously, or stopping and then making perilous surges across the intersection, windows open. A mouth and yellow baseball cap in a Ford truck was yelling: "MOTHERFUCKER." The TV hadn't prepared me for the deafening noise of the riot—breaking glass, engines, sirens, smashing, shouting. Everyone was shouting. The noise of the riot was a shape, and it approached and receded like a wave, surging this way and that.

There was another thing: A lot of people had guns, in the waistbands of their trousers or even in their hands. They weren't firing the guns, they merely had them, but that was frightening enough. In England, people don't carry guns.

Patrol cars must have pulled up because there was now an LAPD sergeant shouting commands, and a line of officers—perhaps fifteen in all— was forming at the far end of the Thrifty Drug Store parking lot. The sudden phalanx of officers had no effect on the looters, and, as it advanced, they tended merely to drift into the next store. One sprinted straight at the police line, yelling, and then swerved off at the last moment, jumping over the low wall of the parking lot. A looter stopped to say cheese for a cameraman wearing a flak jacket. Another, a bearded black in a long white T-shirt, and with a cigarette in his mouth, was pointing to his penis, inviting the officers to suck it. The phalanx of police advanced a few steps farther; they began beating on their riot shields with their batons.

A kid stepped up and hurled a rock into the street. I didn't see if anyone was hit. The kid threw another rock, launching it from low behind his back as if it were a javelin. Suddenly there were lots of kids, all of them throwing rocks, and then more police cars, coming up behind the phalanx. Jake said in his view the situation was about to get nasty.

In my view the situation had gone some way beyond that. This wasn't at all like the quite pleasurable thrill of fear I'd felt at first. I was terrified. A young black, a teenager, stopped in the middle of the street with a bottle of Budweiser which he was getting ready to throw at a car, ours. The bottle was nearly full. He stared at me, saw I was white, glanced at Jake, saw he was black, and made an obvious calculation. He ran on.

It was about two o'clock when Jake dropped me home. I didn't go out again until the early evening. I made a Waldorf salad, thinking: Now I'm making a Waldorf salad. It seemed a startling way to be carrying on. I had to force myself to eat it. The radio said that a fire was being set every three minutes. That night's performance of *The Phantom of the Opera* at the Ahmanson Theatre was canceled; for some reason this piece of information was repeated over and over again. An interview with an analyst from Harvard was cut abruptly short for another repeat of the crucial *Phantom* announcement, and then it was back to the Harvard man, who was interrupted again, but this time for news of yet another fire and looting.

On TV, Tom Bradley, L.A.'s black mayor, appeared, calling for calm. As he spoke, the screen was split, one half showing a respectable black man urging restraint, the other showing the looting of a clothing store. Mayor Bradley urged everyone to stay at home and watch the final episode of *The Cosby Show* that night; perhaps that would help us solve our problems, he suggested. Then Pete Wilson, the governor of California, quoted Martin Luther King. His face wasn't shown, but King's words, spoken by Wilson in a slow and sanctimonious tone, were used as the soundtrack as hundreds of black youths rampaged through a minimall.

A friend called, a little hysterical, having been trapped in a gridlock for over an hour at Century City. It was like a scene from a *Godzilla* movie, she said, with Westsiders heading for hotels in Santa Barbara and San Diego, leaving the city in droves. She often had troubles because of her very blonde hair; it gave her the appearance of a Nazi, she said, and homeboys sometimes took exception. She explained all this as if it were no more remarkable a fact of her life than having a mole on her cheek. She was from Sweden and nothing about America surprised her. She'd been on Olympic when someone threw a rock through the passenger window of her car with such velocity that it passed directly in front of her face and then shattered the window on the driver's side. She'd held the steering wheel so tight on the way home that her arms were still trembling.

At six o'clock on the Thursday night, my girlfriend and I drove to the hills above Silverlake. I wanted the view.

A smart Korean gentleman in his early forties was watching as well. He had on a blue silk shirt and blue linen trousers, baggily cut, and his sunglasses were by Oliver Peoples. He was a *very* smart Korean gentleman, and he remarked with a world-weary air that he had a business in the mid-Wilshire district, right next door to the Sears building, which now appeared to be ablaze. He wasn't going to defend it, though he knew some of his countrymen had armed themselves with shotguns and machine guns in Koreatown. But they were shopkeepers and he — he shrugged, a little apologetically—was not a shopkeeper. "Nor am I Clint Eastwood," he said. "I pay America lots and lots of taxes so I don't have to be."

I asked what line of business he was in.

"I have a gallery," he said. "You're English?"

"That's right."

"Two foreigners together," he said. "And here we are, watching Los Angeles burn." He smiled, revealing his teeth, very white and even. Ah me, he seemed to be saying, the wicked, wicked way of the world.

On a clear day I'd seen the ocean from here, but not this evening; the entire Los Angeles basin was covered in a thick gray haze. The twin towers of Century City, a little more than halfway to the sea, were invisible, and looking south and east, the sky was darker still. Black smoke indicated fires that were out of control; white smoke, those that were now contained. The sound of sirens came from all over, and there was a convoy of army vehicles on the Hollywood freeway,

I said, "Do you think they'll ever feel the same about the city again?"

He asked, "Who?"

"The rich."

"The rich?" he said, and laughed, a sudden explosion. "The *rich?*" He found this very amusing. "Oh my dear, you're so naive. They might feel guilty for a day or two. Some of them might even be panicked into leaving, for good I mean, for Paris or London or Seattle, not just getting the children into the buggy and hightailing it for the Sierras. The rest will pull the wagons in even tighter than before. Watch those security bills soar!"

We were on the way back from Silverlake, driving down Sunset toward a sun that was in fact setting, when I realized that the looting had got very close to my home. I'd been expecting it all day, and I felt a thrill as I saw a pair of homeboys, shouting and jumping, dodging among the cars on Sunset, their arms full of bandannas and Ray-Bans and studded leather jackets, looted, I presumed, from L.A. Roxx, a store which pulled in tourists from the Midwest, relieved them of a couple of hundred dollars, and sent them away looking like clones of the whitebread rockers Guns 'n' Roses. I wondered how the homeboys would manage to dispose of *that* in South Central.

I didn't know why, but I felt a little proud. The riot had reached my neighborhood.

This time I was determined not to be such a wuss. I got out of the car at Highland and walked east along Hollywood. There were people running toward me. There was a small boy, he couldn't have been more than seven years old, with two cartons of Marlboro tucked under his arm; a middle-aged white woman was clutching a boom box still in its box, saying as if she couldn't quite believe it, "For free."

A photographer stood beneath the awning of the Ritz Cinema, shooting down the street. "It's a party now," he said. "It's carnival time."

There was a big crowd between Cherokee and Whitley. They were the type of people I usually saw in the neighborhood, which is to say tourists, teenagers from the Midwest who still dressed like punks, some kids, a few homeboys, even a few young middle-class types in suits. There was a balding fellow who worked in the Hollywood Book City bookstore. They had all gathered round to watch a very bewildered police officer.

The back of a car was hooked to the steel protective shutter in front of an electronic appliance store. The driver was black, about twenty, with a scrubby beard and a woolen hat. The oblong badge on the officer's chest said: *Barraja*. Officer Barraja wore a helmet with the visor down and sunglasses behind it. In any other circumstances, we would all have been very frightened of Officer Barraja. But the moment he walked forward and aimed his shotgun at the head of the driver, I knew, and the crowd knew, and the bearded man certainly knew that Officer Barraja had put himself in an absurd situation; I knew, the crowd knew, and the bearded man certainly knew that Officer Barraja would not shoot. Officer Barraja did not know this yet; he learned it a few moments later when the bearded driver turned and grinned and, gunning his engine, then accelerated until the protective shutter gave way with a groan. Officer Barraja stepped back and shouldered his weapon and then: did nothing. People were hooting and clapping. Someone paused to take his picture. Outside the electronics store a queue was forming, as the people in front ducked through the wrecked fence and stepped inside.

The swapmeet was on fire at the corner of Wilcox, making my eyes smart again, sirens in the distance. I had an exhilarating sense of chaos. I wondered what was going to happen next, when up ahead I spotted a black teenager smashing the door of Frederick's of Hollywood with a hammer. Another pitched a chair and then climbed through the shattered window into the display. Alarm bells sounded, and the crowd, my neighborhood crowd, responded as though to an invitation, and so I went along as well, not trying to resist as I was almost lifted off my feet in the dense mass of bodies that suddenly crushed forward. I had somehow become part of a mob about to loot and trash what passed in Hollywood for a landmark: a lingerie store.

Someone found a switch and turned on the lights. Frederick's was classier than I'd imagined. The floor was slippery marble tile. The lingerie was red and pink and emerald green. As well as black and white, and each piece had its own hanger, its own place in the spacious arrangement of spinners and wall racks.

No one but me appeared to be admiring it. A girl ran to the far corner of the store, ahead of the pack, earning herself just enough time to be a little selective, as she lifted down hangers one by one. A fat lady in white appeared at the back, pushing, shouting at a man, "Let's go, let's go." She, along with the others crushing in behind her, were panicking at the prospect of having arrived too late. The members of this new lot had a strangely fixed expression, concerned perhaps that everything had gone, and were determined to make up for lost time. Broken glass crunched under my feet. Someone had found a ladder and was carefully prising loose an imitation art deco light fixture. There was no anger or fear; just bedlam. A black teenager in a T-shirt with a big cross around his neck made for the door with a mannequin under his arm. Pieces of other mannequins, stripped and smashed, were lying in the window display. The fat lady in white was on her hands and knees, her broad butt swinging in the air, as she rushed to fill up a suitcase. The suitcase had pricetags; she'd just taken it from somewhere else. She looked at me, a round, chubby face, and smiled, nodding, a gesture that I'm sure was supposed to say to me: *Go on.* I wasn't sure how to behave. I must have looked a little odd, standing there. I fingered some silky stuff.

"Hi!" someone shouted. Not at me, I assumed, but then it came again: "Hi, Richard!" It was the not-quite-pretty-enough Texan from the building next to mine, on her way from something called the Lingerie Museum at the back of the store. She picked up an intricate lace bra. "What do you think?" she said, and, without waiting for my reply, folded the bra carefully inside her black leather duffel bag. "I'm having a ball," she said, though she was disappointed that the Madonna bustier — the prize exhibit of the Lingerie Museum—had gone before she got to it; there'd been quite a race. She could have got a leather bra belonging to the pop star Belinda Carlisle, but she didn't care for that sort of music and, in any case, "Definitely a D-cup." She had the same pouty expression I'd seen on her face once before, when a producer of violent action films had brought her home one morning and ridden off on his Harley-Davidson, leaving her without so much as a kiss.

Frederick's, five minutes after being broken into, was picked bare.

A block and a half away, back up on Grace Avenue, a man was wetting the roof of our building with a hose in case somebody set fire to it. Some of our other neighbors were out on the street. They'd formed a vigilante committee, they said.

But of course, I replied, a little dazed, why not? I felt like Bertie Wooster. A fat man I'd never seen before wore a baseball cap that said FUCK EVERYBODY.

The black ex-boxer said, "This town is lost, man. This town is so *lost.*"

The heavy metal musician, standing nearby, opened his jacket to reveal an Ozzy Osbourne T-shirt and, stuffed inside the waistband of his jeans, a gun. "Browning automatic," he said proudly. It turned out he was English too.

"Oh, my God," said my girlfriend. This fellow didn't look like he should be let loose with a water pistol. Was I the only person in Los Angeles who *didn't* have a gun?

"I was in the Falklands, man," said the heavy metal musician. "I've seen this kind of stuff before. Let 'em come."

"Let them not," said the ex-boxer. "I can't afford to move again. I've been moved too many times."

I wondered what he meant by "been moved," but then it was the heavy metal musician again, saying, "The curfew's in force already so you folks had better go home now, okay?" It struck me that he was a strange authority figure. Had he really been in the Falklands? Everything was so extraordinary now I could almost believe he was for real. He walked toward the corner, not without a certain John Wayne swagger. "You all take care now. Okay?"

Nine-thirty, Thursday night, and the death toll was up to thirty. Howard Epstein shot to death at Seventh and Slauson. Jose L. Garcia shot to death at Fresno and Atlantic. Matthew Haines pulled off his motorcycle and shot to death in Long Beach. Eduardo Vela shot to death at 5142 West Slauson. Some of the dead were very young. Fourteen, fifteen. Keven Evanahen died while trying to put out a fire in a check-cashing store at Braddock and Inglewood. At least that made for variety. I blinked and shook my head as soon as that thought popped out. I'd been amazed by the riot, thrilled by it, swept along by it, terrified by it. It wasn't just that events had moved at such speed; the actual nature of what had occurred seemed to be shifting all the time. The riot had started with a particular angry focus: race. It had turned quickly into a poverty riot and then, diffused, became interracial anarchy. I wasn't sure what I'd seen, but I felt changed. Los Angeles itself seemed more tangible, now that everyone, even the players themselves, would have to acknowledge that there was more to the city than the make-believe Medici court of the movie business.

The Gap was being looted on Melrose.

The TV news was replaying a bulletin from earlier in the day. At Third and Vermont an unknown Latino had been shot with his own gun and was lying dead in the back of his car. No ambulance had been able to get there. This was the very intersection where I'd been with Jake. The reporter, talking to the camera, was trying to describe the situation, while black teenagers milled around behind him, clowning it up. At last the reporter gave up. "There's a dead person here and it's a big joke. Back to you at the studio."

At midnight we went for a drive. Hollywood Boulevard was blocked off by National Guardsmen in combat fatigues—they were on every corner—so we got onto the Hollywood freeway. Even at this hour, the freeway was normally crowded; now it was deserted. Los Angeles had become another city. We headed south and just as we were passing L. Ron Hubbard's Church of Scientology Celebrity Center, a police car came up alongside. A voice came through the patrol car's loudspeaker. "*A curfew is in force. You are breaking the law. Go home. Get off the streets. You are breaking the law.*"

In the middle of the afternoon on Friday, it became clear that it was probably over, and, curiously, there was a sense not of relief but of disappointed expectation: People wanted more. The rioting had become an entertainment. Announcers at KWIB — news twenty-four hours a day, all day, give us twenty minutes and we give you the world — actually apologized for the fact that the station was now returning to its true obsession, sport, and it occurred to me that during the time of the riot the city had gathered round a spectacle, as it might during the Super Bowl.

I wanted to see the damage where it had been worst, in South Central, so I went to see Beverley, a black schoolteacher I had recently been introduced to. I was cadging a ride with blacks again, this time so that I wouldn't feel threatened when I looked at their burnt-out neighborhoods.

We started off on Vermont, heading toward South Central. Straight away Beverley's eleven-year-old daughter Maya declared that she was thirsty, so I said I'd keep my eyes peeled for a store still standing to buy her a soda. The task turned out not to be so easy.

"Burned," said Beverley, pointing to one store, and then to another. "Razed . . . looted and burned. See that check store over there? Korean owned, looted and burned." Above it was a bright green sign, still intact:

INSTANT CASH. On top of the sign stood a National Guardsman with his assault rifle.

"Burned," she said, as we continued on our quest. "Leveled to the ground." Delicatessens, liquor stores, furniture stores, a Fedco warehouse where six hundred workers had turned up and found, literally, no job to go to — building after building was burned. Before the riots, there was one store for every 415 residents, less than half the Los Angeles average. That ratio looked pretty good now. On some stores, metal cutters had been used. Solid steel shutters had perfect triangles cut into them, like cans popped with an opener. At the intersection of Vernon and Central all four corners had been wiped out.

"Burned, burned, burned, burned. That's the deli where Latasha Harlins was killed," Beverley said, pointing to the store whose Korean owner Soon Ja Du had been fined $500 for shooting dead a fifteen-year-old black girl in a dispute over a $1.79 bottle of orange juice. It was one of the first stores attacked (nearly one thousand Korean businesses were destroyed, I would learn later). "Homies," Beverley continued, "tried to burn that deli three times, but they were ready. Not open now, of course." In the Watts riots of 1965, many Jewish businesses had been burned in South Los Angeles, and the Jews had left the neighborhood for good; this time the Koreans had been a target. Yet here, ironically, a BLACK OWNED sign had been a less effective guarantee of safety than in other areas of the city, because the destruction had been so general. "See that furniture store over there? A black family ran that for twenty-five years. Razed. Look at the job they did there, that was a liquor store, burned to the ground. Korean owned."

Beverley had been ten in 1965. "This was much worse," she said. "Spread farther and faster. More people died. The abuses that people reacted to in '65 were just the same — police abuse, economic discrimination, lack of jobs, but those riots were about hope. We had hope then. Gone now." It had taken twenty years to get a shopping center built in Watts after 1965. How long would it take to recover from this?

There was graffiti everywhere, on the remains of the buildings that had been burned, on the walls of every one that was still standing:

FUCK THE POLICE
FUCK WHITE PEOPLE
FUCK LAPD
FUCK GATES
FUCK THE LAW
POLICE KILLA
FUCK WHITIES
FUCK THE LAW
FUCK WHITEBOYS
NO JUSTICE, NO PEACE
GATES KILLA
BLOODS 'N' CRIPS TOGETHER FOR EVER
POLICE 187
And then: THIS IS SOUTH CENTRAL.

When I'd first spent time in Los Angeles in the mid-1980s, I'd had no more thought of coming here than to the moon, though I did go with friends to the Los Angeles Coliseum or the Forum, sports arenas close enough to make us very careful about planning the way back to the freeway. Turn a corner, I'd thought, and there I'd be, with bad street lighting and people dreaming of doing me damage. For me, South Central hadn't been just a small, bad neighborhood of the sort that existed in any city; it had been a very big bad neighborhood the size of a small city, and it had existed in my mind not as a real place — with stoplights and movie theaters and stores on the corner — but as a black hole stretching from downtown to Long Beach. I was ashamed of that. It seemed quite possible, now that South Central had had the effrontery to impose itself on the rest of the city, that the rest of the city would respond by turning it into an even grimmer ghetto.

"Security Pacific bank, burned, razed to the ground," said Beverley. "Burning a corner store, that's one thing. But to get into a bank and leave nothing except the empty safe still standing at the back. That takes dedication."

Beverley's daughter Maya reminded me that she was still thirsty, and Beverley said there was a 7-Eleven over on the edge of Inglewood. The rioting hadn't been so bad there, and we drove for another ten minutes only to find another destroyed building. "Looted," said Beverley. "Burned *to the ground.*" She began to laugh, and it did seem funny all of a sudden; we'd spent forty-five minutes driving through the geographical center of America's second largest city, and we'd been unable to buy a Coca-Cola.

I had never seen Simi Valley, the town where the four officers had been found not guilty of beating Rodney King and from where, every morning, more than two thousand LAPD officers, county sheriffs, and other law enforcement personnel commuted to their jobs in distant Los Angeles. I wanted to make the journey myself. My girlfriend and I drove there from South Central.

The journey took us about an hour; in traffic, it could take two hours: the Harbor freeway to the Hollywood freeway, short stretches of the Ventura and San Diego freeways and the bland sprawl of the San Fernando Valley. It was on our last freeway, the Simi Valley, that the landscape changed. This had all been part of Southern California's ranch country; its nineteenth-century history concerned trails and horses and men who did what men had to do. But now housing estates could be seen on most hill-sides, and freeway exit ramps were marked CONSTRUCTION VEHI-CLES ONLY, where new dormitory suburbs were being built. It was like a passage between continents.

At the far end of Los Angeles Avenue, there was a sale of "recreational vehicles," where a short man called Ted said that, while he had been shocked by the verdicts, and horrified by the riots, this was all good news for him. He was a real estate agent. He predicted a boom in Simi Valley, and indeed throughout the whole of Ventura County, as more and more fled black street crime and the Dickensian hell of Los Angeles. "You know the worst thing about the looting all those niggers did down there?" he asked. "*They couldn't afford it.*" Ted paused. "Just kidding," he said.

We drove through the city. Los Angeles Avenue itself consisted of shop-ping malls: Simi Valley Plaza, Mountain Gate Plaza, Madre Plaza, the Westgate Center. In these plazas, huge parking lots were surrounded by stores of all kinds. A cavernous home improvement center issued the smell of wood. Everything else issued the smell of air conditioning. You could buy things here: a new Ford, a taco, a garden hose, an ice cream, an airline ticket to Lake Tahoe, a pair of jeans, a carton of frozen yogurt, a CD player, a haircut, a chili burger, a spade, a doughnut, a bag of enriched soil fertilizer, a vegetarian health sandwich, the *Simi Valley Advertiser,* a novel by Stephen King, a new tie, a bathing suit that dries in minutes, spark plugs, a suit for $250, a nonstick frying pan, a small plastic container of Anacin, the *New York Times*, a set of plastic poker chips. You could collect interest on your savings, wash your car, or go bowling. You could buy beer, Gatorade, and many different kinds of California Chardonnay. You could buy a Coca-Cola. I bought a Coca-Cola.

You could tell who lived in Simi Valley (they were white) and who worked there but lived elsewhere (they were Hispanic). We didn't see any blacks but we may not have stayed long enough. I'm sure there were blacks in Simi Valley.

At the East County Courthouse, where the King verdicts had been reached, I was confronted by a local resident, a middle-aged woman in a beige suit made of an indeterminate fabric. She smiled at me coldly.

"You're not from here, are you?"

"No," I replied, a little surprised. Was I really so obvious? Perhaps I looked a little thin. Simi Valley seemed to be a place where fat people got fatter.

"I thought so," she said. "And you've come because of that Rodney King thing."

I said yes.

"I don't feel guilty," she said, answering a question I hadn't asked. "I refuse to feel guilty. I did everything I could back in the sixties for those people. They just refused to make the most of their opportunities."

"Why was that?"

"Oh, they're lazy," she said. "Those people are just plain lazy.

"Go back to Los Angeles," she said, "and take your issue with you. It has nothing to do with Simi Valley. Those people on the jury did the best job they could, and for you to assume that twelve white people can't hand down a fair verdict in a case like that, well, that's racist in itself, isn't it?"

She was right: If thinking that twelve people like her couldn't be relied upon to hand down a fair verdict was racist, then I was a racist. I hated her. I wanted to hurt her. I didn't want to argue or protest. I wanted her injured. I saw myself doing it. Pow. Pow. Pow.

We returned to Los Angeles.

The riots began on Wednesday, 29 April 1992. Monday, 4 May, was the first day — the first of many — that gun sales topped two thousand in Southern California, twice the normal figure, a gun sale every forty seconds. By that Monday, this was the riot toll: 228 people had suffered critical injuries (second- and third-degree skin burns; blindness; gunshot wounds to the lung, stomach, neck, shoulder, and limbs; knife wounds; life-threatening injuries from broken glass), and 2,383 people had suffered noncritical injuries (requiring hospital treatment); there were more than seven thousand fire emergency calls; 3,100 businesses were affected by burning or looting; 12,111 arrests. Fifty-eight people are dead.

THE BEACH AT SUNSET

Eloise Klein Healy

for Colleen

The cliff above where we stand is crumbling
and up on the Palisades
the sidewalks buckle like a broken conveyer belt.

Art Deco palm trees sway their hula skirts
in perfect unison
against a backdrop of gorgeous blue,

and for you I would try it,
but I have always forbidden myself to write
poems about the beach at sunset.

All the cliches for it sputter
like the first generation of neon,
and what attracts me anyway

are these four species of gulls we've identified,
their bodies turned into the wind,
and not one of them aware of their silly beauty.

I'm the one awash in pastels
and hoping to salvage the day, finally turning away
from the last light on the western shore

and the steady whoosh of waves driving in,
drumming insistently like the undeniable data
of the cancer in your breast.

We walk back to the car
and take the top down for the ride home
through the early mist.

No matter what else is happening,
this is California. You'll have your cancer
at freeway speeds. I'll drive and park

and drive at park. The hospital
when I arrive to visit will be catching
the last rays of the sun, glinting

like an architectural miracle realized.
I realize a miracle is what you need—
a grain of sand, a perfect world

where you live beyond the facts
of what your body has given you
as the first taste of death.

BAD GIRL ON THE CURB

Lisa Glatt

THERE is a bad girl on the curb. It is two in the morning and I, like a good girl, have been sleeping since midnight. My husband has been awake on the couch, reading a book on ghosts, sipping whiskey from a short glass, and it is he who comes into the bedroom to wake me up and let me know about the bad girl. But I know about her already, having been awakened by her crazy brakes and screeching tires. "What happened?" I say, pulling the sheet up over my nightgown, covering the thick scar I haven't yet let him see.

"There's a bad girl on the curb," he says.

"Where?"

"She hit a parked truck, and now she's sitting down surrounded by cops. Come see."

I think about taking the sheet with me onto the balcony, but instead say, "Give me a minute."

He shakes his head, insulted, and walks out of the bedroom. He tips the glass this way and that in the hall, and I hear ice cubes knocking against one another. There were hurtful things I said to him just days after my diagnosis, perhaps as a test, and I think of them now, cranky words falling from my lips, and the expression on his face, a forty-year-old man pouting on a waiting room couch.

I hear the sliding glass door open and know he's standing outside in the wind and cold in just his cotton pajamas. I think of bringing him a sweater, going to the closet and pulling out one of the knits my mother made him six months before she died, the blue one or the brown one, but decide against them both. There are gestures I talk myself out of these days, ones I'm afraid will inspire him to come too close. More than once, he has sat at the breakfast table with half a bagel and a cup of coffee, and I have stood behind him and stopped my own hand midair as it went for his shoulder. There are positions I avoid in sleep; spooning him would mean my one good breast against his back, and him spooning me might mean his palm searching for what's no longer there. I am careful where my feet go. I fold myself into something small and wake with my elbow or shoulder half off the mattress.

I put on my robe and join him. On the dark balcony, I reach for his hand. He pulls it away. "Sure," he says. "Now that we're not in bed."

The bad girl looks bad all right, sitting on the curb in her black dress, her long hair down, pieces of it hanging in her face. The street lights glow orange, and the girl sits with her back against the post directly across from us. We live on the third floor and even from up here, at this hour, there's a lot you can make out. Not quite the look on her face, but the way her thin knees meet, and the high heel shoes she holds with one hand, and her bare feet.

"I bet she's freezing," I say.

"She needs a sweater."

"You need a sweater too." I touch his sleeve. "Let me get you one."

One of the cops is placing flares in the street and another one keeps a watchful eye on the bad girl. Every few minutes, the girl tries to stand or move or escape and the cop comes and steers her back down. I don't know what he says to her, if he calls her Dear or Missy or uses her first name. I don't know the tone of his voice or how hard he grabs her arm. The truck is smashed, bumper thrown off onto the grass, taillight torn and hanging like an earring.

There are things about me my husband does not know: how many nights I was drunk too, running into cars and men I didn't know were there. How I've imagined my own tumors every day for years, fat cherries or plums, how I believe my own worry was the first foul cell. "She must be damn drunk," I say, stating the obvious.

"She was wobbling before you got here."

"I bet her heart is broken," I say. "I bet someone broke her heart tonight."

"Maybe."

"I bet she doesn't care what happens next."

"In the morning she will."

"Yes," I say. "When she's sober."

Then the girl is up, arms out like wings, trying to touch her nose. She is walking a line, tipping left and right. I imagine she wants her bed or mother, a glass of water or one more beer. The cops are big in their dark clothes, towers pointing flashlights at the girl's unsteady feet. Halfway down the block, neighbors have gathered, little groups under trees, a young man and woman leaning against a fence. An old man with a big poodle stands by a fire hydrant.

My husband leans over the ledge to get a better look, and my first impulse is to stop him, to pull him back up where he's safe, but he looks bold and brave bent like that, a human question mark. He stares down at the bad girl and makes sympathetic sounds, tongue hitting the roof of his mouth. "She's in trouble," he says. The cops point the girl toward the police car. The back door is open, a waiting cave. She shakes her head frantically, says no so loud that we hear. "She's feisty," my husband says, just as she's being helped inside by the two officers—one with his hand protecting her head as she dips into the backseat.

The girl's palm is pressed flat against the window as the car pulls away from the curb. She looks anything but feisty now.

"Her hand," my husband says. "Did you see her hand?"

"Yes," I say, leaning over the ledge too, joining him. The groups of people are breaking up. They've seen enough. The poodle lifts his leg to pee. The young couple steps away from the fence. They're holding hands, walking into the apartment building across the street. My husband looks up at me and as he does, his eyes freeze on my chest. My robe has slipped open, revealing what they left me. I stay there with him, looking also. It is ours. Whatever happens next happens to us.

DAY TIME

Bruce Bauman

THIS is how it ended.

"Good luck, then. You can do it now with someone else. You're only forty-one. You've got plenty of time."

I stared at my films, ready, needing to be made *right*. There would be, could be, no one else. Suddenly, there was no time and endless time. Violence and death poured out of me. Winter could not come again in time.

Godfrey Barker, Pulitzer Prize–winning film theorist, pronounced that film is the only art that is not timeless, but out of time.

He was right. I know because I make films out of time.

This happened over many years and one day not long ago.

"The tag is 'How many tanks does it take to make a Panzer?' We go with a panoramic shot of, I don't know, a hundred tanks spelling the word 'Panzer'—and one new luxury Panzer SUV." Rory, the hottest young hotshot at the advertising agency of Amacon, Yorkin, & Stunkle, was trying to sell me on her new campaign. Rory's blond, shoulder-length hair waved away from the collar of her blue suit jacket. Her face reddened under the mask of powder. I stayed in my leather swivel chair. She looked down, hazel eyes begging for approval from me, her boss and hoped-for ally. Rory did not understand she had no allies; not in this business she loved. And I was in the process of leaving.

"I don't get it." I said with disaffected superiority.

"Then we go with the tag 'How many Panzers does it take to conquer a country? . . . One.' It's got strength and it clamps you hard."

"But it doesn't make sense." I knew that commercials did not have to make sense and that her idea would sell.

"It'll be memorable and powerful. Just promise you won't sabotage me. Jason—he's waiting for me to screw up. Please! This could be my Napalm Balm."

Eleven years ago my campaign for the men's cologne Napalm Balm had streaked across the TV sky. Maybe you remember? It featured a couple on a beach. Wearing almost nothing. She, back to the camera, putting on a camisole. He, only in tight jeans. He, glancing at the woman, says, "I love the smell of Napalm Balm in the morning . . . it smells like victory." The lawyers had a field day with that one. We won the lawsuit, and the publicity put me on the advertising map.

The phone rang. "Mr. Day, it's your wife." Gloria, my secretary, dispensed this unwanted information.

"My *estranged* wife, Gloria. Ten seconds and put her through."

Rory motioned toward the door. I nodded. "Okay, Rory, qualified support . . ."

"Thank you," she mouthed, and closed the door behind her.

"Hello there, Winnie." My former wife hated that pet name. Her name was Winter. Winter Riddle Day. Originally of the Riddles of Philadelphia and New Hope, Pennsylvania, and the Winters of Boston, Massachusetts, and Kent, Connecticut. Then she met me, Mark Day of Tenafly, New Jersey. She disliked the idea of being Winter Day, so she kept the Riddle.

"Mark, we have to meet tonight."

"Sounds urgent. Is it about the papers?"

"Yes and no."

"I'm busy tonight, so why don't you tell me now? Or is *Ahn — dre* listening?"

Just before we split, Winter sold a movie she cowrote to Lifetime TV. She swore the producer thought Preston Sturges was an old-time character actor. (Burgess Meredith? Sergeant Preston of the Yukon?) He didn't get the joke of her script because now it's a "Lifetime original drama." Winter used the working title, *How Can I Miss You When You Won't Go Away*. It's been changed to *Go Away, My Lover*.

Then, after thirteen years of marriage, she left me for Andre Mussili, the twenty-six-year-old star of TV movies.

"You can give your project a rest for one night. For an hour. Two at most."

Winter was well aware my films meant more to me than anything.

"That's not it. I have to finish the copy for ReViva."

"ReViva? Never heard of it. And Day, you haven't cared about work in years." She waited for my retort. I didn't have one because she was right. During our marriage, much to her chagrin, I spent many days and weeks working overtime, but I no longer cared a damn about AY&S. Then she slid in the knife. "You haven't cared about anyone in years."

I held my breath, and my tongue—absorbed the blow, until I found the right response.

"I care about ReViva. It is the male multiple orgasm pill. And guarantees 'You'll be a stand up guy within minutes.'. . . It comes too late for us."

"Day, that was never a problem."

"I faked it," I lied. We had a wonderful sex life, up until the day before she left.

"Mark, stop, I don't like this." The trepidation in Winter's voice came through the phone. I knew her too well: A dark smell of cold sweat seeped from her hands. The reliving, the possible rewriting of the past offended her linear view of life.

"Okay, Winnie. My place at eight."

"But you have no furniture. All you have are projectors and miles and miles of tape and film and —"

"—I know what I have. One of us will have to sit on the floor. Or both of us on the bed."

Elias Canetti, Nobel Prize–winning author, wrote near the end of his life, "I have done nothing against time."

This is happening now in Reel Time.

The beginning of most films is the end or the middle because films are made out of sequence. The head honchos claim this method saves money. When we moved to L.A., I learned the real reason. Hollywood is the shiny, ever-altering face of America, which refuses to accept linear time. It refuses aging and death. It believes not in the past or the here and now but in the future. And film is the eternal, possible future, always replayable as if new and immediate. Like it or not, film is America's art. But film is out of time. It is also a lie. I discovered how to make movies into truth. I get the shooting scripts of films. Then I get the films themselves. And I put them back in sequence — recut them piece by piece, frame by frame — until they run the way they were filmed. I make them real.

Day's long journey.

I left my office and walked down the hall to Rory's office. When I knocked and entered, Rory stood, as if dangling and lost.

"Rory, I want to give you some good advice. Stop trying to imitate me. You have your own voice."

She looked hurt. Her luscious lips pouted. Her eyelashes refused to flutter. I stopped trying to advise her. Commercial copywriters and directors who call themselves writers and directors make me laugh, but they take themselves very seriously. I once wanted to make real films. I didn't have the guts or vision. I was going to have a family to support. So, I became a success in commercials. I even had a style named after me. "Day at Dusk." After the yellow smoke-sky of Napalm Balm, all of my commercials had that crepuscular aura. Eat your heart out, François Truffaut.

"Forget it, you're doing fine without me. I'm with you," I said without emotion.

"Thank you. Four o'clock in the conference room."

Rory didn't know that the Stunkles had lost faith in me as a creative force. I'd made them millions, and I knew the business. When they decided to open an L.A. office four years ago, I'd agreed to go and be the subservient mentor to Jason Stunkle, son of cofounder, Cy Stunkle. Winter and

I thought it would reinvigorate our marriage. It was in its death throes. Throes caused by death. Premature death.

This happened three times over many years and happens again every day, like a Nietzschean finger eternally hitting the replay button on a VCR.

"Oh my God, I'm bleeding." Those words were the first I ever heard Winter speak in fear. Instinctually, Winter felt the horror of oncoming death.

That first time, the famed Dr. Apple of Mt. Sinai Hospital in New York said, "It could be nothing. It could be nothing. Come in the morning." And then so painfully, Winter miscarried all through the night. Apple coldly commanding over the phone, while chewing a crunchy unnamed food, "Take some aspirin, there's nothing I can do." He allowed Winter to languish in writhing pain because he was too damn lazy to meet us at the hospital. We were too devastated to know we should've sued him for gross negligence.

The second time I heard those piercing words — "I'm bleeding" — I already knew. I'd smelled the stench of death oozing from her when I licked the lips from where our child would not come. This time we let the sterile machines of modernity do their job of cleaning her womb. But the love between us turned hard, into fear and bitterness. With no one to blame, we blamed each other and ourselves.

We had tests and saw therapists, all to save our marriage. Only a strange combination of tenacity, fear, and inertia kept us together. When the chance came to start over in the city of perpetual starting over, we jumped at it. Instead of growing closer, we grew further apart.

After almost a year in L.A., Winter got pregnant again. We never could relax. Always waiting in fear, fear that now penetrated our every move. And then, one night when I was out on a shoot, the bleeding began. Winter refused to accept the rushing loss. She didn't call the doctors or an ambulance. When I arrived home at nearly midnight, the blood was gushing from her. I carried her to the car and sped to the emergency room.

Not only had another child been lost, but hope.

Then we stopped. And time stopped with us.

Bruce Springsteen, platinum album selling rocker, once screamed at the top of his hoarse lungs as the countdown neared to his thirty-fifth birthday, "Somebody, stop the clock!"

When the first geniuses of film like Eisenstein, the racist Griffith, Chaplin, and Keaton discovered the ability to edit a film and make it new, they must have had the same magical feeling as when the disciples "found" Jesus alive outside the cave. The hope of resurrection, of time reversing, of controlling time, of death before birth is the great myth of the west, the myth of movies. Time beyond itself. But it is a lie as movies are a lie. Like the myth of Jesus, the movies are the trickster's blend of belief and faith. Which is a lie. I make them truth with no trickery allowed.

There are four films I will never remake. *Casablanca* and *Citizen Kane*. And none of the Marx Brothers' movies.

The Marx Brothers really made one long movie. It doesn't matter whether you put the steamer trunk scene from *A Night at the Opera* into *Duck Soup* or the classroom scene from *Horse Feathers* into *A Day at the Races*. It makes no difference — the Marx Brothers were theatrical magicians. Vaudevillians come to the screen. No one has ever matched them.

Casablanca was made in sequence — none of the writers, the actors, director, producers — no one knew from day to day how it would turn out. No actor today could make that movie. Bogie is reborn in life and not in death. That is its secret vitality.

And *Citizen Kane*, not because it was made in sequence — it wasn't — but because it is so set in and against time. Beginning with the tale of the dead Kane, who, no matter how hard others tried to revive him as legend or myth, could not be resurrected. With the burning of the Rosebud sled in the metaphoric embers of hell, Wells stopped time, and denied resurrection not only for Kane but also for himself.

The end of conscious time keeping for Mark Day.

At four-thirty, I sauntered into the conference room. The account executives from Panzer and Jason, Cy, and Amy Yorkin all sat around a huge polished wooden table. Rory stood at the head of the room giving her presentation. I lip-synched an apology for my lateness and took a seat near Rory. She was halfway through. I let her finish. Then Cy asked me, out of policy, what I thought.

"It works. But I want to get into computer imaging instead of tanks. We use an early afternoon shot, we go with a dusk, twilight shot . . ."

Everyone nodded in agreement. Rory sat down.

I waited until the good-byes with the people from Panzer were finished. Then I called Rory, Jason, Amy, and Cy back into the room.

"I should probably do this individually, but since you're all here I have an announcement to make. I'm leaving the firm. No, not for a better offer. I decided, just this afternoon, after months of vacillation to go out and make my films. Cy, you know that's what I've always wanted to do."

Jason's thin lips twitched like a predatory rat trying to hide his pleasure. Cy, his fleshy face unreadable, which helped make him so successful an executive, walked closer to me. Amy acted with indifference. Rory looked truly worried.

"Cy, you talk it over with Jason and Sol. Let me know if you want me to wait for a replacement. I'll do whatever you want. *You* have been good to me."

Alone of the people in the room, Cy knew of the trauma Winter and I had endured. He patted me on the shoulder with one hand while we shook hands with the other, as if I was a pathetic washed-up buffoon. "Call me when I'm back in New York. You and I will talk." He stared at his son Jason with scorn. He believed it was Jason who chased me from his company. It wasn't true, but I wasn't going to disabuse him of that notion either.

My favorite films, and the most dangerous films, are illusions of resurrection in time. The dead body rising in the river in *Deliverance;* the undying cyborg in *The Terminator;* the living hand in *The Hand;* the unkilled Kurtz of the best, unreleased ending of *Apocalypse Now;* the dead sister-mother and living granddaughter in *Chinatown;* the dead King Kong in front of the Empire State Building and then again in front of the Twin Towers, before he ever lived — all "last scenes" defying death — none of them last scenes in time. Now all of them are back where they belong, set between the scenes shot in linear time.

"*Fin du Film. Fin du Cinema,*" says Godard at the end of *Weekend.* Godard understood that even with the longest, linear-based tracking shot in history; a disjointed plot edited purposefully out of sequence and out of time; intentional sloppiness and amateurism; caricatures of historic figures; thorny, now corny, political pontifications that are certainly of their time — he had put time back into film, but he could never recapture time. He could only recreate it as a future — because once on film, the past is always the future. Godard knew that each shot in a movie is like a resurrection and that film is not to be trusted. Film is the false messiah of time.

Day of the dead.

After knocking on the door of my 1920s ramshackle Echo Park rented home — quite a switch from our Brentwood condo — Winter flowed into the house in her long, black dress and purple velvet cape, like a character from *The Scarlet Letter* crossed with *Scream VIII.* Fear and shame came late to Winter, but with her regal bearing, she carried them well. Her small nose sniffed at the mildewed odor in the air, but she refrained from issuing one of her snap-crackle barbs. Instead, she took off her cape and folded it into a pillow on the wooden floor. She did not sit. I turned off the editing machine. She came closer to me. The frailty of her facial bones shrouded an inner core of strength that allowed her to fight off the deaths of her children.

"Mark, I need that divorce." Her face looked paler than usual.

"Some water?"

"Yes."

"Why? You marrying him?" I asked as I walked to the kitchen and took my one clean glass and filled it with water from the tap.

"Maybe . . ." She sat down on her cape. I walked over and handed the glass to her. "But that's not why. I went to a new doctor and found out that I have a strange problem." I knelt down beside her. Close enough to feel each other's warmth, but we did not touch. "Something to do with my auto-immune system. They fixed it with aspirin and cortisone. All those *famous* doctors, and I still can't believe they didn't find it." She tucked her chin into her chest and closed her green eyes. Then she peeked at me, and I saw a spike of satisfaction in her face. Under the grim light of the one lit lamp in the living room, her smile seemed eerie, but I knew her. She couldn't hide her satisfaction. "I'm three months pregnant. I'm fine. The baby is fine."

I stared at her belly. I saw a new, small roundness under her loose-fitting dress. I wanted to punch her till she bled like she bled with my children. Until the would-be child came sliding from her cunt and was nothing but dead DNA — like my three babies, alive but unborn and out of time.

I didn't say another word. I got up and walked solemnly into my bedroom. I picked the papers off the floor. I returned to the living room. She was standing erect, her cape again draped over her shoulders. As I got closer, I saw a vaporous cast in her eyes. In another time, she would have wanted me to hold her. And I would have embraced her with all the immediacy and power of life. Now I reached over and handed her the papers, a cold transaction in the night. A slight, remorseful glaze of memory creased her pale lips and watered her eyes as she sighed ever so quietly. She may have had life in her, but she knew too much death to be happy at that moment in time.

"I'm making my own film, too . . ." I said as she took the papers. "It's called *Winter Riddle: A Marriage Where Almost Nothing Happened.*"

My meanness broke her sadness. "Good luck, then. You can do it now with someone else. You're only forty-one. You've got plenty of time."

I stared at my films, ready, needing to be made *right*. There would be, could be, no one else. Suddenly, there was no time and endless time. Violence and death poured out of me. Winter could not come again in time.

The last film I cannot remake is *Superman*. Not because *Superman* is immortal, but because more than any other movie, despite its mediocrity, it presents the promise of eternal time for us mortals. It promises the future's ability to redo time. Superman, like a master film editor, rewinds the earth and miraculously returns Lois Lane to life. In America, in this time of film and perpetual resurrection, everyone wants the power to bring the dead, even the unborn, back.

This is how it began.

"Mark, we're going to have a baby." And then we made love. It was all before us: a family, our films — happiness! We would live such a wonderful life.

As my seeds gushed into her already welcoming womb, Winter whispered in my ear of her breathless coming.

BIELER'S BROTH

Louise Steinman

PHILIP'S hands are curled around the edges of his blanket. Bird hands. There are vases of daylilies in his room, and the windows are open to the surrounding canyon live oaks and eucalyptus that modify the body smells. Irene is talking quietly to the nurse. I try not react as I walk in, but the change in just over a month is astonishing. Six years shy of forty and Philip looks like an old man. End of June, before he left to see his family in Nebraska, he was joking, he was Philip, ever the actor—punctuating animated conversations with declamatory gestures and rambunctious laughter. Robust and athletic, solid muscles from a childhood doing farm chores. Now Philip is shrinking away, his bones prominent in his face. His eyes blink open. "Why do I have to die?" they ask. He mouths to me, barely, "I'm too exhausted to talk."

I take my sad heart downstairs. I pause on the narrow stairway to look at the framed photograph. Irene has a wonderful picture collection, some from her days working at Magnum Photo in New York. This one is a Russell Lee, two powerful men in overalls. "They look like they're about to brawl," I mumble to no one. Irene is right behind me. "They're square dancing," she says. I look closer and she's right.

Irene and Philip are soul mates, compadres, best friends. When Irene first told me about Philip, I groaned inwardly. My beautiful, single, tender-hearted friend was in love with a gay man who had AIDS. Why shouldn't I have been worried? But I stopped worrying a long time ago; I accepted the rarity of their bond and the mutuality of their devotion and love. Now

Irene has welcomed Philip into her house to live, knowing that he is dying. No one can predict how long it will take. Or if there will be a miracle.

I want to help. "Make Bieler's broth," Irene suggests. "Use the veggies in the fridge." She heads back upstairs with a ceramic pitcher of water. I find a striped denim apron on a hook in a cupboard and put it on. I've never made Bieler's broth before. I know it's that vegetable soup people make when someone's very sick; I think it was invented by some German health food guru. I open Irene's refrigerator and peer into chaos. I gingerly remove several Ziploc bags full of vegetables from the crisper, trying to avoid the ones with brown liquid pooling in the bottoms.

I start chopping. Zucchini and celery, yellow squash and string beans. Okra and green onion. Turnips and Swiss chard. I am grateful there are so many different vegetables to chop, I am grateful to be occupied because it is so excruciating to see Philip dying. When I run out of vegetables, I rummage around to salvage more. A bunch of beets and another of carrots. I chop up every single vegetable in Irene's refrigerator. First I chop them, then I steam them, then I purée them. The yellow squash pales under the heat. The chard wilts. The carrots fade from bright orange to delicate coral. I zap the power button on the blender in short pulses. I don't want to disturb Philip's rest.

Irene is upstairs, sitting on Philip's bed, stroking him. She comes downstairs with tears streaming down her face. In the midst of Philip dying she's supposed to prepare for a radio interview with Susan Sontag. All weekend she's been lugging around Sontag's enormous romantic novel about the nineteenth century. She can't concentrate on reading. I tell her, "Surely Susan Sontag will understand."

I remember trying to carry on "normal life" while my mother was dying of pancreatic cancer. When the time comes, I thought, I'll take a leave from my job. I'll devote myself full-time to caring for Mother, instead of dashing off to a morning appointment, a tech rehearsal, instead of trying to meet an article deadline. I didn't realize until the very end that the time had come. Surely everyone—bosses, lighting designers, editors—would understand. But on the whole, they didn't.

The phone rings, jarring the hush in the house. It's Jeffrey, Philip's friend, calling from a phone booth on Sunset Boulevard. The pharmacy is closed. You can't fill a prescription for Percoset on a Sunday. It's in triplicate. Tomorrow. I go upstairs to tell Irene and Philip.

Philip asks for two Darvocet. The label on the container says "one every four hours for pain." "I'm not giving him two," says Irene, adamant. From Philip, angrily, "Why the fuck not?" Irene wants to do everything right for Philip. She doesn't want to lose him, lose his consciousness, lose his body. But the only rule at this point, it seems to me, is to eliminate pain. The phone again. I rush downstairs—it's the guy from the nursing agency. I ask him about Darvocet. "If he's in a lot of pain, then give him two," he says.

Jeffrey calls again from the corner of Sunset and Doheny. What can he bring Philip to eat? Philip whispers loudly from the bed, "A fish sandwich with a side of fries from Carl's Junior." Irene says no. She is the guardian of Philip's liver, which is functioning at five percent capacity. No fats. No salt. No extra liquids. Philip is really mad, he wants that fish sandwich though he lacks the strength to make a big fuss. "How do I leave him his volition?" Irene groans aloud as she comes downstairs. She stops at the base of the stairs, glances around the room. "I need something Philip can throw up in." I suggest the dishwashing basin, it's easy to aim for. She grabs it and turns to rush upstairs, but first she notices what I've been cooking. Her soft brown eyes startle and widen.

Bieler's broth, I find out too late, is supposed to consist of just three vegetables: string beans, zucchini, and celery. Bieler's broth is supposed to be a comforting pale green.

We eat the shocking scarlet soup for days after Philip dies.

ANAGOGE

Aleida Rodríguez

Rush in from street,
                    drop stuff on desk,
grope   blind   kitchen   dumb   with hunger.

There's Tupperware (sautéed shallots and chanterelles,
broccoli florets and spinach leaves, slivers of roasted red
bell pepper, all splashed with cognac simmering, the whole thing
inverted over agnolotti),

                    but as I'm reaching for it   (the refrigerator light
goes on in my brain)   there shivers last night's takeout Thai green
curry with shrimp and peas in spicy coconut milk and
my hands can't move   fast enough — like when I'm trying
      to corner   a slippery   idea and can't squeeze out the
letters legibly   contents blur into saucepan, curry rises like sea level
and shrimp   bop   green beach balls   among the
Agnolotti Islands,
                    not warm yet but I get my tongue and teeth around it:
fiery spice settles comfortably against pasta cushions,
exotic guest nestling into velvet parlor,
vegetables embrace weeping like old friends separated by war.
Oh, what a great idea this was, I exhale between furious mouthfuls,
standing at the stove, spooning myself into myself.
The table has four legs again.
On the buttery wall

the still life glass of water is infused with sun,
the sated knife lies down beside the halved lemon.
The kitchen chair looks hard and recognizes me.

A NOTE FOR EVERYTHING

Samantha Dunn

SOMETIMES I feel like an interpreter between nations, between the country of musicians and the pay-bills-get-a-nine-to-five-read-the-paper world. By day, I am a copy editor at the UCLA publications office, by night, I review music for local trades when I'm not working as a pen-for-hire for bands who need press packs. According to my calculations, I have spent some 250 evenings in clubs with thin carpets or sawdust or yeast-sticky floors, watery vodka, and the persistent yellow of nicotine air. And those are the ones I remember.

Tonight is another typical Tuesday industry scene at the Troubadour: Wood panel walls and black vinyl seats give the sense of some urban hunting lodge. I sport the nylon badge that will let me into the glass-paneled Loft at the side of the stage, but I stay downstairs instead. The drinks are just as weak up in the Loft, and the conversation more feeble than the booze. I sit at the bar taking notes about the band, even though their psychedelic wah-wah guitar and cry-baby bass are so familiar to me I am sure that if I died in some freak auto accident, the last vain threads of my consciousness would be squandered on this chord progression from a cheap metal act, so long has it been jackhammered into my head. I write the band's name at the top of my notepad and underline it twice, because if I don't, I'll forget it by morning. Still, I sit on the black vinyl stool and listen because, maybe, just on the off chance, I will catch a moment incandescent and chemical.

Writing in a bar is a profane act; it draws the eye of the pack suspiciously toward you. I brace for the question, "What are you writing for?"—sometimes asked with curiosity but more often in a way that makes me feel like I'm shoplifting, like I should put something back. I always want to reply, "I'm writing because I lost my maracas and can't play keyboards," but the timing never seems right.

Now, rising out of the band noise, I hear a voice shouting at me, but I can't understand the words; I've been doing this so long my ears have suffered a certain electric scarring. Finally, I feel a tap on my shoulder and there saying hello is a woman named Barb, the kind of person I run into now and again when we're covering the same gig. Barb works phones for a music publisher and then goes home to edit her own fanzine, specializing in straight-up, Ted Nugent sorts of bands with seemingly endless bolts of hair extensions who find a haven at FM-Station, the North Hollywood venue off Lankershim. With her palomino mane and stiletto black heels, Barb looks as if she could step on a stage herself. If you ask why she doesn't, though, she'll just laugh and tell you, "Honey, I am *way* too smart for that."

"Where's Matt?" She looks to see if my husband is beside me, but as usual, he isn't. My plus-one at the door was given to the guy behind me in line for a ticket, who at first wasn't sure if I was scalping or just friendly.

"In the studio," I say, and Barb nods, needing no elaboration, understanding in a way only those who've lived with a rock musician can. After high school, she had a boyfriend whose band maybe had a shot in L.A. She didn't have anything better to do and, plus, in a pinch she could double as a tour manager.

"But that was a long time ago," she says, the stress on "long" making it sound like a train with too many cars down a straight track. The boyfriend didn't make it and went back to Camden, an irony that makes Barb's mouth twist as if she's got a sweet-and-sour jawbreaker in her mouth.

What a strange sorority we belong to here in California. Like the women who came west during the Gold Rush, we follow men with big dreams. Then a funny thing happens. The guys end up busing tables at Bob's Big Boy or return to Nebraska or New Jersey or wherever. The women stay, and many end up with relatively successful careers in the industry. Maybe it's a question of different expectations when we get to town: The musician arrives wanting Rock Star or nothing, while most of the time, the person who comes with him doesn't have that kind of pressure, so she's willing to work her way up in whatever job she gets. Pulled in as part of a current, we settle, build structures, become the grid of music writers, managers, publicists, secretaries, leather-jacket retail-store clerks on Hollywood Boulevard, the reality that facilitates the fantasy. Across this grid men need only to bring their Anvil cases and fill in the colors.

I came to L.A. about the same time the last Gazzarri girl walked down Sunset Boulevard in her polyurethane-too-shiny-to-be-leather bodysuit, passing out flyers for bands. Parades of adolescents, real and perpetual, still walked the Rainbow-Roxy-Whisky-Teazer strip on weekends; the Whisky and Roxy were just about to upgrade their image from pay-to-play venues for local groups. This was before body piercing got big, before tribal tattooing replaced the old biker fine-line style, before Seattle moved the epicenter of cool to the Northwest, before Metallica cut their hair.

When Matt asked me to marry him, I had no idea I would someday find myself perched on a stool at the Troubadour, fingering the condensation on the curvy glass of my drink, wondering if I needed to stay for more than half the set. I had no idea I would defend myself to friends who'd worry that I spent too much time alone, that I had somehow traded down. I was the student body president, class of 1983. I was not supposed to follow a rock musician to Hollywood. My living room was not supposed to be a repository for black boxes with knobs, drumheads, and guitar stands. "MIT grad" was supposed to mean physicists minted from the Massachusetts Institute of Technology, not Musicians Institute players slightly crusty with a fine sweat layer, more records than clothes, and occasional employment that usually required a name tag. These types of guys were not supposed to sleep drunk on my couch in any sort of consistent intervals, nor was I supposed to know them each by name.

Even before I loaded two orange crates of valuables into a Ford Escort and drove I-10 toward the Pacific all those years ago, I had adopted a new belief system. A line from this gospel would read: *On the first day Les Paul*

created the solid body electric guitar, but it took Leo Fender to make the Strat. One
L.A. morning hung in gray marine layers, I woke up fluent in a dialect I
could speak to no one from my former tribe, in a language that would not
guarantee me safe passage through life.

Matt was not the only reason for this — I was memorizing Frank Zappa's
Joe's Garage, Act I before I graduated out of training bras. But if I were hon-
est, I would admit that Matt is the main reason. In the eyes of women who
like men to wear ties and have business cards, the attraction perhaps would
not be obvious: Sawdust sticks to his hair, it always needs a wash. Long strands
cling to the nubby hairs on his chin, poised near his lips as if he is about to
swallow one. Running like a cable from his right hand is this overdeveloped
forearm muscle, exercised with a plastic pick (a Fender medium; you grab
them by the fistful on the counter when you're in Guitar Center to pick up
GHS Boomers and strap locks). Steel strings ribbed like armadillos have sliced
open his fingers so often the tips are thick as the soles of barefoot runners.
His head always seems angled at the particular tilt of someone listening to the
earth spin, and he defines beauty as a solid rosewood body, bookmatched
flame top, pearl offset dot markers, and a bridge humbucker.

Valerie Bertinelli once said she thought husband Eddie Van Halen was
a genius; I say *selective* genius. When to put gas in his truck, how to read
directions on a boxed macaroni dinner, how to tell county roads from free-
ways on a map are details too mundane to figure out. But this is the same
man who can coax infinite variations out of six metal strings thinner than
spaghetti. He has deciphered the physics of sound, an alchemy of sorts, how
waves press against air, how vibration creates language, understands how
knowledge is formed without words. He also comprehends the rhythm of
touch and how many subtle variations of pressure a human hand has.

For Matt, I put scents of gardenia and tea rose behind my ear, on the
small of my back where I can feel the slight patch of down. I rub my skin
smooth with oil until I know it tastes rich like butter, and I lick the inside
of his mouth starting at the top molar, working my way to the incisors. I
move his scarred fingers down the length of my stomach, against the pulpy
whiteness of it. But more often than not, I also find myself curled up alone

with the "Musician's Friend" catalog Matt leaves near my books on the bedside table, pages folded over strategically in case I want to Christmas shop early. The guitar-effects pedals are my favorite; this year I think he wants the DOD FX-69 Grunge. The ad reads, ". . . level control lets you do damage at any volume, and a two-band EQ shapes output for vicious penetration." I find a certain poetry in this. I have been known to read the catalog out loud to myself, giving dramatic pause to the lines as if I am reading for a crowd. The things you think to do at one in the morning, when the other side of the bed is a boundless arctic tundra, and you wonder if again he will witness how bruised and tender the sky is before dawn.

Rehearsal hours, drum kits to pick up, the gig at Rajis, managers to meet, changing singers again — babe, it's just that rock 'n' roll only happens at night. Something to do with the thinning of the membrane between dream time and waking. I knew that when I signed on. I had, in fact, been warned.

"Avoid musicians. Trust me on this one," my mother once told me. (It didn't sound like advice or admonition, it was spoken in the same tone she talks about laundry. At the time, she was going out with Tuby Llara, this man who played Hank Williams songs on a beat-up hollow-body, had twenty-four hundred acres outside of Hidalgo, New Mexico, and a big-toothed, Dallas-type of brunette wife he saw on weekdays. That was the summer my mother sang along to Johnny Cash on the AM stereo in our Plymouth Fury and pretended to chew wintergreen tobacco.)

How can I explain what I have become? Once Matt and I were walking together in Griffith Park, and he stopped abruptly. His eyes were focused on tall iron sprinklers spaced wide across a lawn, a white mist of water forced out from them.

He put his hand to his lips, telling me to be quiet. "Listen. Hear it? Shug-shug-shug-shug-SHUG," he said, imitating the pattern of the water. "Sprinklers in four-five time."

This taught me that sound is like water, sending ripples, finally building frequency loud enough to hear. From that lesson I too started to hear the syncopation in everyday movement, the way keys strike paper like the flat of a palm strike leather on a tambourine, the way tires hum against pave-

ment with one extended, flat note. Because of Matt, I hear music I was deaf
to, a beat that runs through life's prosaic details and allows me, if only for a
moment, to extend the boundaries of myself.

Standing on the stairs going to the Loft is a young woman with fire-
alarm hair and a velvet choker on her neck that seems wider than her skirt.
The black-capped bouncer will soon tell her to keep moving, but at this
moment her gaze is frozen on the stage, seeming to absorb every movement
the singer makes. This looks strange, positively eighties. Groupies with big
hair and small clothes went out with Mötley Crüe. I feel embarrassed for
her, then mad. She is the reason I started writing under the abbreviation of
my name, "Sam"; I thought the ambiguity would make readers less likely
to dismiss my opinions, to have them say, "Yeah, so who's she fucking?"

Right before I moved to Los Angeles, a girlfriend back home gave me
a copy of *I'm With the Band.* I wondered if she thought Pamela Des Barres's
book about sleeping with the entire rock 'n' roll royal family of the seven-
ties was supposed to be some sort of guide to life in California. Sometimes
still I am haunted by the description of Pamela sitting on stage at a Led
Zeppelin concert in a corner near Jimmy Page's amp, heat from the spot-
light missing her by a fraction. I have an image of her stitching silver-cloth
stars and moons on Jimmy's black bellbottoms; I drew a mental line in the
sand and made a silent vow never to sew for Matt, even if I knew how.

I didn't want Pamela Des Barres's life or an approximation of it. Matt
may have opened my ears, but I did my own homework, learned my own
rock history, bought my own albums, had my own ideas. I wanted to cre-
ate something that was my own and put my name on it.

That's not to say I wanted to make the leap of seeing myself on stage.
For all the occasional Chrissy Hyndes or Debbie Harrys, women who
seized the light for themselves and looked at home there, mostly the image
on stage was male. Maybe the parallel is familiar — wasn't Don McLean
singing "American Pie" twenty years ago? — but rock 'n' roll always has
reminded me of church. On stage, the singer appears porcelain and perish-
able as a father's promise, always in a Christ pose of outstretched arms and

sweat; there is a washing away, purification, sacrifice, and release. He embodies the anger, the joy, the lust collecting in the reptile part of everyone's brain. I have never seen a Virgin Mary do quite the same thing.

Yet in the strip-mall chic of the 5902 Club at Huntington Beach, the warehouse cool of Corona Showcase, Rajis, Jabberjaw, I increasingly notice women, sometimes my age but usually younger, in bands, often the bassist but occasionally singing lead, influenced by Courtney Love, P. J. Harvey, Kim Gordon—women in the rock world who not only own their musical expression but revel in it. Love used to be accused of Yoko Ono-ing her marriage to Kurt Cobain into a record contract, but the truth is she had a major-label deal before Nirvana. Anyone who has heard her spine-ripping howl, seen her dive off stage into a whirling pit of bodies, can testify that Love brought her own ball to the playground. She didn't need to sleep with charisma to have it.

Briefly, I fantasize what Pamela Des Barres would have done for Courtney Love; would she have braided her hair, sewing dresses of white gauze to drape over Courtney's frame? Or would she have seen a part of herself reflected in Courtney's blue eyes that told her she too could learn to hold a six-string?

I have managed to last through the entire Troubadour show and feel as if this is an accomplishment. As I cross Santa Monica at Doheny to get to my car, I catch a glimpse of Jackie, the photographer-by-night-limo-driver-by-day who at one point lived with a bassist. Now that she's single, she's publishing her pictures everywhere; *Spin* even picked up a shot she took of a Red Hot Chili Peppers show.

Jackie and I nod hello, but we don't stop to talk because we don't need to. We both know the essential truth: It doesn't matter if a woman is in the band or married to it, when she pawns her family's silver flatware for a 1978 Hiwatt amp, Mesa Boogie gain mod, and a weekend gig in Phoenix, it ends up having nothing to do with sex. It is all about redemption, a rhythm, kickdrum, cymbal, and bass running in the brain instead of the white noise that used to fill the space between thoughts. Nothing is ever nameless because there is always a note for everything.

NAKED

Susan McMullen

I WAS alone when it happened. Lyle was away for the day over in the next county helping Trip with his car, and mom was at Aunt Vi's for the afternoon playing bridge. It was one of those late August days when summer's settled in and is just hanging around drying things up. I'd come home after playing a good game and was mounting some stamps that my uncle had found in Winchester, pretty ones from Indonesia that had bright butterflies on them that I imagined were the size of kites, and that I could hardly imagine existed in the same world as me. I don't know what drew me out of the back of the house; there wasn't a bell or knock or anything, but there I was at the front door looking through the screen at my father who was standing there naked, like he'd stripped for my birthday and had been wandering around trying to find me. He'd aged much more than the thirteen years since I'd seen him and was clearly crazy with syphilis or scurvy or something. He didn't seem to recognize me at all, but I knew immediately who he was even though he looked a hundred years older than in the picture I had of him on my wall, the one where he's all happy and smiling in his uniform right after winning some big game, and I'm hoisted up on his shoulder, smiling too. It's funny. Whenever I tell this story I feel like I'm lying or something, like I dreamt it and shouldn't be spreading such crazy stories about my father even though I've never heard anyone ever say a nice thing about him other than he sure could play baseball. So there I was, face to face with my father wearing only his skin. I just opened the door and let him walk past me. I called Aunt Vi and told her dad was here. She asked "who" like she'd never heard of him, then "where," and hung up without a word. I knew it would take about five minutes for her and my mom to get there, so I listened to see if I could tell where he was in the house, but all I could hear was the drone of the cicadas getting louder as I circled around to the front porch, where I could see my father walking off again, with my base-ball glove on his right hand like there was somewhere else he'd rather be.

INSIDE MISS LOS ANGELES

Jerry Stahl

I SOMETIMES wonder why every woman I've ever loved was completely insane. But then I think, that's *not right* . . . not really. Not all of them. Just, you know, the ones in the last decade and a half. The ones — how else can I say this? — I've known since I hit Los Angeles.

Not to say that yours truly is any prize. We're talking about an ex-junkie, retired crackhead, failed criminal, erstwhile porn scribe, former big money TV-writing fuckup, and offspring of a suicide by way of a professional electroshock victim . . . but enough bragging. L.A. is the place for guys like me. It's the American Haven for Damaged Goods, the town you come to so you can make enough money to get the fuck out.

Grim but true. One week after sliming into Hollywood in the late seventies, I met a woman named Tammi who had two faces. Literally. Tammi'd hitchhiked to Glitzville "to get in the business," and fallen in with a plastic surgeon who said "he knew people" who'd hire her if she looked like Farrah Fawcett-Majors.

"They wanted Farrahs, for the Asian market," she explained, after two quadruple vodkas in an open-at-six-A.M. Hollywood bar called the Pungee Room. The Pungee was an undusted hideaway decorated with cartoons of has-beens, peripheral talents, and all-around show business mutants of every stripe. Joe Besser, William Bendix, Frank Sinatra Jr., even Rummy Bishop, Joey's uncelebrated brother . . . they were all there, up on the wall, and they didn't seem too happy about it.

In the barroom light, amazingly, Tammi did bear an alarming resemblance to young F. F. It's just that, at the wrong angle, she didn't look like Farrah at all. Sure, her mouth was Farrah's, maybe even her eyes, but everything around and in between was some kind of wasted landscape, a topography of scarred, pitted flesh which, when made up just so, could actually resemble Farrah, but only Farrah after an accident, Farrah after she'd gone through a plate glass window, fallen from a terrace, nose-dived into a kidney-shaped pool from which all water had been drained. Hence, to my jaundiced peepers, she became the GWTF, the Girl With Two Faces, emblem of festive L.A. beauty from that moment on.

"It was Dr. Skippy," Tammi confided, weeping softly into her Wolfschmidt. "He had this cocaine thing . . . I mean, this was in '74, *everybody* did. And I guess he had some kind of seizure, a miniconvulsion, right in the middle of my surgery. I remember, 'cause I was just under a local, and he kept lifting his mask off to get the straw up his nose. But"—and here a tear fell, ever-so-softly, onto the Forrest Tucker coaster—"but he was such a good little soldier, he went ahead and finished my face."

Now came the brave sigh, that extra clutch on the sleeve of my wide-lapeled puce body shirt. For Tammi was, of course, an actress, too. "*And,*" she finished dramatically, "and he almost got it right . . ."

Needless to say, I fell in love up to my earlobes. By day, I labored in Larry Flyntland, down *Hustler* way. My job, for the most part, involved writing sight gags for vagina-shaped squash and rutabagas mailed in from the Dakotas—home, apparently, to a variety of genitally evocative vegetation. While Tammi, God love her, danced topless on tabletops at a strip joint near LAX. Her patrons were middle-management aerospace execs, family men who just wanted a little break from the meat-and-potatoes.

By night, once she'd slapped on her Maybelline, I could forget my troubles and pretend, for one or two gilded hours, that I was the Six Million Dollar Man. Beside my almost-Farrah, I could almost believe that our garage-sized tract in the Hollywood Flats—that region which lies, unglamorously, at the sun-sucked bottom of the chi-chi Hollywood Hills — was really *just* a mini–San Simeon. In the right light, at just the right angle, I could actually convince myself I'd hit the celeb-sex jackpot and nailed down the American dream. That I had, in other words, rolled into Hollywood and rolled onto a Charlie's Angel.

The whole Tammi/Farrah deal was fantasy, of course. But then, this was Los Angeles, the town built on the horrifying reality that reality is so horrifying we need an industry to re-create it, in brighter hues, preferably with spin-off action figures to generate that all-important merchandising revenue.

Fast-forward a few years — we're spleen-deep in the eighties now — and Sweet Tammi's retired to Maui with cash from a settlement on yet another cosmetic casualty: faulty implants that left her right breast the size of a kumquat, the left one a sort of gelid duck pin. While yours truly, ever the rebel, found himself locked down on the famed Cedars Sinai dope ward. In detox I hooked up with a quivering young crystal meth aficionado named Tanya, daughter of a sixties sitcom baron and his Chilean au pair. The combo left her a green-eyed mocha showstopper with a burned-up trust fund and a Medusa's head of auburn dreads. Her own touch were those B & O tracks running north from her dainty wrists to the crook of her banana-black arms.

Naturally, Tanya and I bonded hard during my twenty minutes of posthospital clean time. After which, for better or worse, my entree into the Real L.A., the Inner L.A. — or one particularly cheesy version of it — kicked in like a bang of adrenaline. A So-Cal archetype in her own right, little Tanya left her home in the Hills at sixteen to make her way in the world. Which, this being Hollywood and all, meant she ended up doing freelance dominatrix gigs at a studio called Madame D's, a discreet and well-appointed hideaway catering to high-profile pain devotees.

Beyond the usual spankings and verbal abuse gigs — not to mention the odd electric cattle prod to the testicles, a house specialty — my gal's forte was "The Roman Candle," an arcane practice which involved slipping a match in some whoopee boy's penis and lighting it. Thanks to the monstro powers of concentration unleashed by that IV crank, my sweetheart could slide a fire in a peehole faster than you could say *"Hide the Hibachi!"* This made her a real dream date for clients who wanted the worldly thrill of having their dicks spit flame as they were led around on a leash and bade to light up the mock-Liberace candelabras that lent the dungeon that obligatory Gothic ambiance. Until, that is, they shot their wad, put the match out, then toweled off and hopped in the Jag back to Brentwood to kiss the missus and tuck in the kids.

Here, oddly enough, is where yours truly got to breathe deep of the eau-de-power that keeps America's Entertainment Center on track. By way of extra drug money, I'd help my lovemuffin with a little extracurricular work. And one of her regulars, a hairy-backed producer of afterschool specials, paid five C-notes an hour for the heady thrill of being trussed up in a prom dress and hauled around Orange County in our toast-colored Nissan. Having me hunkered in the backseat made it, for Miss Irv, even more shameful.

Uh huh! No doubt looking to counter the pressure of shaping young minds as they munched their cookies and milk, our man longed to be driven around in drag, sweating till his bouffant slipped sideways, then shoved out at the nearest pod-mall while my vinyl-clad sweetheart called him names in front of horrified shoppers. *"Why you little slut!"* she'd scream at the plump and sweating show business professional. *"You stupid cow! You filthy little pussy-girl!"*

Somehow, between hanging out at Madame D's and riding smacked-out shotgun in my baby's dominatrix-mobile, I came to a strange conclusion regarding the burg I inhabited. It hit me, cruising with Miss Irv, that there exists some slick, subterranean pool of self-loathing and toxic desire from which springs L.A.'s true inspiration. The truth: Everything in this city exists as the opposite of its faux self. So that, despite the hype and blather, it's not about the money, it's not about fame, it's not even about entertainment. Not even close. In this miniature constructed domain of reality called Hollywood, it's about the twisted redemption of hollow visionaries looking to inform their lives with the substance that their very creations, the simulations of life called TV and movies, lack entirely. Hence the bevy of faux-Farrahs (or these days, faux-Julias), the mountains of action scripts written by Ivy Leaguers who've never even been bitch-slapped, the booming traffic in torture subsidized by buns-up Show Biz heavies for whom rank pain is the one real thing they can feel. It all makes sense.

Or maybe not. At least half a decade's passed since most of the unwholesome madness described above. And I think, I *suspect,* that maybe it's *not* the city. Maybe it's *not* the women or the drugs. Maybe, call me a freak-magnet, it's just me. I mean, *I live here.*

And I can't seem to leave.

EZZIE, SWEATING

Cindy Milwe

I.

He is black and fat, new to the class,
and twelve, younger than any of the white girls
with breasts and new blood, the white boys
with strange new heads, clumsy feet.
Sure, they're all awkward, dumbstruck
by the shifts in their cells, growing older
and pained by time pressing through them —
crocus buds, winter snow. They have no idea
they will flower purple, be delicate and beautiful
for too short a time, then trodden or withered
no matter how they began. Maybe Ezzie knows:
the beads of sweat on his cheek to remind him
how hard it will be for him — for anyone —
to rise from the Earth.

II.

He's wearing the same shirt as yesterday
and the day before. Last week, he came
well-dressed, shirt tucked into his corduroys
like an architect. Today, the police come,
ask me questions: "Is he skittish? Is he sad?"
No. Sweating. Wipes his eyes on his wrist
or his dirty white collar, takes off and examines
his glasses. Ezzie lisps when he speaks,

wipes his ears like a cat. But he can't sleep
all day on a window ledge, hide in some tree.
No. He can only let the heat pour out of him
like spirit, and pray for a winter in California,
which he knows — smart as he is — will never come.

TROUBLE MAN

Jervey Tervalon

I MET that Tisha girl on the phone, a wrong number over at Gumbo's, and we kept her on the line and started up a conversation that lasted for weeks. A conversation filled with knee-deep bullshit: "I want you to be my distant lover," or "You oughta be with me," I'd say, quoting song lyrics, filling dead space in long, multihour exchanges. "So, what did you do today?" I'd ask, waiting for the dull itinerary of her day. "Went shopping with my mother. She wouldn't buy me nothing I wanted. I really wanted a bomber jacket, a white one."

We would talk for hours about nothing. And just when I started to lose interest she promised to go out with me, be my girlfriend.

That got me going, a girlfriend, maybe even a girlfriend I could visit, not just a sweet voice coming over the telephone line. Now she had to let me visit, otherwise how could she go with me?

Gumbo had been doing the same thing with Luwanda, Tisha's best friend, and she had an even prettier voice, smooth and seductive and she spoke well, so we knew she wasn't some ignorant tackhead. So we decided to do it, to visit them and see them in the flesh. At first, they didn't seem too interested, especially Luwanda. Maybe she suspected how fat Gumbo really was from the sound of his voice. Gumbo had one of those resounding voices, like an opera singer or the foghorn voiced guy in the Temptations.

"I want to see you. You're my girlfriend, right?" I finally got around to telling Tisha.

"Yeah," she said. "But my Daddy won't let me have boys over."

"He goes to work? I'll come over then."

"No, he ain't working now. . . . But I'll send you my picture."

"Cool!" I said. She was gonna give me a picture even if I didn't get the address. Later Gumbo came by, and we sat on the porch and compared notes and made plans. I found out that Luwanda was also sending him a picture. Gumbo glumly got around to telling me she wanted a picture, too.

"What are you going to do?"

"I'm gonna send my cousin Ricky's. He looks like me."

Yeah, he did, only about a hundred pounds lighter.

"Girls go crazy over Ricky," he said.

"What are you gonna do when we go over there?"

"I'm gonna lose weight," Gumbo said.

"Yeah, right."

"You just worried I'm gonna be thinner than your chunky ass," he said, and took his fat butt elsewhere.

A week later, I received the letter at breakfast. Mama brought it in with the rest of the mail and tossed it on the table. She was short-tempered because she couldn't afford to do as she said she would, and hire a mechanic to fix her car. She resorted to calling Daddy, and he was over in the morning to get a irritatingly bright and early start on her brakes, and to work his way to the table. Daddy was as happy for breakfast as Mama was begrudging.

Even with the tense situation at the table, I couldn't resist opening the envelope. The photo was snugly folded up within the letter. It was one of those school pictures where everybody always looks bad but she looked good. Tisha looked like a Creole Catholic schoolgirl, light-skinned with long hair and big pretty brown eyes. I wondered why would she be talking to me, let alone consent to be my girlfriend. The girl was much too pretty to be meeting guys over the phone.

"Who's that?" Mama said in her gruff voice.

"Nobody," I said.

"It's got to be somebody."

She leaned across the table and snatched the picture.

"Mama!"

"Be quiet," she said, waving me off. She examined the photo longer than I thought she would. Then she passed it to Daddy, who was reading that big book on transmissions again.

"Looks like Martha Dupree's child," Mama said.

"Naw," Daddy said. "She don't have a big nose like those Duprees."

Mama frowned and snatched the photo from Daddy.

"Who is it?"

"Just a friend."

"Friends don't send pictures. Is that the girl you always talking to on the phone?"

Yeah," I gave in and admitted it.

Mama sighed and stood and noisily started clearing the breakfast dishes. I left the kitchen and walked around the corner to Gumbo's house. I knocked at the door and waited for somebody to answer. It always took a long time for the Villabinos to answer the door. They had a big house, two stories and nicely kept. Everything about the house was large, even the porch and the picture window, and all of the Villabinos. There was only one thin Villabino, Gumbo's little sister, and she didn't stay that way long. She gained at least a hundred pounds over one year to keep up with the rest of them. I think she did it in self-defense. I remember when she was a thin little girl of about ten, and Gumbo used to force himself into a moon-wagon and make her pull his fat buttercup butt up and down the alley. I'd watch them pass back and forth of our garage as my Pops worked on Mama's car. Something about watching those two, the shirtless, big-headed Buddha body of Gumbo being pulled up and down the alley by his little pole-thin sister really bugged me, but she didn't seem to mind, as if pulling him was a privilege.

The door finally opened, and there was Mr. Villabino, naked and dripping wet except for a towel wrapped around his tree-trunk waist.

"Sorry, Mr. Villabino. I didn't mean to get you out of the shower."

"Garvy! Oh, hey there . . ." He looked confused as if he were expecting someone else. "I'm looking for somebody," he said and stepped by me onto the porch, his big feet leaving wet footprints on the gray paint. "You see anybody?"

"No," I said.

He walked down the steps and all the way to the sidewalk and, peering in both directions, shook his head.

Usually with people like Mr. Villabino I would get nervous, worried that they would do something weird like eat raw eggs or drive with their car doors open. But it was clear that he was too busy trying to figure out what the world was doing to him to worry about doing something to me. There he was, a white-haired, broad-bodied nut looking for something or somebody.

"What's my Pops doing?"

It was Gumbo. He had finally come to the door sporting a head full of shocking pink curlers, which was becoming an alarmingly popular style.

"I dunno."

Gumbo shrugged. "He's always doing something."

I followed Gumbo inside, through the nice living room with all the furniture covered in plastic, and into the kitchen where his mother, not so fat, but grim and hard-eyed, stood at the sink, shucking peas.

"What you boys doing?" she said.

"None of your business," Gumbo said, reaching into the icebox and taking out a couple of sodas. He handed me one.

Mrs. Villabino slammed the ice-box door shut. "You!" she shouted.

Gumbo ignored her, and I followed him into his small shipman's quarters room. Soon as we were in the room, Gumbo shut the door, pulled out a tired looking cigarette from a shirt pocket, and sat down on a cane stool and started smoking, looking very much like his Daddy, but cool, collected, a roly-poly gangster from one of those 1930s movies who just happened to wear curlers.

"So, you got a picture, too?" he said.

"Yeah," I handed it to him.

He shook the picture out of the letter and gave it an intense going over.

"What does the letter say?" he asked, without looking up.

"She ain't gonna say nothing but some lies. Why should I read it?"

"I'll read it to you . . . 'Garvy, hope you like how I look. Love, your girl-friend, forever.'"

"That's it?"

"Yep."

"She's full of shit."

Gumbo sat up and pulled something out of his back pocket, a letter like mine folded in half.

"Check it out," he said, and tossed it to me.

I unfolded his letter. It was almost identical to mine, same envelope, same school paper, that broad lined stuff we used in elementary school but that teachers continued to give out in junior high if you were too lazy or poor to bring your own. Even the handwriting was similar, but Gumbo's letter was a real letter, it went on to the bottom of the page and halfway down the backside, the side we were told not to write on.

"Gumbo, you supposed to be my boyfriend, but I don't know about that. You don't know how to treat somebody, talking to me like I gotta do what you say 'cause if I don't you gonna drop me. If you want to you oughta do it 'cause I know you ain't gonna find nobody like me around. See, Gumbo, I know I'm somebody who deserves to be treated right . . ."

The letter kept on like that, and ended with, "You said you was going to take me to Magic Mountain. When's that gonna happen? Gonna be no haps on nothing else til that happens."

"Looks like ya'll got something going with this chick."

Gumbo sneered and handed me the photograph. She was just as pretty as Tisha, with light skin and big eyes, but her hair wasn't as straight.

"Yeah, right," he said. "A pootbutt square like me."

"Who's a pootbutt?"

"We are. We don't have cars, we don't got any money. You just about as fat as my ass. What they doing talking to us?"

"You don't know."

"If they're so on the up and up, how come they don't let us come over?"

"I thought you had. From that letter, sounds like you've been creeping over there."

"Hell no. She won't tell me where she lives. Either they're real ugmos or their parents won't let them have no company."

"So what you gonna do?"

Gumbo took a last drag on the butt of his sad looking cigarette. "I wanna see if Luwanda look this good," he said, holding up the picture.

So the next time I talked to Tisha, I mentioned how much Gumbo and I wanted to take them to Magic Mountain. I even lied and said we already had tickets and we would pay for the Greyhound bus. Tisha agreed to everything more quickly than I thought she would. It seemed like a good time to get real since she was going along.

"So maybe I should come check you out."

"What?" she said sweetly, like she hadn't heard.

"Me and Gumbo wanted to come by and visit you and Luwanda."

"Oh," she said.

"Is that cool?"

The phone was very quiet.

"Is it okay?"

"Yeah, that's cool with me."

"Okay," I said. Again the phone was quiet. We had been talking for nearly an hour, me sitting between the twin beds in my bedroom, hiding because sooner or later Mama was going to scream at me to get off the phone.

"What's your address?"

"Address?" she said with that sweet tone in her voice.

"Yeah, you know, if we're going to come over, I'm gonna need your address."

"2364 Normandie," she said, so fast I barely could make it out.

"What?"

"2364 Normandie, before you get to the freeway."

I was glad she was showing a little interest, but that was a part of town I wasn't familiar with. I didn't know the situation, the gang culture.

"So, is it rough around there?"

"Rough?" Her voice didn't sound so pretty, serious more than anything.

"You know, do I gotta watch out for hoodlums?"

"Not if you know what you're doing. Don't act like a punk."

That made me think, but I knew I was going to see her even if it meant I had to go to a new neighborhood, in a direction I normally avoided, east. We were West Coast, whether we liked it or not. Some street was the division between East Coast and West Coast, maybe it was Western or Figueroa, I never found out. To the gangsters it meant a lot. East Coast Crips were harder because the east was the least, past Western, things got funky. Where I lived we supposedly had more money, while folks on the Eastside were so poor they didn't have a pot to piss in, but I didn't know because we didn't go to the Eastside. I had no reason to go east, what was there to see, the Watts Towers? The west had the Crenshaw strip, Baldwin Hills, Fox Hills Mall. We had it way over that other part of town. But I was going east because I had a love situation on my hands.

"So what you think?" I asked Gumbo. I came over to his house just as he was coming home from Catholic school in his grim corduroy pants and stiff white dress shirt with stains beneath the arms.

"Yeah, let's go," he said.

"You gonna change?"

"What the hell you think?" he said and went into the house.

I waited on the crinkly plastic-covered couch while Gumbo changed. I hoped Mr. Villabino wouldn't come walking through the living room, and even more that Mrs. Villabino wouldn't. After a bit, Gumbo returned in Farmer John overalls, and wearing a smartly cuffed beanie. He seemed cool in a robust, country sort of a way.

"I got the address. Normandie and 23rd Street."

"Over there by the freeway?"

"Yeah," I said.

I was ready, committed to seeing to Tisha in the flesh. I'd told her I'd be by and I was coming by. Gumbo though, just kept sitting on the couch, looking away like he was thinking hard about something.

"You think this ain't such a good idea?" I asked.

"I don't know." He paused for a long moment. "But if you down, I'm down."

About two blocks from his house on our way to the Jefferson bus, Gumbo suddenly yanked me from the sidewalk to hide behind a palm tree.

"What?" I said.

"See?" He pointed down the long block to somebody walking in our direction.

"Who's that?"

"Harold! Can't you tell from the goony way he's walking? He's going to want to trip with us."

Harold was new to the block. He came from a huge family straight out of Nickerson Gardens Projects. His whole family acted as though the Westside was Beverly Hills. He even had a gorgeous sister, but he was so friendly and earnest, people either took advantage of him, or they avoided him like he had open sores.

"Maybe he didn't see us," Gumbo said.

Gumbo peeked from behind the tree and just as he did, Harold came sneaking up from the street side. "Hey! What ya'll doing?"

Gumbo looked startled as Harold gave us his loopy-goony smile.

"Nothing," Gumbo said.

Harold nodded, and watched us edge away. When I glanced back, he was still there, waiting like my hound would do before sprinting after me. We got to the corner and turned. Gumbo sighed.

"Glad we ditched his simple butt. He'll hang around like flies."

We passed the five and ten pharmacy where Buelia and Mr. Yamoto worked. I hung out there a lot on my way home from elementary school, looking through their comics and used books. Buelia, a strict, straightforward woman, liked me and let me get to the comics even if she were unwrapping new ones in the tight space between the window and the comics display, but she wouldn't let Onla or Gumbo into the store. She knew they had sticky fingers. I hurried by the pool hall where the police and ambulance seemed to make weekly visits. Gumbo, though, hung back, peering through the grimy window of the upholstered door, the red leatherlike material torn open like a worn couch. I saw Gumbo take a piece of dangling leather and peel it down.

"Come on, man, we gonna miss the bus."

"Look," he said, waving me over.

I didn't want to go, but I knew Gumbo wouldn't leave until I did. Reluctantly, I gave in.

"See," he said, and pulled me in front of the door.

I looked through the filthy window to see the poorly lit pool tables and pool players, all men, except for this fat woman. She looked as if she were going to burst through her skintight jeans, and her halter top couldn't contain her plentiful flesh.

"That's that Mary. Louis's sister. See, I told you she was hooking."

"How you know she's hooking?"

"Hey, any girl go in a place like this got to be hooking."

I took his arm and tried pulling him away, but Gumbo being so heavy, if he didn't want to go somewhere, it was hard to make him.

"Come on, man! I don't see why you always wanting to hang around this dinky-ass pool hall."

He turned leering, wiggling his oddly slender fingers. "Because it's exciting!"

Finally he was ready to go, and we walked the rest of the way to the bus stop. It was crowded with people transferring from the Arlington bus, going east, where we were going. Gumbo went right up to the front of the line, hoping to cut in front of all of those old people, and I was right behind him. Then some skinny backed guy slipped in front of Gumbo. He turned and gave a loopy smile. Harold again.

"Ya'll going downtown? Get some tacos?"

Gumbo shrugged, and we all got onto the bus. Harold stopped at the money well and started coming out of his pockets with change, pennies and stuff, wrappers, rubber bands. Didn't seem like he was ever gonna come up with forty-five cents.

"Here!" Gumbo said, and thrust four or five nickels into the money well.

Harold's rain of pennies went in after and the glowering driver was glad to wave him through.

Harold headed straight for the back of the bus, to the narrow long, last seat. We watched as he slid in past a couple of down-on-their-luck-looking brothers, wearing khakis and biscuits, ugly blunt black prison shoes.

"You going back there?" I asked Gumbo.

"Yeah," he said, like he hadn't hesitated.

The bus started rolling, and the seats were filling up. I decided to stand and sway but Gumbo wanted to go for the gusto. He lurched for the last seat. The two brothers ignored him, not moving an inch to let Gumbo by. Gumbo quickly turned and came back to me.

It was weird, goofy ass Harold who could fit in with those raw brothers. Maybe it's how he sat, with his arms folded, and his legs crossed, and his head hanging low like he was about to nod. Gumbo wanted that, to have that status, but it wasn't something he would ever have.

By the time we arrived at Normandie, the bus was packed and somehow me and Gumbo were back to back like deluxe Siamese twins. I felt ridiculous, and I'm sure we looked ridiculous. When the bus doors opened we went for it, pushing whoever aside. Harold, though, waited to the last moment to escape from that snug seat in the back of the bus. We were already walking north and the bus starting to roll when the folding doors cracked open and Harold slid out.

Damn!" Gumbo said, "I thought he fell asleep."

He hadn't. He just looked like he was asleep because that was too cool, being able to look asleep sitting with dangerous looking guys.

He ran with his straight-knee-no-exertion trot and stopped behind us, as if he was pulling up the rear. Harold was like that, doing things differently, a creature from the east, a good guy from the projects, a mystery nobody wanted to know.

"They live down 23rd Street," I said to Gumbo.

"A couple blocks up," he replied.

Neither one of us said a word to Harold. He just kept trudging along behind us, smiling like we had something great planned. I didn't mind so much that he was tagging along uninvited. The sun setting made me nervous, as if soon something would be stirring and hungry, pulling itself up and out into the night. Maybe it would go for Harold, so I was inclined to increase that pack safety factor by a third.

"Hey, this is it, 23rd Street," Gumbo said and we started west, looking for the house address. I was still nervous but the street didn't seem threatening — so many well-maintained houses and lawns. I thought this Tisha really must have some money.

"Okay, see, the numbers keep getting smaller, we got to go the other way," Gumbo said.

Harold nodded and arched an eyebrow as though Gumbo's change of direction was genius. I thought we had gotten away with something, going through a strange neighborhood without trouble and now we had to backtrack, exposing ourselves all over again. We arrived at busy Normandie and crossed without having to run. Gumbo kind of just waded out there and stopped traffic as we continued east and the neighborhood started to change from middle to lower to rundown, all within three blocks. Some Latinos were outside; a family on the porch, guys working on a truck.

"Where are we?" Harold asked.

"I don't know," I said, and it was true. We continued on another block and saw two black guys about our age. They were up ahead, but they pointed at us.

"Oh no," Harold said, and started inching backward. Gumbo didn't seem to notice or didn't care that Harold had decided to part company.

"I don't get it. We went in both directions, but her number ain't there. You sure you copied it right?"

"Yeah," I said. "Hey, you see those two guys? They're pointing at us."

"Maybe they know us," Gumbo said, and continued examining the nearby addresses. I looked for Harold and caught a glimpse of him doing that weird jog of his toward Normandie. I thought about it. Should I be following Gumbo, this Catholic school kid going for bad, always getting into dumb kinds of trouble, like being thrown out of Holy Name for bringing a boring sex book for kids, the kind where even though it's real naked people they look less sexy than mannequins? On the other hand, Harold must have known something to get out of those rough-ass projects in one piece. Meanwhile, up the street, the two guys were now three, and they were heading in our direction.

"Hey, come on, I don't know those dudes." I didn't wait for him, instead I took off running. That did the trick, and Gumbo finally followed. Neither one of us liked to run, but Gumbo disliked it more.

"Why we running?" he asked. "We can take care of two fools."

"Look behind you!"

"Aw, shit!" he said, and passed me.

The three pursuers were now five. We were running, pretty fast for us, but that was the problem with being slow, you run as fast you can and you still get caught pretty quickly. Then we heard the call, "Get those fools!" and that did it. We got into gear. We reached Normandie and ran right into traffic. Gumbo stuck his arm out like he was going to straight-arm an RTD bus. On the other side, we stopped to catch our breath, but we weren't safe. Plain and simple stupidity, we assumed that our pursuers would stop at a major boulevard like they were sheriffs who wouldn't venture over a state line.

"Here they come!" I said, and tugged Gumbo up from resting. He followed, but barely at a trot.

"Come on, they're gonna kick our asses."

Crack! Something exploded behind us, a bottle shattered to the side. It was good, though, it got us to running again. Still, after about a half mile, that was it. We had to walk the rest of it.

"We lost those idiots," I said, but I don't think Gumbo was listening. He looked sick; even in the light from the streetlamps, I could see the rivulets of sweat down his face. We kept walking, it didn't make sense to catch the bus since we were near Western, more than halfway home. Even so, it was going to take us forever to get to the Avenue. Gumbo was walking like those old ladies trying to make it to the store, one step every four or five seconds, moving but not very much. I wanted to rush him, but it wouldn't do no good, just get him cursing at me. So I fell into step, swaying as much as walking, listening to Gumbo suck air.

"Least we got away without getting stomped," I said.

"Those tackhead bitches, giving us the wrong address," Gumbo said in a harsh, winded voice.

"What ya'll standing around for?" a voice said behind us.

"Who!" Gumbo turned with balled fists, but we already knew, it just took a second for the voice to sink in.

"Harold," I said, and he gave us that loopy grin.

"I knowed you two was gonna get away. You guys know the ropes."

Harold put his hands on both our shoulders. As if we really accomplished something. We walked like that for a bit, me wondering if Harold was going to stop wringing my shoulder. I was sure if Gumbo wasn't so tired he would have flung Harold's hand off.

Slowly, we crossed busy Western, counting on the kindness of rush hour drivers, but now we were relatively safe. We knew most of the thugs around here and were on pretty good terms with everybody. Gumbo sighed, and finally threw off Harold's hand.

"Dumb, really stupid tackheads about got us killed. Tear this number up."

Gumbo pulled out a crumpled ball of paper, tore it in two but didn't fling it like he seemed to want to. Instead, he let it slip out of his hand. Before we got a yard away, Harold turned quickly, bending to pick up the slip. Gumbo didn't notice or didn't care. I guess I didn't care either. All I wanted was to get home, to be able to tell everybody about how we got dogged. Then Harold turned, and pointed to a lowrider creeping along the street. It was weird how slow it was going. I was more interested in how the color bar in the back window was flickering than if I should be worried. How cool could this be having your car looking like Christmas tree lights?

"Who's that?" Gumbo said and started walking to the car. He wanted a ride in a bad way.

Harold and I watched as he approached. The car was deep with heads, no way he could slip in the backseat.

"Yeah, that's them fools," somebody yelled from inside. Everything went crazy. We ran for cover, expecting an explosion. Instead, the heads in the car started to unload, piling out like Keystone Cops.

We were all yelling. Gumbo ran toward a house, and Harold headed for the bushes. I dove, clearing a hedge. Harold kept going to the fence and cleared it with no sweat. I thought I had found a hiding place behind shrubs and wild palms on the side of a house, but Gumbo got caught. I could hear him yelling, "Get off me! What did I do? Leave me alone!"

I imagined the blows, the sound of blubber, fat flesh being struck. And I really wanted to see what was happening to him. It wasn't a heroic thing. No way could I do anything to stop them, but I wanted to see. I came around the hedge, crept to the front of the house, and peeked around the corner. Gumbo was on a porch with a chair in his hand, fending off his attackers, all the while screaming for help. But as soon as I looked, they started yelling.

"Look! There's the other one," and that's when the beating began. Three or four guys rushed to where I was trapped between a fence separating the front yard from the back. The fence wasn't too high but no way could I climb that fast. My one impulse was to not make them mad. I put my arms up to shield my face, but the first guy to reach me, this really big kid, punched right through my weak defense and bashed my jaw.

Lights, stars shaped like cartoon stars, orange, green, and red circled my head. When the stars stopped spinning, I saw him getting ready to swing again. I stumbled through to the front yard, dazed and helpless. This time a little guy ran up on me, but his fist didn't fly, instead he held his palm out.

"I ain't gonna hit you. Got some money?" he asked.

Even though my head was overflowing with noise and colors, his clear, reasonable voice came through like a beacon through the fog. I reached into my pocket hoping for something, dollars to buy my way out of the beating, but I had nothing, just change, nickels and pennies, and a bus transfer. He looked for a second and shook his head.

"Naw, dude, you don't got nothing. You got anything else?"

I pulled my pockets inside out, offering their emptiness to him.

"Naw, that ain't going to do it. You don't got nothing. Nothing I can do for you, man." He turned away, disgusted, and as he did, another two other guys ran up.

More stars, but this go-round didn't hurt. They punched me one way and the other, and I tried to get away, running like a drunk man in wide semicircles until I stumbled out of the yard into the next one. They came again, trying to surround me. Then some guy hit me and another tried to pull me down. I heard Gumbo yelling to me: "Garvy, don't go down!"

At first, I thought he meant he wasn't coming down from the porch to help me and risk getting the shit beaten out of him. That seemed pretty reasonable. Then I realized he was telling me not to let them get me down to the ground. I remembered Lamar, what had happened to him when he fell down after getting coldcocked at that party. Stomped him to death. It worked. The idea that they didn't just want to beat me but stomp me, maybe even kill me, was enough to start me shoving them, grabbing one to shield me, holding him, dragging him into the street and across it, his buddies trying to pry him loose. One of them ran back to the Impala, talking about getting something to make me let go.

That's when Gumbo panicked and bolted from the porch, running for the fence Harold had climbed. The gangsters stopped beating on me to concentrate on the sight of this three-hundred-pound kid, scaling the chain-link fence like an obese spider. He reached the top quickly enough but he stopped there—even the guy I had in a death grip watched to see if all that weight, more precariously balanced than Humpty Dumpty, was going to get down in one huge and intact piece, or if he was going to splat. Then, the guy who had gone to the trunk came out with something in a big dingy pillowcase, and the moment of wonder ended. It was time to go. I flung homeboy down and ran, the last thing I remember Gumbo bellowing, "Help! Help! HELP!"

I cut around the corner and kept going until I passed Holy Name. I was close to home, just four blocks away, but as I walked, I started to worry about Gumbo, and even more importantly what was I going to say to my parents about the knots on my head. I was bleeding, too, my jaw was cut and my knee busted, no missing teeth though, and my head was swelling up in all kinds of places. The closer I got to the house, the sicker I felt, dizzy and nauseated, on the verge of vomiting but not able to.

When I got to the house, I noticed the cars were gone. Mama's Dodge Dart and Daddy's Galaxie 500. The house was quiet. I knocked on the door, but nobody answered. Stuck without keys, I imagined myself lumpy like the Elephant Man.

Then I saw them pull up to the stop sign at the corner in Mama's fairly new Dodge and Daddy's Galaxie 500, both cars loaded with heads, and behind them Winnie's Jag. They turned the corner and stopped in front of the house. It had been and was gonna be a bad night for me, and now my eyes were swelling shut. I felt like a boxer who got a real tattooing.

Mama was the first out of the cars. It was pretty obvious she was going to tear my head off my shoulders. Her stout body looked weird moving so fast.

"Hi, Ma," was all I could think of to say.

The anger in her face was frightening. She had kicked outrage into overdrive.

"You!" She shouted and swung a open-handed right hook at my swollen head. I knew not to block the blow, otherwise she'd come back with a left. Instead, I sidestepped well enough that the blow glanced off my shoulder.

"You're supposed to be dead!"

"Dead? Who said I was dead?"

Realizing Mama wasn't going to club me again, I glanced over to the people coming out of the cars. Sidney's mother and Onla's mother came out of Mama's Dodge. Coming out of Daddy's car was Mr. and Mrs. Villabino, and in Winnie's Jag was Jude, Sidney, and Walter. I was shocked to see Gumbo come out of the backseat also, smiling like he had just got back from Disneyland. I couldn't be sure from the dim streetlights, but it didn't look as though he had any lumps on his head.

"Hey Gumbo! What happened?" I yelled, but he was too busy leaning on the Jag surrounded by the fellas. They were actually listening to him, even hanging on his words.

"Don't be talking to Gumbo. Talk to me!" Mama said, clipping me with a short jab to the ear.

"Sorry, Mama," but I couldn't stop looking at the cars. The other parents started to go. Onla's mother and Mrs. Grierson first, then Mr. and Mrs.

Villabino, Mrs. V. standing almost in that circle around Gumbo, telling him to come home, and Mr. V. pulling at her arm.

"You know what a scare you put in us?" Mama said.

I shrugged. She hit me again.

"Somebody called up and said you were dead in a bush."

"In a bush?"

"That's what they said."

It didn't make sense.

"Who called?"

"Some woman. I don't know. She called screaming you was dead in a bush. You ask Gumbo. Now you get in the house. You're grounded."

Before I could move, Daddy came up with his head low, shoulders back, military man walk.

"Better look at the boy," he said. "They really got him."

"That's what I plan on doing."

Mama grabbed me by the shirt and pulled me inside the house. She led me into the bright light of the bathroom.

"My God! Look at your head!"

When I looked into the mirror, I was about as shocked as she was. Both my eyes were almost closed, my forehead had a knot on it the size of a walnut. It was lumped up almost everywhere else.

"You got to go to the hospital. Whoever beat you was really trying to kill you."

Mama grabbed me again and took me back outside.

"You got to take him to Kaiser. Look at his head."

Daddy grabbed me by the shoulders and hurried to his car. "Come on, you!" he said, but I knew what to expect. He leaned into the car and came out with a spray bottle and a roll of paper towels and started the ritual of window cleaning. He wouldn't move the car until the windows were polished and spotless.

"Get in," he called to me. But I ignored him, knowing it would be at least ten minutes before he was ready to go. He'd just want me to sit there watching him wipe the windows. Instead I walked over to the fellas, who turned away from Gumbo and focused their attention on me. Sidney uncrossed an arm and lightly touched his face.

"Boy gonna need plastic surgery."

"He ain't that messed up," Jude said.

"Yeah, he looks okay," Winnie said.

Walter frowned and spat. "You oughta kill them fools. You can't let them get away with that kind of shit."

Walter's advice made me laugh. What was I supposed to do, throw my father out of the car and drive over to Normandie and 23rd to get my ass kicked all over again? Or maybe I was supposed to steal Daddy's twelve-gauge and light up those pootbutts. I don't know, it could have been all those blows to the head, but I felt exhilarated, as though I had won something.

"How did you get away?" I asked Gumbo.

"Lady heard me yelling and called the police. My line was busy, so I got her to call your house."

"What did you do to keep them from stomping you?"

"Like they stomped you? They knew better than to try that shit with me."

I tried rolling my eyes but it made my face hurt. I felt like thumping him. He must have gotten over the fence and screamed so loud and for so long somebody made calls to get the bellowing fool out of their yard.

I shouldn't have done it. It wasn't right, but he was trying to dog me in front of everybody. Nothing but luck, and now he was claiming all kinds of stuff.

So I pulled back the car antenna he was sitting behind, arcing the thin piece of metal as far as it would go. I heard the voice of my father calling for me to come sit in the car, felt the fellas staring at me, wondering what I planned on doing. Gumbo knew and smirked as if I wouldn't, couldn't let go. I did. Must have struck him ten times in two seconds. The small metal ball at the end of the antenna cracked against his big forehead so fast the smirk on his never changed.

"Wooo!" Sidney said. "Now that must have hurt."

Walter laughed, "That's what he should have done to those punks who jumped him."

"Garvy," Jude said, shaking his head.

Winnie laughed along with the rest of them.

Gumbo rubbed his head and smiled. I smiled. We were putting on a show for them. It's what we all liked, cartoon violence.

"See, I'm gonna get you for that," Gumbo said.

I stood there with them, feeling the pressure build for Gumbo to retaliate, to continue the funny stuff. That's what the fellas liked to see, because that's what they were good at. They'd fight occasionally, argue and insult each other, but they didn't shoot each other, they didn't kill each other. That's what we did. My generation couldn't hold back, would cross any line, stepping off into space. But it made sense, it was even reasonable, if you were frightened like we were, frightened of each other, of ourselves. In our world, it was all or nothing; in theirs, shades of gray.

"Gotta go to the hospital," I finally said. I had to go. Again, I felt sick, dizzy. I walked unsteadily to the Galaxie 500. Somebody grabbed my arm, helping me to the car. It was Gumbo.

"I'm gonna catch you. You'll see."

That was cool. He could catch me later. Hit me in the back with a football, put hot pepper on my ice cream. Steal my phone book and call the few numbers I had.

Right now he was down with me. As those guys who beat me were down for each other. Finally, my father finished with the windows. I opened the car door, pushed the junk tire gauges, jumper cables, screwdrivers cluttering his front seat aside, and slid in. Daddy started the car to a blaring baseball game. I moved the dial to the soul station KGFJ and lowered the volume, hoping he wouldn't notice, but Daddy went back to the ballgame and turned it up again. I tried to ignore Vin Scully's "A man on first, two outs, bottom of the ninth . . ." by looking out the window, watching the streets roll along, hoping Daddy wouldn't start talking. We hadn't gone but a few miles when I felt myself start to cry. I didn't feel too bad, but the tears flowed from my eyes. The beating, I thought, but it wasn't that. I had been stupid, I was crying because I was plain stupid. I stopped myself and wiped my face on my shirt.

Then Daddy started. "Those niggers. I told you about hanging around those people. Liking people like that. But now you can't. You've got to hate them."

"No, I don't."

Daddy harrumphed.

"Don't be no fool, boy. When somebody beat you, you got to hate them."

I guess that was it for him, a notion of fairness.

"It don't matter," I said. "It don't make no difference. They beat me 'cause they're fools."

That's all I said. I didn't have to justify getting my butt kicked, even though it felt like I did.

The doctor checked me out, and determined I had a mild concussion. I liked saying that to everybody when I got home. The word concussion made me think of a mild explosion as though I had a minor blast in my head. The doctor wanted me to be observed for the rest of the night and if I started vomiting or losing consciousness to be rushed back. Mama made me sit on the couch and watch TV with her, my head resting on her big comfortable stomach, as we watched _Star Trek_.

I hoped my face would heal before I had to go back to school. Everybody would ask questions — "Got your butt kicked? Somebody mopped your ass all over the place?" But Monday came, and I went to Foshay, and nobody even noticed. I guess I didn't look that bad. Not like that dude whose Mama whipped him with an extension cord. Anyway, I learned my lesson: Don't get involved with wrong number girls, and most importantly, don't go east or south, stay my butt on the Westside.

AN EMPTY CLASSROOM, LINCOLN HEIGHTS

William Archila

Four dull windows resist the rain outside.
One can hear sirens wailing like a red
angry god. The slamming of lockers and
pencil sharpeners have stopped. One, three, five
crumpled papers, all balled into rocky
planets, circle a trash can. A child has
chalked on the board letters that bend like her
mother at the sewing machine. Others
have laid word after word as if they knew
the exact movements of their fathers, brick
after brick. You can see their small bodies
on these chairs, curve into men and women,
how their eyes pause between a single stroke
of turning a page and finding a word.

THIS YEAR IN LOS ANGELES

David L. Ulin

L ONG and white and formal, the Seder table stretches across the living room like something out of a photograph. A photograph, or a memory, or both—the moment when the picture and the recollection merge. Along its surface sit all the familiar markers of tradition: haggadahs and matzoh, glasses of red wine, and the ceremonial cup for Elijah, as if this year, the old white-bearded prophet might actually descend from heaven to join us for a round. And in the middle, the Seder plate, porcelain like my grandmother's, striated in shades of white and blue, with the Hebrew letters for *pesach* etched across the center, and small blue circles for the egg, bitter herbs, shank bone, parsley, horseradish, and *charoset* that give Passover its peculiar charm.

What scant memories I have of Judaism revolve around a setting just like this one, as ephemeral as a bridge of sighs. When I was a kid, I used to spend Passover at my grandparents' apartment in Brooklyn, where I would sit at the children's table with the cousins I barely knew, grudgingly listening to the story of the Exodus and wondering when I might make my own escape. Back then, all this was just a burden, or even worse, a stigma—a set of peasant superstitions that I couldn't get away from fast enough. Tonight, however, I am taking steps toward adopting those rituals for my own use, as my wife, Rae, and I host our first family Seder here in Los Angeles, the most visible manifestation of my efforts in the last few years to make some contact with my roots.

This process of reconciliation is a tricky one, and even now, I don't know what I think. I'm not the only one; from their places at the table, my parents look bewildered, while my brother and his wife seem more than a little uncomfortable, as if they're not sure why they're here. The only people at ease are Rae and her mother, as well as the handful of friends we've invited to cut the tension, and the kids — my two-and-a-half-year-old son Noah, and his cousins Curtis and Christine — rolling around the floor like wrestlers, blissfully oblivious to any agenda but their own. Perhaps it's true that the whole point of ritual is its reassuring sameness, that by participating in these age-old celebrations, we become connected to our heritage. But my family has never believed that, and in hosting this Seder, I've marked out my own exodus, which to some extent makes Passover a symbol of *dis*connection, of all the things we've tried to put behind us, the fragments of history we could never get to cohere. *Why is this night different from all other nights?* asks the first of the Four Questions, and tonight that takes on added resonance, as my family and I stare at each other across a personal divide. Looking at them, I'm reminded that when I first invited my parents to this Seder, my father laughed and told me, "I never realized you were such a Jew."

My father was joking when he said that, although like most jokes, it carries the small, sharp edge of judgment, as well. Yet perhaps the most appropriate way to read his remark is as another symbol, of the contradictions that beat within my family's hearts like blood. My history is one of assimilation; when I was five, my parents traded our menorah for a Christmas tree, and from then on, I was not taught to respect my traditions, nor even to know them, but to shed them like old skin, after which I might walk bravely, nakedly, unencumbered into a better world. I was never bar mitzvahed, never taught about the Old Testament, and my primary experience of organized religion remains the two years — from ten to twelve — I sang in an Episcopal church choir. Lest this sound more conscious than it's meant to, I should point out that, for me, singing in the choir had less to do with religion than with the twenty-five-dollar-a-month stipend the church paid. But the sheer fact of my having been allowed to do it suggests something fundamental about the way I was brought up, which was to think of faith as fashion, as something that might be useful as a means of self-creation, but was inherently false and empty just the same.

Over the years, I've tried to make sense of this, to reason out a point of view. I've gone through periods of agreeing with my parents, and others when I condemned the depth of their self-loathing, the extent to which they turned their backs on who they were. It's not that I don't understand their logic; growing up on the Upper East Side of Manhattan, aspiring to a certain social status, I always knew it was best to keep my ethnicity well hidden. Yet for all their emphasis on reinvention, my parents never wanted us to become Christian, just to erase the stain of our Jewishness and render ourselves new. For them, it was a matter of transformation through negation, but in the process we were stranded, part of neither the world we wished for nor the one we left behind. Once, when I was eighteen, and working construction in Texas, the foreman asked if I were Jewish, and I said, "No." Even then, though, I'd begun to wonder at my spiritual isolation, the way heritage felt like a box of loose slides in the back of a closet, half-forgotten and largely out of reach. Not only was it all uncataloged, I didn't have the necessary projector, which meant the best I could do was hold each image to the light and squint at it, identifying little more than the odd detail from which I might try to reconstruct the rest.

Half my life later, I'm still piecing together this information, looking to see how it fits. It's a solitary process, lonely even, since, given my background, the simplest accommodations come tinged with capitulation, with the feeling that I've turned my back on the person I was raised to be. It's as if I can't trust my impulses, which keep telling me to seek connection while warning me not to believe in anything larger than myself. This, of course, is the central contradiction, for among the most enduring legacies of my upbringing is a deep-seated distrust of organized religion, of its agendas, its compulsive sense of community, and its insistence on placing the issue of identity in a context broader than my own.

In the end, that may explain why, of all the spasms of ritual, the Seder, with its do-it-yourself aesthetic, is the one I've been most comfortable taking on. It's something that moves me at the most basic level, that there need be no intermediary — no rabbi — to negotiate the ceremony, or tell me what it means. Tonight, if there's an officiating presence, I am it, seated at the head of the table, hiding the *afikoman,* or pouring wine to finger-flick across the crisp white china, ten drops per person for the plagues of Egypt, each in its own way a transubstantiation into blood. For all my uncertainty, it is in these small acts that I sense the fragile tendrils of connection, an understanding that sharpens when Noah and Rae bring a pitcher of water to perform the ritual washing of hands. The moment is hardly solemn; as Noah crawls into my lap and splashes my palms and fingers, his features crinkle and he giggles in high-pitched joy. But in the face of his reaction, I think again about the solace of tradition, and the ways that heritage may leave us not compromised but confirmed.

This is not the first time I've had that realization; when Noah was born, I reluctantly agreed to give him a *bris,* only to find myself moved by what I'd previously excoriated as a "ritual mutilation," a benediction not of love but blood. Then, as now, it was the simple things that touched me, the idea that this was, in the broadest sense, a communal moment, passed down through generations, binding us to our lineage in a way I'd never known. Standing there, holding my infant son's hand as the scalpel cut away his foreskin and left a small, thin ring of exposed flesh, I felt, for a fleeting instant, like part of something, before the feeling faded and I returned to the parameters of my life.

Years ago, I'd have seen this evanescence as proof of religion's inability to sustain us, but these days, such whispers of communion are all I expect. After all, heritage is a hard concept to hold onto, one that slips away each time I turn it over in my mind. There is always an equally opposing impulse; with Judaism, I want both to belong and not to belong. Even at the Seder, I can't avoid that conflict, and when my mother-in-law starts coaching Noah in Hebrew, I clench my fists and glare. Briefly, it's as if time has telescoped, and I'm cast back to my childhood. But then that moment, too, passes, and by the time we reach the closing invocation, "Next Year in Jerusalem," I know that next year in Los Angeles, we will be doing this again.

GOOD WIVES DON'T DRIVE

Joan Jobe Smith

My father refused to teach my mother
how to drive his car, he said it
wasn't ladylike in 1949, a woman driver

was no better than a streetwalker she was
to take the bus and be a good wife like
his mother was so my mother took secret

driving lessons, the instructor man
coming every day in his grey sedan
to show her how to let out the clutch

just right so the car wouldn't jerk, how
to work the choke and the radio, make
turn signals, arm bent up for right

straight out for left, down for slow
me in the backseat watching as we drove
the L.A. streets: Firestone, Rosemead

Sunset Boulevard, Pico, La Brea and
Santa Fe and the day she got her drivers
license she bought herself a green 1939

Ford coupe and waited in the front seat
in the driveway for my father to come home
honked the horn at him when he arrived

and said Hey handsome, need a ride?

LOST

Bia Lowe

As the sight of land is welcome to men who are swimming towards the shore, when Neptune has wrecked their ship with the fury of his winds and waves; a few alone reach the land, and these, covered with brine, are thankful when they find themselves on firm ground and out of danger— even so was her husband welcome to her as she looked upon him, and she could not tear her two fair arms from about his neck.

— Homer, *The Odyssey*

A map can tell me how to find a place I have not seen but often imagined. When I get there, following the map faithfully, the place is not the place of my imagination. Maps, growing ever more real, are much less true.

—Jeanette Winterson, *Sexing the Cherry*

I LOVE maps, and like most people, I throw myself at their mercy when I travel. But it must be said, at the risk of seeming contradictory, that maps lie. Maps of the world are the most bald-faced. They hatch fictions, decorous fibs. Within their counterfeit pages, nations clasp one another as agreeably as hands. Pastel hedgerows softly harmonize. The chaos of ancient rivalries and betrayals, the disorder of homelands seized or surrendered, not to mention blood, human blood, all are masked by a tidy representation of borders— of lines which may be drawn and redrawn, with the steadiest of hands, one year after the next.

Maps of cities conjure a different kind of sham. They claim that the journeyer is not lost; they suggest that life can be serenely viewed from the P.O.V. of an angel, that streets and rivers can be surveyed from a loft as remote as a satellite. Maps can't prepare you for what you'll meet head on. There is nothing on a map of Paris, say, to warn the traveler of aromas, kooks, or beautiful women — any multitude of possible distractions likely to divert the traveler from her course.

There are no guides for the city of the nose, the city of the groin, the city of the raised hackles. There is no signboard to warn you that in your travels, that on your journey, whether actual or figurative, you may encounter something that will change your life forever, that will cause you to become lost to yourself. With map in hand you lose a sense that it might, in fact, be advantageous to be lost — to find yourself by way of the city, rather than to find your way within it. You, and every other Joe, wants to know what comes next, what lurks around the corner. And so we consult the guides: the gamut, advice columns, zodiacs, psychologists, talk show pundits.

There are no maps for being in love either; plenty of clichés, of course, enough well meaning, but fraudulent, accounts of peas tucked happily-ever-after in the pod — enough treacle about folks trying to cleave unto one another, til death do them part. But I ask you, try to wipe some of the syrup away and what could be less known, more scary? bombs in the night? a plague on your own house? a killer at your bedside? Yes, of course. Then why do my glands respond as though I were being pushed out of a 747? Why the sensation of falling, the plunge into panic?

I've been on dangerous turf before. I've stumbled onto riot scorched boulevards, had shouting matches with crackheads, woken at four in the morning with a knife held to my throat. The avenues, the addicts, and the bed are all located in my own neck of the woods, my own turf of Los Angeles. The streets I travel across town are infamous for drug deals, gang wars, drive-by shootings. And the freeways I use rack up their daily obituaries in the form of grisly car crashes. Like Mr. Magoo, I continue, unfettered, while all around me the dangers of urban life rant and rail. I like to think I know danger when I see it, but the fact is I've grown oblivious to much of it, inured to the popping of scattershot at midnight, the clamor of police helicopters (or even to the sneakier perils, the invisible marauders who ravage the air and rob my cells of their potential years).

This isn't to say that my adrenals are underutilized; it's just that, like many humans these days, my scope of dangers includes an interior landscape. Since I fell in love with Rose—*for example*—I've been animal scared. Why should this be?

~

I didn't know much about Ireland a year ago. It was just a place on the map, a place becoming saturated with cliché, what with all the pop music, Celtic New Age hype, all the Americans swilling stout in ersatz pubs.

But Rose, who loves Ireland, and who has been there countless times, took me. She had gone a week before me and was waiting when I arrived at the Dublin airport. We had been together about six months and were falling in love. She threw my bag in the back of the rental car and drove me to a small fishing village. The sea bulged and shone like old green glass. It reminded me, though less green, of childhood haunts in Northern California. We watched the sea in silence, then she drove me to a small thatched cottage nearby. We climbed out of the car, and I knew, with a feeling that gripped my chest and made blood thrum in my ears—was it love? terror? could I tell them apart?—what was coming next. "I just bought it," she said. "It's ours."

How spooky can a cottage be with no attic, no basement, no closets, no darkened recesses? Our cottage (ours, ours!) is about as benign as they come. One story, no steps, floor level with the ground, fireplace in the middle room, sea breeze at the door that never needs to be locked, birds nesting in the thatch. It begs to be lived in. Pretty spooky.

I inferred from the movies that marriage was the end result of love, the achievement, the resolution of doubt. Two people settle in, plumpen, slumber in the cozy buzz of the other's snores. No one told me that love might make me insecure, childish. No one warned me that since Rose and I had fallen deeply and mightily, our plunge into terrors, into fight or flight, would be deep and mighty as well. No one warned me how, being in love, Rose and I would display our fangs to each other in mortal scare.

Let's say you live in a wood. You are a woodsman. You have built your home with the trees you've felled and split with your own ax. There are flowers in the window box, and smoke coils out of the chimney as if drawn with a child's crayon. You know your house and the woods surrounding it like you know the shapes of your own fingernails, the feel of your tongue inside your mouth.

Then one day you hear an unfamiliar sound echo in the wood. A woman's voice stirs the space between the trees in a way that makes the wood feel strangely reconfigured. Because it beckons, you follow the voice, and soon you come upon a beautiful woman in a red cape. At the sight of you, the woman drops her basket and flees deeper into the forest. "Please don't go!" you cry. "I won't hurt you!" You pursue her, confident that another look at your affable face, your dependable workman's hands, will reassure her. You cry out to her again, but your voice has become desperate, hoarse. She is swift on her feet and has led you into a part of the woods you've never been. Brambles scrape and snag you. You shred their canes with your nails, wail at the thorns that tear the pads of your feet. Your boots! Where are your boots? And there on the ground, on the damp leaves, her cape spread out like a pool of fresh blood. Whose feet are yours? Whose hands, all covered with fur? Whose strange claws? Whose long tongue curls inside your panting mouth?

And who is the creature who now crouches before you, ready to strike? Who is she?

~

In the land of drama, a tragedy ends when the protagonists die; a comedy ends when the protagonists marry. The credits scroll, the houselights brighten, people head back to their frozen dinners, known quantities, and insurance policies. But where is the drama that opens with marriage? Where are the scripts and maps outlining its plot? It must be, like the Eleusinian Mysteries or the Eucharist, an esoteric and safely guarded process. Or else it is wholly improvised. Marriage is a drama that ends when the protagonists emerge from the maze, blinking into the sunlight, a drama that ends when the protagonists are found.

Or let's say you are a beautiful woman in a red cape and you are lost in a wood. You come to a house with flowers in the window box and smoke curling out of the chimney. It is everything you've imagined a house should be, and you imagine perhaps it might be your own. Chairs. Porridge. Beds. Let's say you realize this is the house that was promised to you. The house you are to share with your betrothed, a woodsman you recently met while walking in the woods. You are longing for him to return to your house now, for him to hang up his hat and for the two of you to begin the business of happiness. You open the closet to take comfort in the smells and textures of his clothes. But he is there in the dark, waiting, and so are the others.

The monsters storm about the house, claiming to be father, mother, and child. "Who's been sitting in *my* chair!?" each demands. It is a tantrum on a grand scale. The baby screams, the father scolds, the mother threatens. Mine. Mine. Mine. Chairs. Porridge. Beds. This is the house of your nightmares that you and your beloved have become lost inside of. There is no place to sit and think, nothing to eat, no place to sleep. You could not possibly have wanted this, no.

~

Pain is the stuff by which Westerners know themselves. Small jabs of electricity are aimed into the body, and the nerves are described by the routes and velocities through which the resulting pain is transported. Suffering, like some radioactive isotope, is the substance that is visible to us, that leaves its tracks and maps who we are. Even animals are judged worthy of humane concern, based on their ability to be sentient, i. e., their ability to feel pain.

It would seem that pleasure and love go about their business in an unseen dimension, if at all. I do not want to suggest that pleasure and love are one and the same, though they do keep company, and it is true that through pleasure love creates its greatest dangers. Love and pleasure undo us, working their invisible mischief like worms in the soil. They aim to corrupt the ego, like Vedic avatars, until we are no longer ourselves, but more like transparencies that emit more light, less definition. And that, of course, is cause for panic. Definition is what we crave: lines, shadings, borders. We want to be in order, not in love.

But then, of course, our definitions are always changing. I was advised, for example, not to kiss Rose until our fifth date; later, to spend at least one night apart. I've prayed for a satellite's perspective on all our hissing and scratching and been handed guidelines for "active listening." I've also been advised, only thirty years ago, by people equally as well wishing, that love between women is a disorder, that Negroes are less than human, etc. DON'T GO THERE! urge our protectors. They love us; they see us trembling at the threshold of the maze; they know the interior is bloody. Why should we risk danger? Don't go.

~

A week after our visit to Ireland, we were in Istanbul. Our sleep was furtive, the calls to prayer from a loudspeaker at the nearby mosque blared, it seemed, incessantly. On our first day we stood inside that mosque and watched as a hundred or so of the devout knelt in the direction of Mecca, and prayed.

Later we stood on a hill near the Grand Bazaar and tried to orient ourselves by a map. We were lost, but the thought of being lost in such a foreign city was simply unacceptable to me—I had, I believed, an impeccable sense of direction. As I stood, map in hand, the vista I claimed to recognize was not the corresponding territory I saw on the page before me. That is east, I proclaimed, down there is the Bosphorus. So, down we went to the water, which was not the Bosphorus. Down we went farther and farther, the streets more difficult to descend into. Narrower and narrower, steeper and steeper. We had not come to the Golden Horn as we wished. I still insisted that the Bosphorus was just beyond the wall, and Rose, who had indulged my delusion up until then, had obviously lost patience. We followed the wall, through a fog of coal smoke, but the ruse was up — I had no idea where we were.

It was rush hour when we finally emerged onto a boulevard. The street suddenly filled with belching cars and busses, and people, hundreds and hundreds. "Look around," said Rose. "Do you notice anything unusual?" As far as the eye could see, we were the only women. All the men were swarthy, many looked like Islamic fundamentalists. Were we in danger? We were lost, we were out of place, we did not belong. I could feel myself starting to unhinge. Would we be harassed? raped? stoned? taken into white slavery?

It is true that the threat of civil war is a palpable sensation in Istanbul, that it hisses and shudders just below the surface. Young men gripping Uzis guard civic buildings. Scores of women show their support for a less secular government by covering their heads in public. The ingredients are incendiary: poverty, fundamentalism, immigration, and a militaristic lid holding down the boil. Nevertheless, despite the burble of civil unrest, despite the hazards of a medieval infrastructure, our biggest threat might have come in the form of an Armenian gigolo, or a Russian pickpocket. Were we in danger? Compared to being a female pedestrian lost in Los Angeles, piece of cake. We were lost, simply, but my reaction carried with it the tremors of greater dangers.

Like Kurtz, I bring my perils with me.

Each time I return to our house in Ireland, I check the lock on the door. I worry about the ground movement, as though the San Andreas runs under the hearth. The odd kindness of our neighbors makes me suspicious, and even the birds, which I can't identify without a guidebook, conspire in my disorientation. I feel out of my element, turned around, lost at sea, not simply because I've begun to orient myself east — toward Ireland — but because I have embarked on a journey for which there is no compass, other than love.

James Baldwin:

> *It is necessary, while in darkness, to know that there is a light somewhere, to know that in oneself, waiting to be found, there is a light. What the light reveals is danger, and what it demands is faith. Pretend, for example, that you were born in Chicago, and have never had the remotest desire to visit Hong Kong, which is only a name on a map for you; pretend that some convulsion, sometimes called accident, throws you into a connection with a man or a woman who lives in Hong Kong; and that you fall in love. Hong Kong will immediately cease to be a name and become the center of your life. And you may never know how many people live in Hong Kong. But you will know that one man or woman lives there without whom you cannot live. And this is how our lives are changed, and this is how we are redeemed.*

~

Ireland has begun to make her own map inside me. I know the road from the airport, imagine myself driving in the evening light to the cottage. It's almost dark as we pass through the village. We'll pass Flynn's, the pub where last December, Mr. Flynn, of nimble foot and bulging paunch, waltzed me around the dance floor. We'll stop by Fionna's store for milk and tea. "Were you gone?" she'll ask. We'll talk about her daughter and the weather, children and sunshine, the two Irish obsessions. We'll climb back in the car and drive toward the sea.

I know the cottage will be cold but dry. Rose goes to fetch coal. Then our neighbor Kate knocks on the door. When I open it, I find her teasing smile. "So," she growls, "she's back now, is she?" And looking for Rose: "And where's Herself? Left you to unpack, has she?" Her nine-year-old, Eamonn, beams beside her. He is, to condense great matters of the heart into a simple clause, the child I wish I'd had. Kate catches the look that passes between Eamonn and me, and knows it for what it is, and likes what it bodes for the both of us. "Come over later after ye get settled in. Welcome home!"

It's not easy to leave what is familiar. I have lived twenty-seven years in the same city. I have friends and peers, and most of them are gay and child-less, writerly and fortyish. Suddenly, I feel the gravitational pull of a nine-year-old boy; and of his parents who seem to enjoy the company of two spinster Yanks; and of a bawdy village where an elderly publican teaches me to dance; and of unfamiliar birds who require my naming; and of course, of Rose, who needs me to adventure this with her.

Nothing is certain. How do I proceed?

Let's say you are a hero named Odysseus and you have sailed home to your island. You have come home to your wife, your beloved, to live hap-pily ever after. For that reason this tale must be a comedy, and therefore what comes next is yet unwritten.

You have killed the monsters: the wolves, the bears, and the Cyclops. You and wifey know how monsters — if they are true monsters and worthy of their monstrosity — never die, they transform themselves and reappear. A home, too, continually alters itself, defies maps: One day it's all gingerbread confection, next thing you know, a witch is stoking your oven, eyeing you like a pair of clove-studded hams. You are home, at last, but this is just the beginning.

You have only yourselves as guides for what is to come. Bread crumbs. String. Prayers. She slips the red cape from your shoulders, wraps her arms around your neck, licks the brine from your cheek . . . welcome home.

NOTES ON CONTRIBUTORS

Luis Alfaro was born and raised in downtown Los Angeles. A poet, play-wright, fiction writer, performer, and director, he co-directs the Latino Theatre Initiative at the Mark Taper Forum. He received a MacArthur Fellowship in 1997.

William Archila was born in Santa Ana, El Salvador. His work has appeared in *Americas Review, Drum Voices Revue, Rattle*, and the anthologies *New to North America: Writing by Immigrants* and *The Practice of Peace*. He is a 1999 PEN Center USA West Emerging Voices fellow, and the winner of Poetry in the Windows II and III, a project of the Arroyo Arts Collective.

Bruce Bauman became a writer-in-residence at Santa Monica's 18th Street Arts Complex in 1997. In 1999, he was awarded a UNESCO Laureate fellowship in literature and spent three months at the Sanskriti Foundation for the Arts in New Delhi, India.

Aimee Bender is the author of a short story collection, *The Girl in the Flammable Skirt*, and a novel, *An Invisible Sign of My Own*, both published by Doubleday. She's had short stories appear in *Granta, GQ, Story, Harper's, The Paris Review*, and other journals.

michael datcher is the Director of Literary Programs at the World Stage Writer's Workshop and the author of *Raising Fences: A Black Man's Love Story* (Putnam/Riverhead).

Jacqueline De Angelis is a poet and prose writer. Her work has most recently appeared in *Paterson Review, International Quarterly*, and *Agni* mag-azine. She has won the Crossing Boundaries Award for innovative and experimental writing and was a finalist for both the Allen Ginsberg and Emily Dickinson Awards.

Samantha Dunn is the author of the novel *Failing Paris* (Toby Press), and the memoir *Not By Accident* (Henry Holt).

Bart Edelman is an English professor at Glendale College, where he edits *Eclipse*, a literary journal. His poetry has appeared in newspapers, journals, textbooks, and anthologies. Collections of his work include *Crossing the Hackensack* (Prometheus Press), *Under Damaris' Dress* (Lightning Press), *The Alphabet of Love* (Red Hen Press), and *The Gentle Man* (Red Hen Press).

Sesshu Foster is the author of *City Terrace Field Manual* (Kaya Press). He has taught composition and literature in East Los Angeles for a dozen years.

Lynell George is a staff writer for the *Los Angeles Times*, where she writes about culture, the arts, and social issues. She is the author of *No Crystal Stair: African Americans in the City of Angels* (Verso/Anchor). Her work has also appeared in *LA Weekly*, *The Boston Globe*, *Vibe*, *Essence*, and *The New Left Review*. A native of Los Angeles, she happily resides one long block away from Dodger Stadium in Echo Park.

Amy Gerstler's most recent book of poems, *Medicine*, was published by Penguin Putnam in 2000. Her previous books include *Crown of Weeds* (Penguin), *Nerve Storm* (Penguin), and *Bitter Angel* (North Point Press), which won the National Book Critics Circle Award in poetry. She teaches writing in the MFA program at Antioch University Los Angeles, and is a graduate advisor in the Fine Arts Department at Art Center College of Design.

Lisa Glatt teaches in the Writers Program at UCLA Extension and at California State University, Long Beach. Her two collections, both published by Pearl Editions, are *Monsters and Other Lovers* and *Shelter*.

Eloise Klein Healy is the author of four books of poetry, the founding chair of the MFA in Creative Writing Program at Antioch University Los Angeles, and the Associate Editor/Poetry Editor of *The Lesbian Review of*

Books. Artemis In Echo Park (Firebrand Books), her most recent collection, is also available as a spoken word recording from New Alliance Records. Her poetry is widely anthologized, notably in *The Geography of Home: California's Poetry of Place* and *The World In Us: Gay and Lesbian Poetry of the Next Wave*.

David Hernandez is the author of two volumes of poetry, *Man Climbs Out of Manhole* (Pearl Editions) and *Donating the Heart* (Pudding House Publications). His poems have appeared in *Poet Lore, Quarterly West, Southern Poetry Review, Passages North*, and *Crab Orchard Review*.

Erik Himmelsbach has spent his adult life running from his San Fernando Valley roots. He has written about music and pop culture for *Rolling Stone, Spin, Revolver*, the *Los Angeles Times Magazine, LA Weekly*, and other publications.

Tara Ison's novel, *A Child Out of Alcatraz* (Faber & Faber), was a finalist for the *Los Angeles Times* Book Awards.

Diane Lefer's books include *The Circles I Move In* (Zoland Books), *Very Much Like Desire* (Carnegie Mellon University Press), and *Radiant Hunger* (Authors Choice Press). She teaches creative writing in the MFA programs at Antioch University Los Angeles and Vermont College of Norwich University, and serves on the animal behavior observation team for the Research Department of the Los Angeles Zoo.

Russell Charles Leong is a poet, fiction writer, and book editor. His book of poems, *The Country of Dreams and Dust* (West End Press), received a PEN Josephine Miles Literature Award in 1993. His most recent book, *Phoenix Eyes and Other Stories*, was published by the University of Wash ington Press in 2000 and is forthcoming in a Chinese translation. He is an adjunct professor of English at UCLA, and editor of *Amerasia Journal* at the UCLA Asian American Studies Center.

Judith Lewis has been on staff at *LA Weekly* since 1991. Her work has appeared in *Elle*, *Wired*, and *American Theatre* magazines.

Gerald Locklin is the author of ninety or so books and chapbooks of poetry, fiction, and criticism, including *Go West, Young Toad: Selected Writings* (Water Row Press), *Candy Bars: Selected Stories* (Water Row Press), and *The Firebird Poems* (Event Horizon Press). He has taught at California State University, Long Beach, since 1965.

Bia Lowe's first book *Wild Ride* (HarperCollins) won QPB's 1996 New Visions Award for groundbreaking nonfiction. Her essays have appeared in *Harper's*, *The Kenyon Review*, and *Salmagundi*, and been anthologized in *In Short: A Collection of Brief Creative Nonfiction* and *Helter Skelter: L.A. Art in the 1990s*. She lives in California and Ireland.

Ellyn Maybe is the author of *The Cowardice of Amnesia* (2.13.61), *Putting My 2¢ In* (Sacred Beverage), and *The Ellyn Maybe Coloring Book* (Sacred Beverage). She can be seen reading her work in Michael Radford's film *Dancing at the Blue Iguana*.

Jeffrey McDaniel is the author of *Alibi School* and *The Forgiveness Parade*, both published by Manic D Press. His poems have appeared in *The Best American Poetry 1994*, *New (American) Poets*, *The Outlaw Bible of American Poetry*, *Ploughshares*, and on NPR's *Talk of the Nation*. He has performed his work at venues throughout Europe and North America.

Susan McMullen was born and raised in Canada. She now lives in Santa Monica, and this is her first published story.

Cindy Milwe is a writer and teacher living in Venice, California. Her work has appeared in *Poet Lore*, *The New York Quarterly*, and *Alaska Quarterly Review*, among others. She teaches English and yoga at Santa Monica High School.

Richard Rayner has written for *The New Yorker, Granta, The New York Times*, and various other publications. He is the author of *Los Angeles Without a Map* (Mariner Books), *The Blue Suit* (Houghton Mifflin), and, most recently, *The Cloud Sketcher* (HarperCollins).

Aleida Rodríguez has lived in Los Angeles since 1967. Her collection of poetry *Garden of Exile* (Sarabande Books) has won both the Kathryn A. Morton Prize and the PEN Center USA West 2000 Literary Award.

Rob Roberge's fiction has appeared in *ZYZZYVA, Chelsea, Other Voices, Alaska Quarterly Review,* and *Fatal Embrace.* His plays have been produced in Los Angeles by Empire Red Lip and Wolfskill Theater, and he wrote the screenplay for the feature-length film *Worst Case Scenario.*

Marjorie Gellhorn Sa'adah is a former director of public health programs in Los Angeles; she holds a Masters degree in Ethics from Episcopal Divinity School. Her writing has been supported in part by PEN Center USA West's Emerging Writers Fellowship, the Sundance Institute's Writing Program, and the Jolt Cafe at Grand Central Market.

Erika Schickel is a writer, performer, and teacher. Her play *Wild Amerika* was produced as part of L.A. Theatre Works' "The Play's the Thing" and broadcast on KCRW; it has also been selected as the United States submission for the "World Play" radio series. Currently, she is working on a collection of essays, one of which will be featured as part of NPR's "Spoken Interludes."

Joan Jobe Smith has published seventeen collections of poetry, including *Jehovah Jukebox* (Event Horizon), *The Pow Wow Café* (The Poetry Business), and *Bukowski Boulevard* (Pearl Editions). Her work has recently appeared in *The Outlaw Bible of American Poetry* and *The Forward Book of Poetry 1999.*

Jerry Stahl is the author of a memoir, *Permanent Midnight* (Warner Books) and two novels, *Perv — A Love Story* and *Plainclothes Naked*, both published by William Morrow.

Louise Steinman is the author of *The Knowing Body: The Artist as Storyteller in Contemporary Performance* (North Atlantic) and *The Souvenir: A Daughter Discovers Her Father's War* (Algonquin). She curates literary programs for the Los Angeles Public Library. Her book on the Pacific War and its effect on both an American and a Japanese family will be published by Algonquin Books in Fall 2001.

Jervey Tervalon's first novel *Understand This* (University of California Press) won QPB's 1994 New Voices Award. He is also the author of *Living for the City* (Incommunicado Press), a collection of stories, and a second novel, *Dead Above Ground* (Pocket Books). His work has appeared in the *Los Angeles Times*, *Details*, and other publications, and he teaches writing at California State University, Los Angeles.

Amy Uyematsu is a sansei (third-generation Japanese American) poet and teacher from Los Angeles. She has two published books, *30 Miles from J-Town* and *Nights of Fire, Nights of Rain*, both available from Story Line Press.

Benjamin Weissman is the author of *Dear Dead Person* (High Risk/ Serpent's Tail). He is a graduate advisor at Art Center College of Design, where he also teaches writing.

David L. Ulin was born and raised in Manhattan, but has lived in Los Angeles since 1991. He is the author of *Cape Cod Blues* (Red Dust), a chap-book of poems, and from 1993 to 1996 was book editor of the *Los Angeles Reader*. A member of the Board of Directors of the National Book Critics Circle, he writes frequently for *LA Weekly*, the *Chicago Tribune*, *Newsday*, and the *Los Angeles Times*. His work has also appeared in *The Nation*, *The New York Times Book Review*, *GQ*, *The Village Voice*, and *Ruminator Review*.